ALSO BY ERIC BROWN

NOVELS
Helix
New York Dreams
New York Blues
New York Nights
Bengal Station
Penumbra
Engineman
Meridian Days

NOVELLAS
Starship Summer
Revenge
The Extraordinary Voyage of Jules Verne
Approaching Omega
A Writer's Life

COLLECTIONS
Threshold Shift
The Fall of Tartarus
Deep Future
Parallax View (with Keith Brooke)
Blue Shifting
The Time-Lapsed Man

FOR CHILDREN
An Alien Ate Me for Breakfast
Crazy Love
Space Ace
British Front
Firebug
Twocking
Walkabout
Untouchable

AS EDITOR
The Mammoth Book of New Jules Verne Adventures
(with Mike Ashley)

KÉTHANI

ERIC BROWN

SOLARIS

First published 2008 by Solaris
an imprint of BL Publishing
Games Workshop Ltd,
Willow Road,
Nottingham
NG7 2WS
UK

www.solarisbooks.com

Trade Paperback
ISBN-13: 978-1-84416-473-8
ISBN-10: 1-84416-473-X

Portions of this novel appeared in the following publications: "Ferryman" first appeared in *New Worlds*, "Onward Station" first appeared in *Interzone* 135, "The Kéthani Inheritance" first appeared in *Spectrum* 7, "Thursday's Child" first appeared in *Spectrum* 9, "The Touch of Angels" first appeared in *Threshold Shift*, "The Wisdom of the Dead" first appeared in *Interzone* 186, "A Heritage of Stars" first appeared in *Constellations*, "A Choice of Eternities" first appeared in *Postscripts* 1 and "The Farewell Party" first appeared in *The Solaris Book of New SF*.

Cover illustration: John Harris

10 9 8 7 6 5 4 3 2 1

A CIP catalogue record for this book is available from the British Library.

Designed & typeset by BL Publishing.

To Stratford A. Kirby
friend & poet

The Coming of the Kēthani

Everyone remembers what they were doing on the day the Onward Stations, those towering monuments to the fact of extraterrestrial intelligence, appeared on Earth.

I was in my mid-twenties, finishing my internship at Bradley General Hospital in the wild moorland of West Yorkshire. Life was good; I enjoyed my work, and the prospect of specialisation. I had met a wonderful woman a year earlier—Zara, whom I would marry in eighteen months—and I was adapting well to life in the country after twenty-five years of living in Bradford.

And then the Kéthani came, and for a while everything was in turmoil.

On the day planet Earth was made aware that sentient alien life existed out there beyond the solar system, I had the privilege of witnessing the appearance of the strange alien construct on the harsh winter landscape of the moorland above the village of Oxenworth.

It was midday on a freezing Monday in mid-January, and I had set off early for a late shift at the hospital. What was in my head as I drove from the village and climbed the narrow lane onto the brow of the moors, from it seemed the entire world could be viewed?

Well, as ever I was thanking my lucky stars, and no doubt enjoying the panorama. After the cramped shabbiness of my life in Bradford, the unspoilt landscape of the moorland, giving way to rolling farmland in the distance, seemed pristine and limitless. Not unlike my future—though little did I realise this at the time.

I was slowing down to appreciate the view to my right when it happened.

To my left, something flashed. It was so bright that it caused me to brake and peer through the side window, giving an involuntary cry of surprise.

The crest of the moorland, perhaps half a mile above me, was shimmering—the kind of corrugated effect produced by heat haze above a road in summer, except that this shimmer extended vertically perhaps five hundred metres into the clear blue winter sky.

I just sat and stared.

The shimmer vanished, and in its place I made out a slim obelisk fashioned, I thought instantly, from ice. It reflected the sun in golden bursts, and where its steep planes did not coruscate with the winter sunlight, they had a dazzling silver aluminium sheen.

I know it's a cliché, but I did not believe my eyes.

I was convinced that I was seeing things, that the needle-slim tower was an effect of the sunlight on the snow, or perhaps an icicle in the foreground which my brain processed as much larger than it was... which was ridiculous, of course. But at the time I was dazed and shaken, to say the least.

I started the car and drove on 100 metres, to be as close to the thing as the road would take me. Then I climbed out and began walking towards it, leaving the tarmac and wading through the snow-covered heather.

I was filled with wonder. I could not analyse my feelings then, though I've had plenty of time since to work out why I felt what I did. The inexplicable arrival of the obelisk was sufficient in itself to rouse awe from the most sceptical of people, and, if that were not enough, then the actual physical beauty of the construct, its alien perfection, tugged something in the heart. I say *alien* perfection, but this is not the wisdom of hindsight: the strange architecture of the tower spoke of a design never dreamed up by a human mind. As I drew closer and stared up, craning my neck to peer at its summit some five hundred metres above me, I made out the odd swirling patterns etched into the material of its rearing flanks—ice, I mistakenly thought of the material then. There was something ineluctably *other* in the curlicue whorls that climbed the needle, something random like an abstract pattern, and yet obeying a logic that spoke almost of some kind of language.

At the base of the tower was a rectangular block, and set into its sides was what appeared to be a triangular door, and to either side long, horizontal viewscreens. These were the most identifiable aspect of the tower, and yet still possessed a strangeness not of this world.

I fumbled with my mobile and got through to Zara. She was still on holiday, preparing lessons for the start of the new term.

"Khalid?" She sounded worried. I rarely used the mobile. "What is it?"

"Zara. Drop what you're doing and look out of the front window."

"What...? Khalid, are you—?"

"Do it!"

A silence of five seconds, then a soft, "Oh, my... Khalid, what is it? Oh... oh, it's so *beautiful*."

"I'm standing right beside it. Can you see my car on the road? Look, get yourself up here."

"I'm coming, Khalid." She cut the connection.

My heart was beating fast. I just wanted to hold Zara and cry. Perhaps it was some odd effect of the tower, its alien influence. Perhaps the Kéthani were manipulating us, even then.

I heard a car on the road behind me, and then another. Within a minute there were half a dozen cars lined up in the lane, their owners making their way through the snow and heather, gazing up in silent wonder. Behind them, I made out the roads leading from Oxenworth. The sun dazzled on a dozen car windscreens.

I recognised a couple of people in the small group: Richard Lincoln, who I'd chatted to a few times in the Fleece, and Jeff Morrow, a local teacher. They joined me.

I said, "It just appeared. Like magic. It wasn't there... and then... the air shimmered and it just... *appeared*." I realised I was babbling and shut up.

Richard stepped forward, leaving the group and approaching the silver building that formed the base of the tower. He reached out tentatively, touched the material with his fingertips and didn't take his hand away.

I often wonder what drew him to the construct, if it were some knowledge that soon, very soon, he would be in the employ of our alien visitors.

He looked back at us, still connected to the wall by his fingertips. "It's warm," he whispered.

We all approached then and touched the silver flank, and Lincoln was right. The material seemed... well, *alive*. I swore I felt, other than warmth, a pulse beneath my hand. I tried to peer through, but the material was opaque and nothing of the interior could be seen.

Jeff Morrow said, almost to himself, "And now this..."

It took a few seconds before I realised what he meant. Caroline, his wife, had been killed in a car accident a couple of weeks before Christmas... and as if that were not enough for him to cope with, the questioning that accompanies grief was compounded by this mystery.

Later, when the Kéthani explained their mission on Earth, Jeff Morrow's grief would be tested even further. Perhaps he intuited this even then, or perhaps the dead light in his eyes as he beheld the tower was merely sadness that he could not share the moment with his wife.

I heard a sound behind me, my name. It was Zara, tramping through the snow, her sari hitched up to her knees. In her other hand she clutched, incongruously, a transistor radio.

"Khalid," she called. "It's not the only one! There are reports coming in... there's hundreds of them... thousands, all over the world."

She joined us and upped the volume. The tinny voice of an on-the-scene reporter filled the air. "... standing beside the tower on the south downs a mile west of Lewes. Reports are that the tower just appeared out of the blue at midday precisely. I have with me an eyewitness..."

I listened, but with only half an ear, to a largely incoherent account of the wonder that had occurred in Sussex.

I held Zara to me, a strange emotion welling in my chest.

Ten minutes later it seemed that the entire population of Oxenworth and the surrounding villages had poured out and were massed at the foot of the tower. We stood in a crowd five deep, staring up and listening to Zara's radio as reports flooded in from around the world. The story was the same from Austria to Zaire, Australia to Zanzibar: at the same time, all around the globe, the towers had appeared in relatively unpopulated areas beside small villages or towns. There were no reports of their appearing in cities, nor in uninhabited areas like deserts. The initial estimate, garnered in the first hour by the BBC, was that tens of thousands had appeared across the face of the Earth. The actual figure, it eventuated, was precisely 110,000.

The government had issued warnings that under no circumstances must citizens approach the towers. The army had been mobilised, and experts were being called in—though experts in precisely what was never explained.

One hour after the arrival of the towers, the next stage of the phenomenon occurred.

A bright white light, arching through the heavens in a vast parabola, fell and hit the summit of the obelisk. The light dazzled, and drew gasps from the surrounding crowd, but was in itself completely silent. It lasted merely seconds, and then was gone.

But I swore that the tower changed.

It had possessed some kind of life before, but— and maybe this was my imagination, playing tricks, or again a trick of retrospect— I was convinced that now the tower was possessed of intelligence.

We flocked to touch the surface of the tower, and I was flooded with a strange sense of well-being. I felt as if something, or someone, had attempted to communicate with me.

The arc of light had descended on the towers at the same instant all around the world, apparently. The radio reporter near Lewes was almost speechless as he tried to convey the effect.

One hour later, the cold getting to us, Zara and I made our reluctant way home, turned on the TV—every channel was carrying the story live—and watched the unfolding of the greatest event in the history of the world.

Over the course of the next day we watched reports from hundreds of locations around the globe. It was as if the towers had been positioned systematically, equal distances apart, on every continent, country and island. We watched a succession of fazed politicians attempt the reassure their citizens that everything was under control, that there was no danger or threat from the towers. In some instances, it was obvious that the politicians were not believed, as angry mobs in Malaysia and Sudan rioted and attempted to burn down their respective towers. When the flames and embers died, it was revealed that not the slightest damage had been done to the unearthly constructions.

Precisely one day after the arrival of the towers, the heads of every country in the world appeared live on television and gave more or less the same address.

They had, they reported, been contacted by the agents responsible for the imposition of the towers. The agents were extraterrestrial in origin, and hailed from the planet orbiting the star Delta Pavonis, almost twenty light years from Earth. They called their planet Kéthan. They had come in peace, and reassured the citizens of Earth that there was absolutely no cause for concern.

It was not reported how the aliens had made the contact and communicated their message, which fuelled wild speculation in the press for twenty-four hours. Sources close to the world governments let slip that officials had been in meetings with impeccably dressed humanoids shortly before the Kéthani, as they came to be known, issued their communiqué to the world. Later, government officials across the world denied that they had had face-to-face meetings with the Kéthani, and the accepted story now is that all communications were via televisual links.

Two days after the arrival of the towers, newspapers, television and radio were running stories that asked the obvious question: what did the Kéthani want from Earth?

The answers, depending on the quality of the paper you read, ranged from scare stories straight from B-movies along the lines of *The Invasion of the Body Snatchers* to more peaceful scenarios that cast the aliens as Messiah figures come to put the planet to rights.

Three days after that fateful noon arrival, a tired-looking prime minister went on air and addressed the British nation.

Something in the expression on the man's face, a kind of manic euphoria combined with exhaustion and perhaps a dash of disbelief, told me that this was what we had been waiting for.

I gripped Zara's hand as we sat side by side on the sofa and watched with mounting incredulity as the leader of our country stared into the camera and told his citizens why the Kéthani had come to Earth.

Over the course of the next fifteen years I came to know a group of people in the village of Oxenworth who became dear to me. It is through the eyes of these people that I wish to tell the story of how the coming of the Kéthani affected the lives of everyone on Earth. Much has been written about the gift of the elusive aliens, and I cannot claim that what follows is in any way original. What is special about this document, I think, is that it concentrates on the small-scale lives of ordinary, everyday people during this unique time of change.

A long time after the coming of the Kéthani, I approached my friends and asked them to describe, in their own words, their stories in the light of the Kéthani's gift to humanity. For the most part I have reproduced their stories in full, with only minor corrections and emendations. In a couple of instances my friends, for whatever reasons, were unable or unwilling to record their reactions, and I have taken the liberty of producing documents recounting their stories, having of course first obtained their permission. I have included two of my own first-hand accounts of life during the period of transition, for the sake of completeness.

Nothing was ever the same again, after the Kéthani came. It is safe to say that the life of everyone on Earth was changed irrevocably from that momentous day. This is the story of how my life and the lives of my friends were transformed, for ever and ever…

INTERLUDE

Every Tuesday night, come rain or shine, Zara and I headed for the Fleece at nine o'clock and settled ourselves in the main bar. Over the years the circle of our friends grew to become a crowd, but at that point—a year after the coming of the Kéthani—we were a group of four: Zara, myself, Richard Lincoln and Jeff Morrow. Lincoln was a ferryman, employed by the local Onward Station, Morrow a teacher at Zara's school over in Bradley. I had known Lincoln a little before the Kéthani came—he was a fixture in the Fleece—and over the past few months we had come to know him better. He was a big, quiet, reserved man who gave the air of harbouring a sadness it was not in his nature to articulate.

That particular night he seemed even more subdued than normal. A television set was playing in the corner of the room, the sound turned low. It was not a regular fitting in the main bar, but the landlord had installed it because Leeds had been playing in Europe that night, and no one had bothered to turn it off.

Lincoln nursed his pint and stared at the flickering images, as if in a daze.

He was married to a big, red-headed woman called Barbara, who had left him that summer and moved down south. She had never, in all my time in the village, accompanied him to the Fleece. In fact, I had never seen them out together. When I had come across her in the village, she had always seemed preoccupied and not particularly friendly. It was an indication of Lincoln's reserve that, when Barbara walked out that summer, he told us that she was taking a long holiday with her sister, and never again mentioned his wife.

Zara and I were living together at the time, and planning our marriage in the summer. We were at that stage of our relationship where we were consumed by mutual love; I felt it must have been obvious to all our friends, like a glow. I held complex feelings for Richard Lincoln; I did not want to flaunt my happiness with Zara, when his relationship with his own wife had so obviously failed—and oddly, at the same time, I felt uneasy in his company, as if what he had gone through with Barbara compromised the possibility of my lasting happiness with my bride-to-be. I received the impression that the older, more experienced Lincoln was watching me and smiling to himself with the wry tolerance of the once-bitten.

"My God," he said suddenly, apropos of nothing. "I sometimes wonder..."

His pronouncement startled us. He was staring at the TV screen. Zara stopped talking to Jeff about their school and said, "What, Richard?"

He nodded towards the news programme. "Look at that. Chaos. How will it end, for Godsake? I sometimes wonder why I became a ferryman..."

In silence we turned to the screen and watched. A year of turmoil had followed the coming of the Kéthani. The human race, suspicious and hostile at the best of times, did not trust the alien race that had arrived unannounced bearing its gift from the stars.

There had to be a catch, some said. No race could be so altruistic. We were, of course, judging the Kéthani by our own standards, which is always a mistake when attempting to understand the motivating forces of others.

The report showed scenes of rioting in the Philippines. Manila was ablaze. The government, pro-Kéthani, had been toppled by the anti-Kéthani armed forces, and a bloody coup was in progress. Three thousand citizens were reported dead.

The scene shifted to a BBC reporter in Pakistan. There, the imams had declared the Kéthani evil and the implants an abomination. Hundreds of implanted citizens had been attacked and slaughtered.

The world was in chaos. Hundreds of thousands of citizens had lost their lives in the rioting. Two camps were emerging from the chaos: those opposed to the Kéthani and those who embraced the gift of the aliens with whole-hearted enthusiasm. The divide happened on a global level: some countries accepted the gift, while others rejected it. Many nations were torn by internal opposing forces.

"Do you mind?" Lincoln asked, gesturing to the screen. "I don't think I can take much more."

Perhaps sensing that his disquiet had its source much closer to home, we murmured that of course he could turn it off.

He downed his pint and turned to us. "Did I tell you that Barbara was... *is*... fervently opposed to the Kéthani?" he asked.

The divide was repeated on a smaller scale, splitting families, even husbands and wives.

"I was fifty years old when the Kéthani came," Lincoln said now, staring into his empty glass, "and I'd felt that something was wrong for years. When they came, I thought that was obviously the answer." He gestured at the screen. "I wonder now how things will end?"

Little by little, over the next few months, I came to understand what Richard Lincoln was going through.

ONE

Ferryman

Lincoln sat in the darkened living room and half-listened to the radio news. More unrest in the East; riots and protests against the implantation process in India and Malaysia. The president of France had taken his life, another suicide statistic to add to the growing list. The news finished and was followed by a weather report: a severe snowfall was forecast for that night and the following day.

Lincoln was hoping for a quiet shift when his mobile rang. It was his controller at the Station. She gave the name and address of the dead subject, then rang off.

Despite the weather and the inconvenience of the late hour—or rather the early hour: it was two in the morning—as ever he felt the visceral thrill of embarkation, the anticipation of what was to come.

He stepped into the hall and found his coat, already planning the route twenty miles over the moors to the dead man's town.

He was checking his pocket for the Range Rover's keys when he heard the muffled grumble, amplified by the snow, of a car engine. His cottage was a mile from the nearest road, serviced by a potholed cart track. No one ever turned down the track by mistake, and he'd had no visitors in years.

He waited, as if half expecting the noise to go away, but the vehicle's irritable whine increased as it fought through the snow and ice towards the cottage. Lincoln switched on the outside light and returned to the living room, pulling aside the curtain and peering out.

A white Fiat Electra lurched from pothole to pothole, headlights bouncing. It came to a stop outside the cottage, the sudden silence profound, and a second later someone climbed out.

Lincoln watched his daughter slam the car door and pick her way carefully through the snow.

The doorbell chimed.

He envisaged the tense confrontation that would follow, thankful for the call-out that would reduce his contact with Susanne to a minimum.

He pulled open the door. She stood tall in an expensive white mackintosh, collar turned up around her long, dark, snow-specked hair.

Her implant showed as a slight bulge at her temple.

She could hardly bring herself to look him in the eye. Which, he thought, was hardly surprising.

She gave a timid half-smile. "It's cold out here, Richard."

"Ah... Come in. This is a surprise. Why didn't you ring?"

"I couldn't talk over the phone. I needed to see you in person."

To explain herself, he thought; to excuse her recent conduct.

She swept past him, shaking the melted snow from her hair. She hung her coat in the hall and walked into the living room.

Lincoln paused behind her, his throat constricted with an emotion he found hard to identify. He knew he should have felt angry, but all he did feel was the desire for Susanne to leave.

"I'm sorry. I should have come sooner. I've been busy."

She was thirty, tall and good-looking and—*damn them*—treacherous genes had bequeathed her the unsettling appearance of her mother.

As he stared at her, Lincoln realised that he no longer knew the woman who was his daughter.

"But I'm here now," she said. "I've come about—"

He interrupted, his pulse racing. "I don't want to talk about your mother."

"Well I do," Susanne said. "This is important."

"Look, it's impossible right now. I've just had a call from the Station."

"You're going? Just when I get here?"

"I'm sorry, Susanne. Thing is, it's quite a way—Hebden Bridge. I should really be setting off. Look… make yourself at home. You know where the spare room is. We can… we'll talk in the morning, okay?"

He caught the flash of impatience on her face, soon doused by the realisation that nothing came between him and his calling.

She sighed. "Fine. See you in the morning."

Relief lifting from his shoulders like a weight, Lincoln nodded and hurried outside. Seconds later he was revving the Range Rover up the uneven track, into the darkness.

The main road had been gritted earlier that night, and the snow that had fallen since had turned into a thin grey mush. Lincoln drove cautiously, his the only vehicle out this late. Insulated from the cold outside, he tried to forget about the presence of Susanne back at the cottage. He half-listened to a discussion programme on the World Service. He imagined half a dozen dusty academics huddled in a tiny studio in Bush House. Cockburn, the Cambridge philosopher, had the microphone: "It is indeed possible that individuals will experience a certain disaffection, even apathy, which is the result of knowing that there is more to existence than this life…"

Lincoln wondered if this might explain the alienation he had felt for a year, since accepting his present position. But then he'd always had difficulty in showing his emotions and consequently accepting that anyone else had emotions to show.

This life is a prelude, he thought, a farce I've endured for fifty years—the end of which I look forward to with anticipation.

It took him almost an hour to reach Hebden Bridge. The small town, occupying the depths of a steep valley, was dank and quiet in the continuing snowfall. Streetlights sparkled through the darkness.

He drove through the town and up a steep hill, then turned right up an even steeper minor road. Hillcrest Farm occupied a bluff overlooking the acute incision of the valley. Coachlights burned orange around the front porch. A police car was parked outside.

Lincoln climbed from the Range Rover and hurried across to the porch. He stood for a second before pressing the doorbell, composing himself. He always found it best to adopt a neutral attitude until he could assess the mood of the bereaved family: more often than not the atmosphere in the homes of the dead was one of excitement and anticipation.

Infrequently, especially if the bereaved were religious, a more formal grief prevailed.

He pressed the bell and seconds later a ruddy-faced local constable opened the door. "There you are. We've been wondering if you'd make it, weather like it is."

"Nice night for it," Lincoln said, stepping into the hall.

The constable gestured up a narrow flight of stairs. "The dead man's a farmer—silly bugger went out looking for a lost ewe. Heart attack. His daughter was out with him—but he was dead by the time she fetched help. He's in the front bedroom."

Lincoln followed the constable up the stairs and along a corridor. The entrance to the bedroom was impossibly low; both men had to stoop as if entering a cave.

The farmer lay fully dressed on the bed, rugged and grey like the carving of a knight on a sarcophagus. Half a dozen men and women in their twenties and thirties were seated around the bed on dining chairs. An old woman, presumably the farmer's widow, sat on the bed itself, her husband's lifeless blue hand clutched in hers.

Lincoln registered the looks he received as he entered the room: the light of hope and gratitude burned in the eyes of the family, as if he, Lincoln himself, was responsible for what would happen over the course of the next six months.

An actor assuming a role, Lincoln nodded with suitable gravity to each of the family in turn.

"If anyone has any questions, anything at all, I'll be glad to answer them." It was a line he came out with every time to break the ice, but he was rarely questioned these days.

He stepped forward and touched the implant at the dead man's temple. It purred reassuringly. The nanomechs had begun the initial stage of the process upon the death of the farmer—the preparation of the body for its onward journey.

"I'll fetch the container," Lincoln said—he never called it a coffin—and nodded to the constable.

Together they carried the polycarbon container from the back of the Range Rover, easing it around the bends in the stairs. The family formed a silent huddle outside the bedroom door. Lincoln and the constable passed inside and closed the door behind them.

They lifted the corpse into the container and Lincoln sealed the sliding lid. The job of carrying the container down the stairs— attempting to maintain dignity in the face of impossible angles and improbable bends—was made all the more difficult by the presence of the family, watching from the stair landing.

Five minutes of gentle coaxing and patient lifting and turning, and the container was in the back of the Range Rover.

The constable handed over a sheaf of papers, which Lincoln duly signed and passed back. "I'll be on my way, Mr Lincoln," the constable said. "See you later." He waved and climbed into his squad car.

One of the farmer's daughters hurried from the house. "You'll stay for a cup of tea?"

Lincoln was about to refuse, then had second thoughts. If he returned home early, there was always the chance that Susanne would have waited up for him. "Yes, that'd be nice. Thanks."

He followed her into a big, stone-flagged kitchen, an Aga stove filling the room with warmth.

He could tell that she had been crying. She was a plain woman in her mid-thirties, with the stolid, resigned appearance of the unfortunate sibling left at home to help with the farm work.

He saw the crucifix on a gold chain around her neck, and only then noticed that her temple was without an implant. He began to regret accepting the offer of tea.

He sat at the big wooden table and wrapped his hands around the steaming mug. The woman sat down across from him, nervously meeting his eyes.

"It happened so quickly. I can hardly believe it. He had a weak heart—we knew that. We told him to slow down. But he didn't listen."

Lincoln gestured. "He was implanted," he said gently.

She nodded, eyes regarding her mug. "They all are, my mother, brothers and sisters." She glanced up at him, something like mute appeal in her eyes. "It seems that all the country is, these days."

When she looked away, Lincoln found his fingers straying to the outline of his own implant.

"But..." she whispered, "I'm sure things before were... I don't know... *better*. I mean, look at all the suicides. Thousands of people every month take their lives..." She shook her head, confused. "Don't you think that people are less... less concerned now, less caring?"

"I've heard Cockburn's speeches. He says something along the same lines."

"I agree with him. To so many people this life is no longer that important. It's something to be got through, before what follows."

How could he tell her that he felt this himself?

He said, "But wasn't that what religious people thought about life, before the change?"

She stared at him as if he were an ignoramus. "No! Of course not. That might have been what atheists *thought* religious people felt... But we love life, Mr Lincoln. We give thanks for the miracle of God's gift."

She turned her mug self-consciously between flattened palms. "I don't like what's happened to the world. I don't think it's *right*. I loved my father. We were close. I've never loved anyone quite so much." She looked up at him, her eyes silver with tears. "He was such a wonderful man. We attended church together. And then the Kéthani came," she said with venom, "and everything changed. My father, he..." she could not stop the tears now, "he believed what they said. He left the Church. He had the implant, like all the rest of you."

He reached out and touched her hand. "Look, this might sound strange, coming from me, but I understand what you're saying. I might not agree, but I know what you're experiencing."

She looked at him, something like hope in her eyes. "You do? You really do? Then..." She fell silent, regarding the scrubbed pine tabletop. "Mr. Lincoln," she said at last, in a whispered entreaty, "do you really have to take him away?"

He sighed, pained. "Of course I do. It was his choice. He chose to be implanted. Don't you realise that to violate his trust, his choice..." He paused. "You said you loved him. In that case respect his wishes."

She was slowly shaking her head. "But I love God even more," she said. "And I think that what is happening is wrong."

He drained his tea with a gesture of finality. "There'll be a religious service of your choice at the Station tomorrow."

She looked up and murmured, "What do they want with our dead, Mr. Lincoln? Why are they doing this to us?"

He sighed. "You must have read the literature, seen the documentaries. It's all in there."

"But you... as a ferryman... surely you can tell me what they really want?"

"They want what they say—nothing more and nothing less."

A silence came between them. She was nodding, staring into her empty mug. He stood and touched her shoulder as he left the kitchen. He said goodbye to the family in the living room—gathered like the survivors of some natural catastrophe, unsure quite how to proceed—and let himself out through the front door.

He climbed into the Range Rover, turned and accelerated south towards the Onward Station.

He drove for the next hour through the darkness, high over the West Yorkshire moors, cocooned in the warmth of the vehicle with a symphony by Haydn playing counterpoint to the grumble of the engine.

Neither the music nor the concentration required to keep the vehicle on the road fully occupied his thoughts. The events at the farmhouse, and his conversation with the dead man's daughter, stirred memories and emotions he would rather not have recalled.

It was more than the woman's professed love for her dead father that troubled him, reminding him of his failed relationship with his own daughter, Susanne. The fact that the farmer's daughter had forgone the implant stirred a deep anger within him. He had said nothing at the time, but now he wanted to return and plead with her to think again about undergoing the simple process of implantation.

In July, at the height of summer, Lincoln's wife had finally left him. After twenty-five years of marriage she had walked out, moved to London to stay with Susanne until she found a place of her own.

In retrospect he was not surprised at her decision to leave; it was the inevitable culmination of years of neglect on his part. At the time, however, it had come as a shock—verification that the increasing disaffection he felt had at last destroyed their relationship.

He recalled their confrontation on that final morning as clearly as if it were yesterday.

Behind a barricade of suitcases piled in the hall, Barbara had stared at him with an expression little short of hatred. They had rehearsed the dialogue many times before.

"You've changed, Rich," she said accusingly. "Over the past few months, since taking the job."

He shook his head, tired of the same old argument. "I'm still the same person I always was."

She gave a bitter smile. "Oh, you've always been a cold and emotionless bastard, but since taking the job…"

He wondered if he had applied for the position because of who and what he was, a natural progression from the solitary profession of freelance editor of scholastic textbooks. Ferrymen were looked upon by the general public with a certain degree of wariness, much as undertakers had been in the past. They were seen as a profession apart.

Or, he wondered, did he become a ferryman to spite his wife?

There had been mixed reactions to the news of the implants and their consequences: many people were euphoric at the prospect of renewed life; others had been cautiously wary, not to say suspicious. Barbara had placed herself among the latter.

"There's no hurry," she had told Lincoln when he mentioned that he'd decided to have the operation. "I have no intention of dying, just yet."

At first he had taken her reluctance as no more than an obstinate stance, a desire to be different from the herd. Most people they knew had had the implant; Barbara's abstention was a talking point.

Then it occurred to Lincoln that she had decided against having the implantation specifically to annoy him; she had adopted these frustrating affectations during the years of their marriage: silly things like refusing to holiday on the coast because of her dislike of the sea, or rather because Lincoln loved the sea; deciding to become a vegetarian, and doing her damnedest to turn him into one, too.

Then, drunk one evening after a long day of sneaking shots of gin, she had confessed that the reason she had refused the implant option was because she was petrified of what might happen to her after she died. She did not trust their motives.

"How... how do we know that they're telling the truth? How do we know what... what'll happen to us once *they* have us in their grasp?"

"You're making them sound like B-movie monsters," Lincoln said.

"Aren't they?"

He had gone through the government pamphlets with her, reiterated the arguments both for and against. He had tried to persuade her that the implants were the greatest advance in the history of humankind.

"But not everyone's going along with it," she had countered. "Look at all the protest groups. Look at what's happening around the world. The riots, political assassinations—"

"That's because they cling to their bloody superstitious religions," Lincoln had said. "Let's go over it again..."

But she had steadfastly refused to be convinced, and after a while he had given up trying to change her mind.

Then he'd applied to become a ferryman, and was accepted.

"I hope you feel pleased with yourself," Barbara said one day, gin-drunk and vindictive.

He had lowered his newspaper. "What do you mean?"

"I mean, why the hell do you want to work for *them*, do their dirty work?" Then she had smiled. "Because, Mr. Bloody

Ferryman, you'd rather side with *them* than with me. I'm only your bloody wife, after all."

And Lincoln had returned to the paper, wondering whether what she had said was true.

Over the next few weeks their relationship, never steady, had deteriorated rapidly. They lived separate lives, meeting for occasional meals when, depending on how much she had drunk, Barbara could be sullenly uncommunicative or hysterically spiteful.

Complacent, Lincoln had assumed the rift would heal in time.

Her decision to leave had initially shocked him. Then, as her decision turned from threat to reality, he saw the logic of their separation—it was, after all, the last step in the process of isolation he had been moving towards for a long, long time.

He had pleaded with her, before she left, to think again about having the implant operation.

"The first resurrectees will be returning soon," he told her. "Then you'll find you have nothing to fear."

But Barbara had merely shaken her head and walked out of his life.

He wrote to her at Susanne's address over the next couple of months, self-conscious letters expressing his hopes that Barbara was doing okay, would think again about having an implant. Reading the letters back to himself, he had realised how little he had said— how little there was to say—about himself and his own life.

Then last autumn, Lincoln had received a phone call from Susanne. The sound of her voice—the novelty of her call—told Lincoln that something was wrong.

"It's your mother—" he began.

"Dad... I'm sorry. She didn't want you to know. She was ill for a month—she wasn't in pain."

All he could say was, "What?" as a cold hollow expanded inside his chest.

"Cancer. It was inoperable."

Silence—then, against his better judgement, he asked, "Did—did she have the implant, Susanne?"

An even longer silence greeted the question, and Lincoln knew full well the answer.

"She didn't want a funeral," Susanne said. "I scattered her ashes on the pond at Rochester."

A week later he had travelled down to London. He called at his daughter's flat, but she was either out or ignoring him. He drove on to Rochester, his wife's birthplace, not really knowing why he was going but aware that, somehow, the pilgrimage was necessary.

He had stood beside the pond, staring into the water and weeping quietly to himself. Christ, he had hated the bitch at times—but, again, at certain times with Barbara he had also experienced all the love he had ever known.

As if to mock the fact of his wife's death, her immutable non-existence, the rearing crystal obelisk of this sector's Onward Station towered over the town like a monument to humankind's new-found immortality, or an epitaph to the legion of dead and gone.

He had returned home and resumed his work, and over the months the pain had become bearable. His daughter's return, last night, had reopened the old wound.

By the time he arrived at the Station a silver dawn was breaking over the horizon, revealing a landscape redesigned, seemingly inflated, by the night's snowfall. The Onward Station appeared on the skyline, a fabulous tower of spun glass scintillating in the light of the rising sun.

He visited the Station perhaps four or five times a week, and never failed to stare in awe—struck not only by the structure's ethereal architecture, but by what it meant for the future of humankind.

He braked in the car park alongside the vehicles of the dozen other ferrymen on duty today. He climbed out and pulled the polycarbon container from the back of the Range Rover, the collapsible chromium trolley taking its weight. His breath pluming before him in the ice-cold air, he hurried towards the entrance set into the sloping walls.

The interior design of the Station was arctic in its antiseptic inhospitality, the corridors shining with sourceless, polar light. As he manoeuvred the trolley down the seemingly endless corridors, he felt as ever that he was, truly, trespassing on territory forever alien.

He arrived at the preparation room and eased the container onto the circular reception table, opening the lid. The farmer lay unmoving, maintained by the host of alien nanomechs that later, augmented by others more powerful, would begin the resurrection process. They would not only restore him to life, strip away the years, but make him fit and strong again: the man who returned to Earth in six months would be physically in his thirties, but effectively immortal.

In this room, Lincoln never ceased to be overcome by the wonder, as might a believer at the altar of some mighty cathedral.

He backed out, pulling the trolley after him, and retraced his steps. To either side of the foyer, cleaners vacuumed carpets and arranged sprays of flowers in the greeting rooms, ready to receive the day's returnees, their relatives and loved ones.

He emerged into the ice-cold dawn and hurried across to the Range Rover. On the road that climbed the hill behind the Station, he braked and sat for ten minutes staring down at the diaphanous structure.

Every day a dozen bodies were beamed from this Station to the starship in geo-sync orbit, pulses of energy invisible during the daylight hours. At night the pulses were blinding columns of white lightning, illuminating the land for miles around.

Lincoln looked up, into the rapidly fading darkness. A few bright stars still glimmered, stars that for so long had been mysterious and unattainable—but which now, hard though it was sometimes to believe, had been thrown open to humankind by the beneficence of beings still mistrusted by many, but accepted by others as saviours.

And why had the Kéthani made their offer to humankind?

There were millions upon millions of galaxies out there, the aliens said, billions of solar systems, and countless, literally countless, planets that sustained life of various kinds. Explorers were needed, envoys and ambassadors, to discover new life, and make contact, and spread the greetings of the civilised universe far and wide.

Lincoln stared up at the fading stars and thought what a wondrous fact, what a miracle; he considered the new worlds out there, waiting to be discovered, strange planets and civilisations, and it was almost too much to comprehend that, when he died and was reborn, he too would venture out on that greatest diaspora of all.

He drove home slowly, tired after the exertions of the night. Only when he turned down the cart track, and saw the white Fiat parked outside the cottage, was he reminded of his daughter.

He told himself that he would make an effort today: he would not reprimand her for saying nothing about Barbara's illness, wouldn't even question her. God knows, he had never done anything in the past to earn her trust and affection. It was perfectly understandable that she had complied with her mother's last wishes.

Still, despite his resolve, he felt a slow fuse of anger burning within him as he climbed from the Range Rover and let himself into the house.

He moved to the kitchen to make himself a coffee, and as he was crossing the hall he noticed that Susanne's coat was missing from the stand, and likewise her boots from beneath it.

From the kitchen window he looked up at the broad sweep of the moorland, fleeced in brilliant snow, to the gold and silver laminated sunrise.

He made out Susanne's slim figure silhouetted against the brightness. She looked small and vulnerable, set against such vastness, and Lincoln felt something move within him, an emotion like sadness and regret, the realisation of squandered opportunity.

On impulse he fetched his coat, left the cottage and followed the trail of her deep footprints up the hillside to the crest of the rise.

She heard the crunch of his approach, turned and gave a wan half-smile. "Admiring the view," she whispered.

He stood beside her, staring down at the limitless expanse of the land, comprehensively white save for the lee sides of the drystone walls, the occasional distant farmhouse.

Years ago he had taken long walks with Susanne, enjoyed summer afternoons with her on the wild and undulating moorland. Then she had grown, metamorphosed into a teenager he had no hope of comprehending, a unique individual—no longer a malleable child—over whom he had no control. He had found himself, as she came more and more to resemble her mother and take Barbara's side in every argument, in a minority of one.

He had become increasingly embittered, over the years. Now he wanted to reach out to Susanne, make some gesture to show her that he cared, but found himself unable to even contemplate the overture of reconciliation.

In the distance, miles away on the far horizon, was the faerie structure of the Station, its tower flashing sunlight.

At last she said, "I'm sorry," so softly that he hardly heard.

His voice seemed too loud by comparison. "I understand," he said.

She shook her head. "I don't think you do." She paused. Tears filled her eyes, and he wondered why she was crying like this.

"Susanne..."

"But you *don't* understand."

"I do," he said gently. "Your mother didn't want me to know about her illness—she didn't want me around. Christ, I was a pain enough to her when she was perfectly well."

"It wasn't that," Susanne said in a small voice. "You see, she didn't want you to know that she'd been wrong."

"Wrong?" He stared at her, not comprehending. "Wrong about what?"

She took a breath, said, "Wrong about the implant," and tears escaped her eyes and tracked down her cheeks.

Lincoln felt something tighten within his chest, constrict his throat, making words difficult.

"What do you mean?" he asked at last.

"Faced with death, in the last weeks... it was too much. I... I persuaded her to think again. At last she realised she'd been wrong. A week before she died, she had the implant." Susanne looked away, not wanting, or not daring, to look upon his reaction to her duplicity.

He found it impossible to speak, much less order his thoughts, as the realisation coursed through him.

Good God. *Barbara*...

He felt then love and hate, desire and a flare of anger.

Susanne said, "She made me swear not to tell you. She hated you, towards the end."

"It was my fault," he said. "I was a bastard. I deserved everything. It's complex, Susanne, so bloody damned complex—loving someone and hating them at the same time, needing to be alone and yet needing what they can give."

A wind sprang up, lifting a tress of his daughter's hair. She fingered it back into place behind her ear. "I heard from her three months ago—a kind of CD thing delivered from my local Station. She told me that she'd been terribly cruel in not telling you. I... I meant to come up and tell you earlier, but I had no idea how you'd react. I kept putting it off. I came up yesterday because it was the last chance before she returns."

"When?" Lincoln asked, suddenly aware of the steady pounding of his heart.

"Today," Susanne said. She glanced at her watch. "At noon today—at this Station."

"This Station?" Lincoln said. "Of all the hundreds in Britain?" He shook his head, some unnameable emotion making words difficult. "What... what does she want?"

"To see you, of course. She wants to apologise. She told me she's learned a great many things up there, and one of them was compassion."

Oh, Christ, he thought.

"Susanne," he said, "I don't think I could face your mother right now."

She turned to him. "Please," she said, "please, this time, can't you make the effort—for me? What do you think it's been like, watching you two fight over the years?"

Lincoln baulked at the idea of meeting this resurrected Barbara, this reconstructed, *compassionate* creature. He wanted nothing of her pity.

"Look," Susanne said at last, "she's leaving soon, going to some star I can't even pronounce. She wants to say goodbye."

Lincoln looked towards the horizon, at the coruscating tower of the Station.

"We used to walk a lot round here when I was young," Susanne said. There was a note of desperation in her voice, a final appeal.

Lincoln looked at his watch. It was almost ten. They could easily make it to the Station by midday, if they set off now.

He wondered if he would have been able to face Barbara, had she intended to stay on Earth.

At last, Lincoln reached out and took his daughter's hand.

They walked down the hill, through the snow, towards the achingly beautiful tower of the Onward Station.

INTERLUDE

It was a freezing Tuesday evening and I was hurrying to the Fleece, anticipating the roaring fire and a pint or three of creamy Landlord ale, when I saw the muffled figure up ahead. It was a man, lagged in a greatcoat with a scarf bandaged around his ears. Only his eyes showed, as he leaned against the farm gate and stared over the snow-covered landscape at the bypass far below.

He turned when I approached, and I realised with surprise that it was Jeffrey Morrow. "Jeff," I said, "What the hell are you doing?"

Something about his posture, the way he was slumped against the gate, alarmed me, and when I drew close enough to look in his eyes I saw the unshed tears there.

In reply, he just turned to the bypass and pointed a gloved finger. "It happened there, Khalid. Two years ago tomorrow. That bend, right there."

I gripped his arm. "Jeff. Come on, I'll get you a pint."

"I was at home, doing some marking. I was expecting Caroline around six... Six came and went, and she didn't phone. I knew something was wrong, then. You see, she always phoned. I tried her mobile, of course. It was switched off. At seven, Khalid, I was about to phone the police. Then Richard came to the door and told me..."

A single tear trickled down his cheek, freezing before it reached his mouth. He dashed it off as if in denial, as if to leave it there would be an admission of weakness.

"And a month later, a sodding month later, Khalid, the Kéthani came..."

I gripped his arm even tighter and felt an incredible wave of compassion for my friend. "Come on, Jeff. It's freezing out here. Let's get inside. You need a drink."

He straightened up and took a deep breath, then looked at me and smiled. "I'm fine, Khalid. Yes. A pint. My round, okay?"

I smiled as we set off side by side. "I won't argue, Jeffrey."

The main bar of the Fleece greeted us with warmth and the hum of conversation. We settled ourselves around our usual table and Jeffrey got the pints in. The usual faces were there, warming themselves before the open fire: Richard Lincoln and Ben Knightly.

"No Zara tonight?" Richard asked.

"Ploughed under with work, " I said. "I told her I'd have a pint or two for her."

Jeffrey returned from the bar with a tray of Taylor's Landlord. He smiled at me. There was no sign of the emotion he had experienced minutes earlier.

At one point that evening, he said, "I've been having... I suppose you'd call it counselling... about what happened to Caroline."

Ben said, "Haven't the Kéthani set up... I don't know what you'd call them—clinics? Anyway, places you can go to talk about what's happened, how it affects you personally..." He stopped there. Ben, alone in our group, was not implanted, and he had never told us the reason why—but that's another story.

All across the world, stricken citizens remembered life before the Kéthani, grieving over loved ones who had died—died and gone to oblivion everlasting—while accepting the gift for themselves and suffering the consequences of renewed grief and guilt. I'd read about the psychiatric clinics set up to help us…

Richard Lincoln said, "Representatives of the Kéthani, humans recruited to do the administrative work of the aliens, have started counselling stations. The thing is, there are rumours."

I looked at him. "What do you mean?"

He shrugged. "Look, this is just hearsay. But I've heard that these counsellors… well, that they're actually representatives of the Kéthani race."

We stared at him. As a ferryman, his words on these matters carried a certain weight.

"You've heard that at the Station?" I asked.

"Unofficially, of course. Personally, I don't know what to think…"

Jeffrey said, with a distant look in his eyes, "To think of it, I might have been pouring out my woes to an extraterrestrial."

For the rest of the night, we chatted about the pros and cons of this idea.

The thought of the Kéthani amongst us…

Jeffrey said, "Whether I've been talking to a human or an alien," he smiled, "I know that it's done me some good. Some things just can't be handled alone."

I was to remember these words, a few weeks later, when Jeffrey suffered another tragic loss.

TWO
Onward Station

That winter was the coldest in living memory, and January saw a record fall of snow across the north of England. On the last Monday of the month I sat in the warmth of the staffroom and gazed out across the snow-sealed moorland, my mind completely blank. Miller, Head of Maths, dropped himself into the opposite seat, effectively blocking my view.

"Jeffrey," he said. "You take year thirteen for Film Studies, don't you?"

"For my sins."

"What do you make of the Hainault girl?"

"I was away when she started," I said. It had been mid-December, and I'd had other things on my mind.

"Oh, of course. Sorry. Well, you take them today, don't you?"

"Last period. Why?"

He had the annoying habit of tapping the implant at his temple with a nicotine-stained finger, producing an insistent, hollow beat.

"Just wondered what you'd make of her, that's all."

"Disruptive?"

"The Hainault girl?" He grunted a laugh. "Quite the contrary. Brilliant pupil. Educated privately in France before arriving here. She's wasted at this dump. It's just…"

"Yes?"

He hesitated. "You'll see when you take the class," he said, and stubbed out his cigarette.

I watched, puzzled, as he stood and shuffled from the room.

"Tomlinson, Wilkins—if you want to turn out for the school team on Wednesday, shut it now."

Silence from the usually logorrhoeic double act. I stared around the class, challenging.

"Thank you. Now, get into your study groups and switch on the screens. If you recall…" I glanced at my notes, "last week we were examining the final scenes of *Brighton Rock*. I want you to watch the last fifteen minutes, then we'll talk."

I glanced around the room. "Claudine Hainault?"

The new girl was sitting alone at the back of the class, already tapping into her computer. She looked up when I called her name, tossed a strand of hair from her eyes, and smiled.

She was blonde and slim, almost impossibly pretty. She appeared older than her eighteen years, something about her poise and confidence giving her a sophistication possessed by none of her classmates.

I moved to her desk and knelt. "Claudine, I'll run through what's happened so far, then leave you to it."

"It is okay, Mr. Morrow." She spoke precisely, with a slight accent. "I know the film."

Only then did I notice that she was not implanted.

I returned to my desk, sat down, and willed myself not to stare at the girl.

The lesson progressed. Once, when I sensed that she was not looking, I glanced over at Claudine Hainault. The skin of her right temple was smooth, without the square, raised outline of the implant device.

With five minutes to go before the bell, a boy looked up from the screen. He shook his head. "But Mr. Morrow... he *died*. And this was before... before the implants. How did people live without going mad?"

I felt a tightness in my throat. "It was only two years ago," I said. "You'll learn all about that in Cultural Studies."

The class went silent. They were all staring at Claudine Hainault. To her credit, she affected an interest in the screen before her.

Then the bell shattered the silence and all was forgotten in the mad scramble to be the first to quit the classroom.

At four I followed the school bus as it crawled along the gritted lane between snow-drifted hedges. I lived in a converted farmhouse five miles from the school, and Claudine Hainault, I discovered with a pang of some emotion I could not quite define, was my neighbour—our houses separated by the grim, slate-grey expanse of the reservoir.

The bus braked and the girl climbed down and walked along the track towards an isolated farmhouse, a tiny figure in a cold and inhospitable landscape. I watched her until she disappeared from sight, then I restarted the engine and drove home.

I pulled into the driveway minutes later, unlocked the front door and stepped into a freezing house. The framed photographs of Caroline glimmered, indiscernible, in the twilight. I turned on the lights and the heating, microwaved an instant meal and ate in the lounge while listening to the radio news. I washed it down with a bottle of good claret—but even the wine made me think of the Hainault girl.

For a long time I sat and stared out through the picture window. The Onward Station was situated only a mile away, a breathtaking crystalline tower, scintillating in the moonlight like a confection of spun ice. Tonight it illuminated the landscape and my lounge, a monument to the immortality of humankind, a tragic epitaph to all those who had suffered and died before its erection.

The following Friday at first break, Miller approached me in the staffroom. "So what do you make of the Hainault girl, Jeff?"

I shrugged. "She's very able," I said non-committally.

"I'm worried about her. She seems withdrawn... depressed. She doesn't mix, you know. She has no friends." He tapped the implant at his temple. "I was wondering... you're good at drawing the kids out. Have a word with her, would you? See if anything's troubling her."

He was too absorbed in relighting his cigarette to notice my stare. *Troubling her?* I wanted to ask; the poor girl isn't implanted—*what do you think is troubling her?*

I had spent the week doing my best not to think about Claudine Hainault, an effort that proved futile. I could not help but notice her every time I took year thirteen; how she always sat alone, absorbed in her work; how she never volunteered to answer questions, though I knew full well from the standard of her written work that she had the answers; how, from time to time, she would catch my eye and smile. Her smile, at these times, seemed at odds with her general air of sadness.

At lunchtime I was staring out of the staffroom window when I noticed a knot of kids gathered in the corner of the schoolyard. There were about six of them, confronting a single girl.

I rushed out and crossed the tarmac. The group, mainly girls, was taunting Claudine. She faced them, cursing in French.

"That's quite enough!" I called. "Okay, break it up." I sent the ringleaders off to visit the head-teacher and told the others to scarper.

"But we were just telling Claudine that she's going to die!" one of the girls said in parting.

When I turned to Claudine she had her back to me and was staring through the railings at the distant speck of the Onward Station. I wanted to touch her shoulder, but stopped myself.

"Are you alright?"

She nodded, not looking at me. Her long blonde hair fell to the small of her back, swept cleanly behind her ears. When she finally turned and smiled at me, her expression seemed carved from ice, imbued with fortitude.

That afternoon I remained at school an extra hour, catching up on some marking I had no desire to take home. It was dark when I set off, but at least I wasn't trapped behind the school bus, and the lanes were free of traffic. A couple of miles from school, my headlights picked out a quick, striding figure, silhouetted against the snow. I slowed down and braked, reached over and opened the passenger door.

She bent her knees and peered in at me.

"Claudine," I said. "What on earth are you doing walking home? Do you realise how far...?"

"Oh, Mr. Morrow," she said. "I missed the bus."

"Hop in. I'll take you home."

She climbed in and stared ahead, her small face red with cold, diadems of melting snow spangling her hair.

"Were you kept back?" I asked.

"I was using the bathroom."

I didn't believe her. She had missed the bus on purpose, to avoid her classmates.

We continued in silence for a while. I felt an almost desperate need to break the ice, establish contact and gain her confidence. I cleared my throat.

"What brought you to England?" I asked at last.

"My mother, she is English," she said, as if that were answer enough.

"Does your father work here?"

She shook her head minimally, staring straight ahead.

I concentrated on the road, steering around the icy bends. "Couldn't you have phoned your mother to come for you?" I said. "She does drive?" Private transport was a necessity this far out.

"My mother, she is an alcoholic, Mr. Morrow," she said with candour. "She doesn't do anything."

"Oh. I'm sorry." I felt myself colouring. "Look," I said, my mouth dry, "if you don't want to catch the bus in future, I'll drive you home, okay?"

She turned and smiled at me, a smile of complicity and gratitude.

I was aware of the pounding of my heart, as if I had taken the first irrevocable step towards founding a relationship I knew to be foolhardy but which I was powerless to prevent.

I looked forward to our short time together in the warmth of my car at the end of every school-day. I probed Claudine about her life in France, wanting to know, of course, why she was not implanted. But with an adroitness unusual in one so young, she turned around my questions and interrogated me. I found myself, more often than not, talking about my own past.

At one point I managed to steer the conversation away from me. "I've been impressed with the standard of your work," I said, aware that I sounded didactic. "Your grades are good. What do you plan to study at university?"

She wrinkled her nose. "Oh, I thought perhaps philosophy. I'm interested in Nietzsche and Cioran."

I glanced at her. "You are?"

She smiled. "Why not?" she replied. "They seem to have all the answers, I think."

"Do they?" I said, surprised. "I would have thought that a young girl like you…"

We came to a halt at the end of the track leading to her house, and the sudden silence was startling. She stared at me. I could see that she had half a mind to tell me not to be so patronising. Instead she shook her head.

"Life is awful, Mr. Morrow," she said. "It always has been. And it hasn't improved since *they* arrived. If anything, it has made things even worse."

Tentatively, I reached out and took her hand. I wondered for a second if I had misjudged the situation completely; if she would react with indignation and fright, or even report me.

"If there's anything I can do to help..." I said. Did she realise, in her teenage wisdom, that my words were just as much a cry for help as an offer of the same?

She smiled brightly, filling me with relief. "Thanks, Mr. Morrow. It's nice to be able to talk to someone." She climbed out and waved to me with a mittened hand before setting off down the farm-track.

That night I set out to get seriously drunk. I placed three bottles of claret on the coffee table before the fire and sat in the darkness and drank. I would be lying if I claimed that I was trying to banish the painful memories of Caroline that Claudine stirred in me. More truthfully, I wanted to banish the knowledge of the failure I had become through inaction and fear. A lonely man has the capacity for self-pity so much greater than his ability, or desire, to change the circumstances that brought about such self-pity in the first place.

I was drinking because I realised the futility of trying to seek solace and companionship from a mixed-up eighteen year-old schoolgirl.

I awoke late the following day, lost myself in a book for a couple of hours, and later that afternoon watched the live match on television. Leeds had a returnee playing up front, but after the year's lay-off he had yet to find his previous form, and the game ended in a dull nil-nil draw. At six, as a new snowfall created a pointillistic flurry in the darkness outside, I started on the half bottle of claret remaining from the night before.

I was contemplating another drunken evening when I heard a call from outside and seconds later a frenzied banging on the front door.

Claudine stood on the doorstep, wet, bedraggled, and frozen. She began as soon as I pulled open the door, "She has fallen and hit her head. The lines are down and I can't call the ambulance. We don't have a mobile."

"Slow down," I said, taking her hand and pulling her across the threshold. "Who's fallen?"

"My mother. She was drinking. She fell down the stairs. She is unconscious."

She was wearing a thin anorak, a short skirt, and incongruously bulky moon-boots. Her legs were bare and whipped red from the frozen wind.

"I've a mobile somewhere." I hurried into the lounge, dug through the cushions of the settee for the phone, and called an ambulance.

Claudine watched me, teeth chattering. With her hair plastered to her forehead, and her bare knees knocking, she looked about twelve years old.

I took her hand, hurried her from the house to my car. She sat in silence as I drove past the reservoir and turned down the track to her house.

She had left the front door wide open in her haste to summon help. I rushed inside. "In the lounge," Claudine said. "Through there."

The lounge was a split-level affair, with three steps leading from the higher level to a spacious area with a picture window overlooking the water. Claudine's mother sprawled across the floor, having tumbled and struck her head on the edge of a wrought-iron coffee table. She was a thin, tanned woman with bleached-blonde hair. In her unconscious features I saw the likeness of Claudine, thirty years on.

The reek of whisky, spilt from the glass she had been carrying, filled the room.

I rolled her onto her side and did my best to staunch the flow of blood from her forehead, noticing as I did so that she, unlike her daughter, was implanted.

The ambulance arrived fifteen minutes later. The paramedics examined Claudine's mother, then eased her onto a stretcher. I watched them load her into the back of the vehicle, my arm around Claudine. One of the medics asked Claudine if she wanted to accompany her mother in the ambulance.

"I'll take her in the car," I said before she had time to reply.

The ambulance backed up the track and raced, blue light flashing, down the lane into town. I made for the car.

Behind me, Claudine said, "I don't want to go."

"What?"

She stood, pathetic and frozen, in the snow. She shook her head. "I don't want to go to the hospital. I'll stay here."

"On your own?"

She gave an apathetic shrug.

"Look... there's a spare room at my place. You can stay there until your mother's released, okay?"

She stared at me through the falling snow. "Are you sure?"

"Go get some clothes and things. And lock the door. I'll be waiting here."

I climbed into the car and watched as the lights in the house went out one by one. Claudine appeared at the front door, carrying a holdall and fumbling with a key ring. She climbed into the passenger seat and I set off up the track, turned right and continued along the lane until we reached my place.

I showed Claudine to the bathroom, and while she showered and changed I prepared a simple pasta dish. I had experienced a rush of adrenalin while attending to her mother and waiting for the ambulance, and I realised that something of the anxiety was with me still. My hands were shaking as I set two places at the table. I went over and over what I would say during dinner.

I was wondering what was taking her so long when I heard a voice from the lounge. "This is really a beautiful place." There was a note of surprise in her voice, as if she thought that the domicile of a washed-up forty year-old teacher would prove to be an inhospitable dump.

I crossed the kitchen and stood in the doorway, watching her as she moved around the lounge. She was barefoot, dressed in flared jeans, which were back in fashion, and a white T-shirt that had either shrunk in the wash or was designed to reveal a strip of slim stomach.

She paused before the photographs of Caroline on the wall. She looked at me.

"My wife," I said.

She said, casually, "I didn't know you were married."

"I'm not," I said. "Any longer. She died in a car accident two years ago."

She winced, ever so slightly. "Before they came?" she asked.

"Just a month before," I said.

I joined her and stared at the photograph. Caroline smiled out at me. "She looked like a lovely person," Claudine said.

I nodded. "She was."

As if she feared that the subject might move us on to the reason why she was not implanted, Claudine drifted across the room to inspect the bookshelves.

I returned to the kitchen and served dinner.

We chatted as we ate, going over things we'd talked about before, school, local attractions, novels and films we admired.

"You can phone the hospital later," I said at one point. "I'll drive you over tomorrow if you like."

She shook her head, not meeting my gaze. "It doesn't matter. I'm not that bothered. She'll come back when she's better."

I paused. "What happened between you two?" I asked at last.

She smiled up at me. She was so pretty when she smiled; then again, she had a certain sullen *hauteur* that was equally as attractive when she deigned not to smile.

"Oh, we have never got on," she said. "I was always my father's favourite. I think she was jealous. They fought a lot—it might have been because of me. I don't know."

"Are they separated?"

Claudine looked at me with her oversized brown eyes. She shook her head. "You might have heard of him—Bertrand Hainault? He was a philosopher, one of those popular media intellectuals you don't have over here, I think."

I shook my head. "Sorry. Not up on philosophy."

"My father took his life last year," she said quietly. "He and mother were fighting constantly, but I think it was more than that... I don't know. It was all so confusing. I think it might have been a protest, too—a protest at what *they* were doing."

Something caught in my throat. "He wasn't implanted?"

"Oh, no. He was opposed to the whole process. He argued his position in televised debates and in a series of books, but of course no one took any notice."

Except you, I thought, beginning at last to understand the enigma that was Claudine Hainault.

She changed the subject, suddenly brightening. "I'll help you with the dishes, then can we watch a DVD?"

Later we sat on the settee, drank wine and watched a classic Truffaut. Claudine curled up beside me, whispering comments on the film to herself. She fell asleep leaning against me, and I watched the remainder of the movie accompanied by the sound of her breathing and the pleasant weight of her shampooed head against my shoulder.

Rather than wake her, at midnight I carefully lowered her to the cushions and covered her with a blanket. In the pulsing blue light from the TV, I sat for a while and watched her sleeping.

In the morning I was woken by the unfamiliar sound of someone moving about the house. Then the aroma of a cooked breakfast eddied up the stairs. I had a quick shower and joined Claudine in the kitchen. She was sliding fried eggs and bacon onto plates. The coffee percolator bubbled. She could hardly bring herself to meet my eyes, as if fearing that I might consider this rite of domesticity an unwelcome escalation of the intimacy we had shared the night before.

Over breakfast, I suggested that we go for a long walk across the moors. It was a dazzling winter's morning, the sky blue and the snow an unblemished mantle for as far as the eye could see.

I drove Claudine back to her house to change into walking boots and a thick coat. We left the car at my place and started along the bright, metalled lane. Later we struck off across the moors, following a bridleway that would take us, eventually, to the escarpment overlooking the valley, the reservoir and a scattering of farmhouses.

Somewhere along the way her mittened hand found my cold fingers and squeezed. She was smiling as I exaggerated the misfortunes of the school football team, which I organised. I would never have thought that I could be so cheered by something as simple as her smile.

Claudine looked up, ahead, and her expression changed. I followed the line of her gaze and saw the sparkling pinnacle of the Onward Station projecting above the crest of the hill.

Her mouth was open in wonder. "God... This is the closest I've been to it. I never realised it was so beautiful."

She pulled me along, up the incline. As we climbed, more and more of the Station was revealed in the valley below. At last we stood on the lip of the escarpment, staring down. My attention was divided equally between the alien edifice and Claudine. She gazed down with wide eyes, her nose and cheeks red with the cold, her thoughts unguessable.

It was not so much the architecture of the Station that struck the onlooker, as the material from which it was made. The Station—identical to the thousands of others situated around the world—rose from the snow-covered ground like a cathedral constructed from glass, climbing to a spire that coruscated in the bright winter sunlight.

As we watched, a pale beam—weakened by the daylight—fell through the sky towards the Station, bringing a cargo of returnees back home.

I put my arm around Claudine's shoulders. She said, "The very fact of the Station is like the idea it promotes."

I made some interrogational noise.

"Beguiling," she said. "It is like some Christmas bauble that dazzles children, I think."

"For ages humankind has dreamed of becoming immortal," I said, staring at her. "Thanks to the Kéthani..."

She laid her head against my shoulder, almost sadly. "But," she said, gesturing in a bid to articulate her objection. "But don't you see, Jeff, that it really doesn't *matter*? Whether we live seventy years, or seven thousand—it's still the same old futile repetition of day-to-day existence."

Anger slow-burned within me. "Futile? What about our ability to learn, to experience, to discover new and wondrous things out there?"

She was shaking her head. "It is merely repetition, Jeff—a going through the motions. We've done all these things on Earth, and so what? Are we any happier as a race?"

"But I think we are," I said. "Now that the spectre of death is banished—" I stopped myself.

Claudine just shook her head.

Into the silence, I said, "I honestly don't understand why you aren't implanted."

She looked up at me, so young and vulnerable. "I'll tell you why, Jeff. I've read the philosophical works of the Kéthani and the other races out there—or at least read summaries of them. My father and I... in the early days we went through them all. And do you know what?"

I shook my head, suddenly weary. "No. What? Tell me."

She smiled up at me, but her eyes were terrified. "They understand everything, and have come to the realisation that the universe and life in it is just one vast mechanistic carousel. It doesn't *mean* anything."

"Claudine, Claudine. Of course it doesn't. But we must live with that. There never were any answers, unless you were religious. But you must make your own meaning. We have so much time ahead of us to live for the day, to love—"

She laughed. "Do you know something? I don't believe in love, very much. I saw my parents' relationship deteriorate, turn to hate. I can feel it," she looked at me, "but I can't believe that it will last."

"It changes," I began, then fell silent.

She squeezed my hand. "Let's go home," she said. "I'm hungry. I'll prepare lunch, okay?"

We set off down the hillside, passing the Station. A ferryman driving a Range Rover pulled into the car park, delivering another dead citizen. Tonight, the darkness would pulse with white light as the bodies were transported to the Kéthani starship in orbit high above.

After lunch that afternoon we lounged before the roaring fire and talked. When the words ran out it seemed entirely natural, an action of no consequence to the outside world, but important only to ourselves, that we should seek each other with touches and kisses, coming in silence to some mutual understanding of our needs.

That night, as we lay close in bed, we stared through the window at the constellations. The higher magnitude stars burned in the freezing night sky, while beyond them the sweep of the Milky Way was a hazy opaline blur.

"Hard to believe there are hundreds of thousands of humans out there," she said, close to sleep.

I thought of the new planets, the strange civilisations, that I would some day encounter—and I experienced a sudden surge of panic at the fact that Claudine was willingly forgoing the opportunity to do the same. I wanted to shake her in my sudden rage and demand that she underwent the implantation process.

It was a long while before I slept.

The following day an ambulance brought Claudine's mother home, and I drove her over to the farmhouse. She kissed me before climbing from the car, suddenly solemn. "See you at school," she said, and was gone.

Suddenly, the routine of school seemed no longer a burden. I could put up with the recalcitrance of ignorant teenagers and the petty infighting between members of staff. The sight of Claudine in the schoolyard, or seated at her desk, filled me with rapture. Her swift, knowing smile during lessons was an injection of some effervescent and exhilarating drug.

After school I would pull off the road, up some lonely and abandoned cart track, and we would make love in the little time we had before I dropped her off at home. She told me that she would spend the following weekend at my place—she'd tell her mother that she was staying with a friend—and the days until then seemed never-ending.

On the Friday, just as I was about to leave the building, Miller buttonholed me in the corridor. "What the hell's going on, Jeffrey?"

My heart hammered. "What do you mean?"

"Between you and the Hainault girl, for Chrissake. It's glaringly obvious. They way you look at each other. You're a changed man."

"There's nothing *going on*," I began.

"Look," he said. He paused, as if unsure whether to go on. "Someone saw you with her yesterday—in your car on the moors." He shook his head. "This can't continue, Jeffrey. It's got to stop—"

I didn't let him finish. I pushed past him and hurried out and across to the car park. Claudine was standing by the bus stop on the main road, and as I let her in she gave me a dazzling smile that banished the threat of Miller's words and the consequences if I ignored them.

On the Saturday night we lay in bed and talked, and I told her what Miller had said to me.

"It doesn't matter," she whispered in return. "They can't do anything. We'll be more careful in future, I think. Now forget about bloody Miller."

We went for a long walk on the Sunday afternoon, avoiding the Station as if mutually fearing the argument it might provoke. Claudine was quiet, withdrawn, as if Miller's words were troubling her.

She wept quietly after we made love that night. I held her. "Claudine—I've decided to resign, quit school. I'll find a job in town. There's plenty of work about. You can move in here, okay?" I babbled on, a love-struck teenager promising the world.

She was silent for a time. At last she whispered, "It wouldn't work."

Something turned in my stomach. "What?" I said.

Kéthani

"Love doesn't last," she said quietly. "It would be fine at first, and then..."

At that moment the room was washed in a blinding beam of light as the dead were beamed from the Onward Station to the Kéthani starship. I was appalled at what I saw in the sudden illumination. Claudine's eyes were raw from crying, her face distorted in a silent grimace of anguish.

"Like everything," she sobbed, "it would corrupt."

I held her to me, unable to respond, unable to find the words that might convince her otherwise.

At last I said, "But I can still see you?" in desperation.

She smiled through her tears and nodded; touched, perhaps, by my naïve hope.

In the early hours she slipped from the bed and kissed me softly on the cheek, before dressing and hurrying home.

Next day at school I desperately sought from Claudine some sign that I had not spoiled our relationship with my demands of the night before. In class, she smiled at me with forced brightness, a smile that disguised a freight of sadness and regret.

We had agreed that I would no longer drive her home, to scotch the rumours flying about the school, and that evening her absence during the journey was painful. I looked ahead to the weekend when we would be together, and the days seemed endless.

On Tuesday Claudine was not at school. I assumed that she had slept in and missed the bus.

During the first period I saw the police car pull into the school grounds, but thought nothing of it.

Fifteen minutes later the secretary tapped on the classroom door and entered. I should have guessed that something was amiss by the way she averted her gaze as she handed me the note—but what seems obvious in retrospect is never apparent at the time. The Head had called a staff meeting at first break.

57

When the bell went I crossed the hall to the staffroom. I recall very well what I was thinking as I pushed open the door. My thoughts were full of Claudine, of course. The next time I saw her in private, I would plead with her to live with me once I had resigned my post at the school; to her claim that love never lasted I would counter that at least we should give it a try.

The room was crowded with ashen-faced teachers, and a dread silence hung in the air. Miller made his way to my side, his expression stricken.

"What?" I began, my stomach turning.

The Head cleared his throat and began to speak, and I heard only fragments of what he said.

"Claudine Hainault... Tragic accident... Her body was found in the reservoir..."

I felt myself removed from proceedings, abstracted through shock from the terrible reality unfolding around me.

Teachers began to weep. Miller gripped my arm, guided me to the nearest chair.

"The police think she slipped... went under... It was so cold she was paralysed and couldn't get out."

I wanted to scream at the injustice, but all I could do was weep.

"Such a terrible tragedy..." The head paused and stared around the room. "As you know, she refused to be implanted."

I made myself attend the funeral.

I drank half a bottle of whisky before leaving the house, and somehow survived the service. It brought back memories of another funeral, just over two years ago. Claudine was buried in the Oxenworth village churchyard, just three graves along from Caroline, beneath a stand of cherry trees which would flower with the coming of spring.

A television crew was present, along with reporters and photographers from the national press. So few people really died these days, and and at the same time censorious, unable to condone my love for Claudine's being young and attractive made the story all the more sensational. Relatives flew in from France. Her mother was an inconsolable wreck. I tried to ignore Miller and his begrudging words of commiseration; his attitude was consoling and at the same time censorious, unable to condone my love for Claudine.

I watched the coffin being lowered into the black maw of the grave, finding it impossible to accept that Claudine was within it. Then I slipped away and walked to the reservoir. A pathetic spread of wind-blown flowers, left by pupils and stricken locals, marked the spot on the bank where she had fallen.

That night I wrote a letter of resignation to the school authorities. It would be impossible to go back to the place where I had first met Claudine, to the classrooms haunted by her absence. I considered selling the house and moving from the area. Claudine still seemed present, as if she might at any second emerge from another room, smiling at me.

That night I drank myself unconscious.

In the morning, waking from oblivion to face the terrible fact of her death anew, I dressed and made my way downstairs and saw the letter lying on the doormat.

I read my name and address in Claudine's precise schoolgirl hand.

With trembling fingers I ripped open the envelope and pulled out the single folded sheet.

I sank to the floor, disbelieving. I moaned with grief intensified, made more painful than I ever imagined possible.

I read her note a second time, then again and again, as if by doing so I might change what she had written, and what it meant.

My Dear Jeff, she began, and continued with words I would never forget, *I'm sorry. I'm so very sorry—but I can't go on. I love you, but it can't last, nothing lasts. I've known joy with you and perhaps it is best to end that joy at its height, rather than have it spoil.*

And I wanted to cry, *no!* I wanted the chance to vent my anger and tell her how very wrong she was.

You know I don't want immortality. Life is so very hard to bear at the best of times. To face life everlasting... I feel at peace when I contemplate what I'm going to do—please try to understand.
She was going to leave her house—*had* left her house—and walk to the reservoir, and give herself to the frigid embrace of the water... How could I understand *that*? How could I understand an act so irrational, an act of violence provoked by fears and pressures known only to herself? How often since have I wished I had known her better, had been a lover capable of being there when she needed me most?

I can hear you asking how could I do this to you. But, Jeff, you will survive—you have all the time in the universe. In a hundred years I will be a fleeting memory, and in a thousand...
They say that time heals all wounds.
And she had finished, *With all my love, Claudine.*

I spend a long time contemplating the events of the past, going over my time with Claudine and wondering where I went wrong. I blame myself, of course, for not persuading her to undergo the implantation process; for not being able to show her how much I loved her. I blame myself for not giving her reason enough to go on living.

I am haunted by her words, *You have all the time in the universe...*

At night I sit in the darkened lounge and stare out at the rearing edifice of the Onward Station, marvelling at its beauty and contemplating the terrible gift of the Kéthani.

INTERLUDE

Five years had passed since the coming of the Kéthani, and after the first two years of turbulent change—two years of rioting and protest around the world—order had been restored. Hundreds of thousands of returnees came back to Earth, and though they had been subtly changed by the experience of dying and being reborn, none were the zombies or monsters that the Jeremiahs and prophets of doom had forecast.

Slowly, things began to change on Earth. So slowly, so gradually, that it was almost unnoticeable.

That evening—after a long day on the ward where I worked as an implant surgeon—I was enjoying a pint in the Fleece when Jeffrey Morrow said, "I don't know if you've noticed, but over the past few years things have got better on Earth, don't you think?"

We looked at him. Jeffrey had greyed in the years since I first got to know him, which wasn't at all surprising, considering what he'd undergone. He was a quiet man, much given to introspection and thoughtful silences. After Claudine's death, we had persuaded him to remain in the area, to stay on at the school in Bradley, to face the terrors of his past and not to run away.

Considering what Jeffrey had experienced in recent years, this latest pronouncement was a little unexpected, to say the least.

"Got better?" I said. "How do you mean?"

"I came across an academic paper the other day," Jeffrey said, "by some high-up in the UN." He was on his fourth pint, and his eyes were distant. "It was a breakdown of the incidences of conflict around the world. And do you know something—since the coming of the Kéthani, cases of armed conflict have decreased globally by almost seventy per cent."

Richard Lincoln nodded. "I've heard the same. Not only that, violence in general has fallen around the world. For instance, murder rates are in decline."

That led us to speculate about the reasons for this gradual amelioration of the human condition...

Richard said, "Well, you know what I think—"

Zara laughed and hummed the spooky opening bars of the *Twilight Zone*. "The aliens are amongst us, Richard?"

He pointed at her, mock stern. "Oh, ye of little faith. The Kéthani have powers which we can't even dream of, so it stands to reason that they'd come among us to help us along the way."

I thought about that, then said, "I'm not saying you're wrong, Richard. But I think that that might be unnecessary."

Richard downed half his pint. "Go on."

"Think about it. We die. They transport us to their homeworld. They bring us back to life. And we come back—changed. I've heard it said that people come back... I don't know... *better*, improved."

Richard objected, "But that doesn't disprove my thesis, Khalid!"

"No—what I'm saying is that if things have got better on Earth, if there is less conflict, then maybe it's caused less by the activity of the Kéthani down here and more by what the Kéthani did to us up there. Maybe it's the mentality of the returnees that is changing things." It was a nice thought—and how was I to know that, in a few years time, I would have first-hand knowledge of just how the resurrection process could render change in an individual?

Zara said, "Whichever it is, we have the Kéthani to thank."

For the first time that night, Ben spoke up. He was the only one among our group who was not implanted, and we had never questioned him as to why this was so. Some things, we thought, were just too personal to share.

"Perhaps," he said, "the people who come back, the returnees, aren't really the people they were. Perhaps," and he smiled as he said this, making me think that he wasn't entirely serious, "perhaps they're aliens in disguise?"

We laughed and argued amongst ourselves for a while, and then Ben said, "I've often wondered about the bastards who die and come back. I mean, the really evil people. Killers, despots, psychotics. They come back changed—I know that. But who's to say that they are who they once were?"

Zara smiled. "You don't really think...?"

Ben laughed. "Of course not. I've read enough to realise that the maniacs are somehow mentally altered up there, for the better. Made humane." He shook his head, his gaze lost in the leaping flames of the open fire. "It makes you wonder, though, exactly what does happen..."

Talk drifted onto other subjects.

Ben remained quiet for the rest of the evening. It was only later—a year later, to be precise—that he told us the reason why he was not implanted, and why he wondered at the process of transformation undergone by the returnees.

THREE

The Kēthani Inheritance

That winter, two events occurred that changed my life. My father died and, for the first time in thirty years, I fell in love. I suppose the irony is that, but for my father's illness, I would never have met Elisabeth Carstairs.

He was sitting in the lounge of the Sunny View nursing home that afternoon, chocked upright in his wheelchair with the aid of cushions, drooling and staring at me with blank eyes. The room reeked of vomit with an astringent overlay of bleach.

"Who're you, then?"

I sighed. I was accustomed to the mind-numbing, repetitive charade. "Ben," I said. "Benjamin. Your son."

Sometimes it worked, and I would see the dull light of recognition in his rheumy eyes. Today, however, he remained blank.

"Who're you, then? What do you want?"

"I'm Ben, your son. I've come to visit you."

I looked around the room, at the other patients, or "guests" as the nurses called them; they all gazed into space, seeing not the future, but the past.

"Who're you, then?"

Where was the strong man I had hated for so long? Such was his decrepitude that I could not bring myself to hate him any longer; I only wished that he would die.

I had wished him dead so many times in the past. Now it came to me that he was having his revenge: he was protracting his life purely to spite me.

In Holland, I thought, where a euthanasia law had been passed years ago, the old bastard would be long dead.

I stood and moved to the window. The late afternoon view was far from sunny. Snow covered the hills to the far horizon, above which the sky was mauve with the promise of evening.

I was overcome with a sudden and soul-destroying depression.

"What's this?" my father said.

I focused on his apparition reflected in the plate-glass window. His thin hand had strayed to his implant.

"What's this, then?"

I returned to him and sat down. I would go through this one more time—for perhaps the hundredth time in a year—and then say goodbye and leave.

His frail fingers tapped the implant at his temple, creating a hollow drumming sound.

"It's your implant," I said.

"What's it doing there?"

It sat beneath the papery skin of his temple, raised and rectangular, the approximate size of a matchbox.

"The medics put it there. Most people have them now. When you die, it will bring you back to life."

His eyes stared at me, then through me, uncomprehendingly.

I stood. "I'm going now. I'll pop in next week…" It would be more like next month, but, in his shattered mind, all days were one now.

As I strode quickly from the room I heard him say, "Who're you, then?"

An infant-faced Filipino nurse beamed at me as I passed reception. "Would you like a cup of tea, Mr. Knightly?"

I usually refused, wanting only to be out of the place, but that day something made me accept the offer.

Serendipity. Had I left Sunny View then, I might never have met Elisabeth. The thought often fills me with panic.

"Coffee, if that's okay? I'll be in here." I indicated a room designated as the library, though stocked only with Mills and Boon paperbacks, *Reader's Digest* magazines and large-print Western novels.

I scanned the chipboard bookcases for a real book, then gave up. I sat down in a big, comfortable armchair and stared out at the snow. A minute later the coffee arrived. The nurse intuited that I wished to be left alone.

I drank the coffee and gazed at my reflection in the glass: I felt like a patient, or rather a "guest".

I think I was weeping when I heard, "It is depressing, isn't it?"

The voice shocked me. She was standing behind my chair, gripping a steaming mug and smiling.

I dashed away a tear, overcome with irritation at the interruption.

She sat down in the chair next to mine. I guessed she was about my age—around thirty—though I learned later that she was thirty-five. She was broad and short with dark hair bobbed, like brackets, around a pleasant, homely face.

"I know what it's like. My mother's a guest here. She's senile." She had a direct way of speaking that I found refreshing.

"My father has Alzheimer's," I said. "He's been in here for the past year."

She rolled her eyes. "God! The repetition! I sometimes just want to strangle her. I suppose I shouldn't be saying that, should I? The thing is, we were so close. I love her dearly."

I found myself saying, "In time, when she dies and returns, her memory will—" I stopped, alarmed by something in her expression.

It was as if I had slapped her.

Her smile persisted, but it was a brave one now in the face of adversity. She shook her head. "She isn't implanted. She refused."

"Is she religious?"

"No," she said, "just stubborn. And fearful. She doesn't trust the Kéthani."

"I'm sorry."

She shook her head, as if to dismiss the matter. "I'm Elisabeth, by the way. Elisabeth Carstairs."

She reached out a hand, and, a little surprised at the forthright gesture, I took it. I never even thought to tell her my own name.

She kept hold of my hand, turning it over like an expert palm-reader. Only later did I come to realise that she was as lonely as I was: the difference being, of course, that Elisabeth had hope, something I had given up long ago.

"Don't tell me," she said, examining my weather-raw fingers. "You're a farmer, right?"

I smiled. "Wrong. I build and repair dry-stone walls."

She laughed. "Well, I was almost there, wasn't I? You do work outdoors, with your hands."

"What do you do?" I would never have asked normally, but something in her manner put me at ease. She did not threaten.

"I teach English. The comprehensive over at Bradley."

"Then you must know Jeff Morrow. He's a friend."

"You know Jeff? What a small world."

"We meet in the Fleece every Tuesday." I shrugged. "Creatures of habit."

She glanced at her watch and pulled a face. "I really should be getting off. It's been nice talking..." She paused, looking quizzical.

I was slow on the uptake, then realised. "Ben," I said. "Ben Knightly. Look, I'm driving into the village. I can give you a lift if you—"

She jangled car keys. "Thanks anyway."

I stood to leave, nodding awkwardly, and for the first time she could see the left-hand side of my face.

She stared, something stricken in her eyes, at where my implant should have been.

I hurried from the nursing home and into the raw winter wind, climbed into my battered ten-year-old Sherpa van and drove away at speed.

The following evening, just as I was about to set off to the Fleece, the phone rang. I almost ignored it, but it might have been a prospective customer, and I was going through a lean spell.

"Hello, Ben Knightly? Elisabeth here, Elisabeth Carstairs. We met yesterday."

"Of course, yes." My heart was thudding, my mouth dry: the usual reactions of an inexperienced teenager to being phoned by a girl.

"The thing is, I have a wall that needs fixing. A couple of cows barged through it the other day. I don't suppose...?"

"Always looking for work," I said, experiencing a curious mixture of relief and disappointment. "I could come round tomorrow, or whenever's convenient."

"Sometime tomorrow afternoon?" She gave me her address.

"I'll be there between two and three," I said, thanked her and rang off.

That night, in the main bar of the Fleece, I was on my third pint of Landlord before I broached the subject of Elisabeth Carstairs.

Jeff Morrow was a small, thoughtful man who shared my interest in football and books. An accretion of sadness showed in his eyes. He had lost two people close to him, over the years; one had been his wife, killed in a car accident before the coming of the Kéthani; the other a lover who had refused to be implanted.

He had never once commented on the fact that I was not implanted, and I respected him for this.

The other members of our party were Richard Lincoln and Khalid and Zara Azzam.

"I met a woman called Elisabeth Carstairs yesterday," I said. "She teaches at your school, Jeff."

"Ah, Liz. Lovely woman. Good teacher. The kids love her. One of those naturals."

That might have been the end of that conversation, but I went on, "Is she married?"

He looked up. "Liz? God no."

Richard traced the outline of his implant with an absent fore-finger. "Why 'God, no', Jeff? She isn't—?"

"No, nothing like that." He shrugged, uncomfortable. Jeff is a tactful man. He said to me, "She's been looking after her mother for the past ten years. As long as I've known her, she's never had a boyfriend."

Khalid winked at me. "You're in there, Ben." Zara dug her husband in the ribs with a sharp elbow.

I swore at him. Jeff said, "Where did you meet?"

I told him, and conversation moved on to the health of my father (on his third stroke, demented, but still hanging on), and then by some process of convoluted logic to Leeds United's prospects this Saturday.

Another thing I liked about the Tuesday night group was that they never made digs about the fact that I'd never had a girlfriend since they'd known me—since my early twenties, if the truth be known.

I'd long ago reconciled myself to a life mending dry-stone walls, reading the classics, and sharing numerous pints with friends at the Fleece.

And I'd never told anyone that I blamed my father: some wounds are too repulsive to reveal.

It was midnight by the time I made my way up the hill and across the moors to the cottage. I recall stopping once to gaze at the Onward Station, towering beside the reservoir a mile away. It coruscated in the light of the full moon like a stalagmite of ice.

As I stared, a beam of energy, blindingly white, arced through the night sky towards the orbiting Kéthani starship, and the sight, I must admit, frightened me.

"I tried repairing it myself," Elisabeth said, "but as you can see I went a bit wrong."

"It's like a jigsaw puzzle," I said. "It's just a matter of finding the right piece and fitting it in."

It was one of those rare, brilliantly sunny November days. There was no wind, and the snow reflected the sunlight with a twenty-four carat dazzle.

I dropped the last stone into place, rocked it home, and then stood back and admired the repair.

"Thirty minutes," Elisabeth said. "You make it look so easy."

I smiled. "Matter of fact, I built this wall originally, twelve years ago."

"You've been in the business that long?"

We chatted. Elisabeth wore snow boots and a padded parka with a fur-lined hood that that made her look like an Eskimo. She stamped her feet. "Look, it's bitter out here. Would you like a coffee?"

"Love one."

Her house was a converted barn on the edge of the moor, on the opposite side of the village to my father's cottage where I lived. Inside it was luxurious: deep pile carpets, a lot of low beams and brass. The spacious kitchen was heated by an Aga.

I stood on the doormat, conscious of my boots.

"Just wipe them and come on in," she said, laughing. "I'm not house-proud, unlike my mother."

I sat at the kitchen table and glanced through the door to a room full of books. I pointed. "Like reading?"

"I love books," she said, handing me a big mug of real coffee. "I teach English, and the miracle is that it hasn't put me off reading. You?" She leaned against the Aga, holding her cup in both hands.

We talked about books for a while, and I think she was surprised at my knowledge.

Once I saw her glance at my left temple, where the implant should have been. I felt that she wanted to comment, to question me, but couldn't find a polite way of going about it.

The more I looked at her, and the more we talked, the more I realised that I found her attractive. She was short, and a little overweight, and her hair was greying, but her smile filled me with joy.

Romantic and inexperienced as I was, I extrapolated fantasies from this meeting, mapped the future.

"How often do you visit your mother?" I asked, to fill a conversational lull.

"Four times a week. Monday, Wednesday, Friday, and Sunday."

I hesitated. "How long has she been ill?"

She blew. "Oh... when has she ever been well! She had her first stroke around ten years ago, not long after we moved here. I've been working part-time and looking after her ever since. She's averaged about... oh, a stroke every three years since. The doctors say it's a miracle she's still with us."

She hesitated, then said, "Then the Kéthani came, and offered us the implants... and I thought all my prayers had been answered."

I avoided her eyes.

Elisabeth stared into her cup. "She was a very intelligent woman, a member of the old Labour Party before the Blair sellout. She knew her mind. She wanted nothing to do with afterlife, as she called it."

"She was suspicious of the Kéthani?"

"A little, I suppose. Weren't we all, in the beginning? But it was more than that. I think she foresaw humanity becoming complacent, apathetic with this life when the stars beckoned."

"Some people would say she was right."

A silence developed. She stared at me. "Is that the reason you...?"

There were as many reasons for not having the implant, I was sure, as there were individuals who had decided to go without. Religious, philosophical, moral... I gave Elisabeth a version of the truth.

Not looking her in the eye, but staring into my empty cup, I said, "I decided not to have the implant, at first, because I was suspicious. I thought I'd wait; see how it went with everyone who did have it. A few years passed... It seemed fine. The returnees came back fitter, healthier, younger. Those that went among the stars later, they recounted their experiences. It was as the Kéthani said. We had nothing to fear." I looked up quickly to see how she was taking it.

She was squinting at me. She shrugged. "So, why didn't you...?"

"By that time," I said, "I'd come to realise something. Living on the edge of death, staring it in the face, made life all the more worth living. I'd be alone, on some outlying farm somewhere, and I'd be at one with the elements... and, I don't know, I came to appreciate being alive."

Bullshit, I thought. It was the line I'd used many a time in the past, and though it contained an element of truth, it was not the real reason.

Elisabeth was intelligent; I think she saw through my words, realised that I was hiding something, and I must admit that I felt guilty about lying to her.

I thanked her for the coffee and made to leave.

"How much for the work?" she said, gesturing through the window at the repaired wall.

I hesitated. I almost asked her if she would like to go for a meal, but stopped myself just in time. I told myself that it would seem crass, as if she had to accept the invitation in payment. In fact, the coward in me shied away from escalating the terms of our relationship.

"Call it fifty," I said.

She gave me a fifty euro note and I hurried from the house, part of me feeling that I had escaped, while another part was cursing my fear and inadequacy.

I found myself, after that, visiting my father on Monday, Wednesday, Friday, and Sunday. Sunny View seemed a suitably neutral venue in which to meet and talk to Elisabeth Carstairs.

I even found myself looking forward to the visits.

About two weeks after I repaired her wall, I was sitting in the lounge with my father. It was four o'clock and we were alone. Around four-thirty Elisabeth would emerge from her mother's room and we would have coffee in the library.

I was especially nervous today because I'd decided to ask her if she would like to come for a meal the following day, a Thursday. I'd heard about a good Indonesian place in Bradley.

I'd come to realise that I liked Elisabeth Carstairs for who she was, her essential character, rather than for what she might represent: a woman willing to show me friendship, affection, and maybe even more.

We had a lot in common, shared a love of books, films, and even a similar sense of humour. Moreover, I saw in Elisabeth a fundamental human decency, perhaps born out of hardship, that I detected in few other people.

"Who're you, then?"

"Ben," I said absently, my thoughts miles away.

He regarded me for about a minute, then said, "You always were bloody useless!"

I stared at him. He had moments of lucidity: for a second, he was back to his old self, but his comment failed to hurt. I'd heard it often before, when the sentiment had been backed by an ability to be brutal.

"Dry-stone walls!" he spat.

"Is that any worse than being a bus driver?" I said.

"Useless young…" he began, and dribbled off.

I leaned forward. "Why don't you go to hell!" I said, and hurried from the room, shaking.

I sat in the library, staring out at the snow and shaking. I wondered if, when my father was resurrected and returned, he would have any memory of the insult.

"Hello, Ben. Nice to see you."

She was wearing her chunky primrose parka and, beneath it, a jet-black cashmere jumper.

"You don't look too good," she said, sitting down and sipping her coffee.

I shrugged. "I'm fine."

"Some days he's worse than others, right? Don't tell me. Mum's having one of her bad days today."

More than anything I wanted to tell her that I cared nothing for my father, but resisted the urge for fear of appearing cruel.

We chatted about the books we were reading at the moment; she had loaned me Chesterton's *Tales of the Long Bow*, and I enthused about his prose.

Later, my coffee drunk, I twisted the cup awkwardly and avoided her eyes. "Elisabeth, I was wondering… There's a nice Indonesian restaurant in Bradley. At least, I've heard it's good. I was wondering—"

She came to my rescue. "I'd love to go," she said, smiling at me. "Name a day."

"How about tomorrow? And I'll pay."

"Well, I'll get the next one, then. How's that sound? And I'll drive tomorrow, if you like."

I nodded. "Deal," I said, grinning like an idiot.

I was working on a high sheepfold all the following day, and I was in good spirits. I couldn't stop thinking about Elisabeth, elation mixed equally with trepidation. From time to time I'd stop work for a coffee from my Thermos, sit on the wall I was building, and stare down at the vast, cold expanse of the reservoir, and the Onward Station beside it.

Ferrymen came and went, delivering the dead. I saw Richard Lincoln's Range Rover pull up and watched as he unloaded a container and trolleyed it across the car park and into the Station.

At five I made my way home, showered and changed and waited nervously for Elisabeth to pick me up.

The meal was a success. In fact, contrary to my fears, the entire night was wonderful. We began talking from the time she collected me and never stopped.

The restaurant was quiet, the service excellent, and the food even better. We ate and chattered, and it seemed to me that I had known this friendly, fascinating woman all my life.

I could not see in Elisabeth the lonely, loveless woman that Jeff had described; she seemed comfortable and at ease. I feared I would appear gauche and naïve to her, but she gave no indication of thinking so. Perhaps the fact was that we complemented each other: two lonely people who had, by some arbitrary accident, overcome the odds and discovered each other.

Elisabeth drove us back through a fierce snowstorm and stopped outside her converted barn. She turned to me in the darkness. "You'll come in for a coffee, Ben?"

I nodded, my mouth dry. "Love to," I said.

We sat on the sofa and drank coffee and talked, and the free and easy atmosphere carried over from the restaurant. It was one o'clock by the time I looked into my empty mug and said, "Well, it's getting on. I'd better be…"

She reached out and touched my hand with her fingers. "Ben, stay the night, please."

"Well… If it's okay with you."

"Christ," she said, "what do you think?" And, before I knew it, she was in my arms.

I had often wondered what the first time would be like, tried to envisage the embarrassment of trying to do something that I had never done before. The simple fact was that, when we undressed each other beside the bed, and came together, flesh to soft, warm flesh, it seemed entirely natural, and accomplished with mutual trust and affection—and I realised that I'd never really had anything to fear, after all.

I was awoken in the night by a bright flash of light. I rolled over and held Elisabeth to me, cupped her bottom in my pelvis and slipped a hand across her belly.

The window overlooked the valley, the reservoir, and the Station.

High-energy pulse beams lanced into the stratosphere.

"You 'wake?" she murmured.

"Mmm," I said.

"Isn't it beautiful?" she whispered. Shafts of dazzling white light bisected the sable sky, but more beautiful to me was holding a warm, naked woman in my arms.

"Mmm," I said.

"I always keep the curtains open," she whispered. "I like to watch the lights when I can't sleep. They fill me with hope."

I watched the lights with her. Hard to conceive that every beam of energy contained the newly dead of Earth.

"Elisabeth," I said.

"Hmm?"

"Have you read much about the Kéthani?"

She turned to face me, her breasts against my chest. She stroked my face and lightly kissed my lips. "Just about everything there is to read."

"Something I don't understand," I said. "Millions of humans die, and are taken away and resurrected. Then they have a choice. They can either come back and resume their lives on Earth, or they can do the bidding of the Kéthani, and go among the stars, as explorers, ambassadors..."

"Or they can come to Earth, live a while, and then leave for the stars."

I hesitated, then said, "And we trust them?"

"We do now. At first, millions of us didn't. Then the reports started to come back from those who had died, been resurrected, and gone among the stars. And the stories they told, the accounts of a wondrous and teeming universe..."

I nodded. "I've seen the documentaries. But—"

"What?"

"What about all those humans who are..." I tried to think of a diplomatic phrase, "let's say, unsuited even for life on Earth. I mean, thugs and murderers, dictators, psychopaths."

My father...

"Hard to imagine Pol Pot or Bush acting as an ambassador for an enlightened alien race," I said.

She stroked my hair. "They're changed in the resurrection process, Ben. They come back... *different*. Altered. Still themselves, but with compassion, humanity." She laughed, suddenly.

"What?" I asked.

"The irony of it," she said. "That it takes an alien race to invest some people with humanity!"

She reached down and took me in her fingers, and guided me into her. We made love, again, bathed in the blinding light of the dead as they ascended to heaven.

Our parents died the following week, within days of each other.

On the Monday afternoon I was working on the third wall of the sheepfold when my mobile rang. "Hello, Ben Knightly here," I called above the biting wind.

"Mr. Knightly? This is Maria, from Sunny View. Your father was taken into Bradley General at noon today. The doctor I spoke to thinks that it might only be a matter of hours."

I nodded, momentarily at a loss for words.

"Mr. Knightly?"

"Thanks. Thank you. I'll be there as soon..." I drifted off.

"Very well, Mr. Knightly. I'm so sorry."

I thanked her again and cut the connection.

I continued the section of wall I was working on, placing the stones with slow deliberation, ensuring a solid finish.

I had anticipated this day for months: it would mark the start of a temporary freedom, an immediate release from the routine of visiting the nursing home. For six months I would be free of the thought of my father on Earth, demanding my attention.

It was perhaps two hours after receiving the call that I drove into the car park at Bradley General and made my way along what seemed like miles of corridors to the acute coronary ward. My father had suffered a massive heart attack. He was unconscious when I arrived, never came round, and died an hour later.

The sudden lack of a regular bleep on his cardiogram brought me from my reverie: I was staring through the window at the snow-covered fields, thinking that a few walls out there could do with attention.

Then the bleep changed to a continuous note, and I looked at my father. He appeared as he had before death: grey, open-mouthed, and utterly lifeless.

A ferryman came for him, asked me if I would be attending the farewell ceremony—I declined—and took him away in a box they called a container, not a coffin. I signed all the necessary papers, and then made my way to Elisabeth's house.

That night, after making love, we lay in bed and watched the first energy beam leave the Onward Station at ten o'clock.

"You're quiet," she said.

I hesitated. "My father died today," I told her.

She fumbled for the light, then turned and stared at me. "Why on earth didn't you say something earlier?"

I reached out for her and pulled her to me. "I didn't think it mattered," I said.

She stroked my hair. I had never told her of my relationship with my father, always managed to steer the subject away from our acrimony.

She kissed my forehead. "He'll be back in six months," she soothed. "Renewed, younger, full of life."

How could I tell her that that was what I feared most?

The following Thursday I finished work at five and drove to Elisabeth's. The day after my father died, she had asked me to move in with her. I felt that our relationship had graduated to another level; I often had to pause and remind myself how fortunate I was.

We settled into a routine of domestic bliss. We took turns at cooking each other meals more daring and spectacular than we would have prepared for ourselves alone.

I was expecting, that night, to be assailed by the aroma of cooking meat when I entered the kitchen, but instead detected only the cloying fragrance of air freshener. The light was off.

Then I made out Elisabeth. She was sitting on the floor by the far wall, the receiver of the phone cradled redundantly in her lap.

I saw her look up when I came in, and I reached instinctively for the light.

Her face, revealed, was a tear-stained mask of anguish.

My stomach flipped, for I knew immediately.

"Oh, Ben," she said, reaching for me. "That was the nursing home. Mum died an hour ago."

I was across the room and kneeling and hugging her to me, and for the first time I experienced another person's heartfelt grief.

The funeral was a quiet affair at the village church—the first one there, the vicar told me, for years. A reporter from a national newspaper was snooping, wanting Elisabeth's story. I told him where to go in no uncertain terms. There was less I could do to deter the interest of a camera crew from the BBC, who kept their distance but whose very presence was a reminder, if any were required, of the tragedy of Mary Carstairs's death.

Every day we walked up to the overgrown churchyard, and Elisabeth left flowers at the grave, and wept. If anything, my love for her increased over the next few weeks; I had never before felt needed, and to have someone rely on me, and tell me so, made me realise in return how much I needed Elisabeth.

One evening I was cooking on the Aga when she came up behind me very quietly, slipped her arms around my body and laid her head between my shoulder blades. "God, Ben. I would have gone mad without you. You're the best thing that's ever happened to me."

I turned and held her. "Love you," I whispered.

I introduced her to the Tuesday night crowd, where she became an instant hit. I think my friends were both surprised and delighted that I'd found someone at last.

We were in the Fleece, three months after my father's death, when Richard Lincoln entered the main bar and handed me a package. "Special delivery from the Onward Station."

I turned the silver envelope over. It was small and square, the size of the DVD I knew it would contain. My name and address were printed on both sides, below the double star logo of the Kéthani.

"A message from your father, Ben," Richard said.

I could not bring myself to enjoy the rest of the evening: the package was burning a hole in my pocket.

When we returned home, Elisabeth said, "Well?"

I laughed, wrestling her towards the bedroom. "Well, what?"

"Aren't you going to play it?"

"Don't think I'll bother."

She stared at me. "Aren't you curious?"

"Not particularly."

"Well, if you aren't, I am. Come on, we'll play it on the TV in the bedroom."

I lay in bed, staring out at the rearing obelisk of the Station, while she inserted the DVD into the player. Then, with Elisabeth in my arms, I turned and stared at the screen.

My father had decided against a visual recording: only his broad, bluff Yorkshire voice came through, while the screen remained blank. I was relieved that I would be spared the sight of his new, rejuvenated image.

"Ben, Reg here. I'm well. We still haven't seen the Kéthani—can you believe that? I thought I'd catch a glimpse of them at least." He paused. The fact that his voice issued from a star twenty light years away struck me as faintly ridiculous. "I'm in a group with about a dozen other resurrectees, all from different countries. We're learning a lot. I still haven't decided what I'm doing yet, when I get back..." He hesitated, then signed off. His murmured farewell was followed by a profound silence.

And that was it, as casual as a postcard from Blackpool; except, I told myself, there was something almost human in his tone, an absence of hostility that I had not heard in years.

But that did nothing to help lessen my dread of the bastard's return.

Whenever Elisabeth broached the topic of implants, however tenuously, I managed to change the subject. In retrospect, I was ashamed at how my reluctance to undergo the implantation process affected her; at the time, selfishly, I could apprehend only my own frail emotions.

More than once, late at night, when we had made love, she would whisper that she loved me more than anything in the world, and that she did not want to lose me.

A week before my father was due to return, she could no longer keep her fears to herself.

She was sitting at the kitchen table when I returned from work. She indicated the letter I'd received that morning from the Onward Station. My father was returning in seven days; he had asked to meet me at a reception room in the Station.

It was the meeting I had dreaded for so long.

She was quiet over dinner, and finally I said, "Elisabeth, what is it?" I imagined that the news of my father's return had reminded her again of her mother's irrevocable demise.

She was silent for a while.

"Please don't avoid the issue this time," she said at last. "Don't change the subject or walk off." Her hand was shaking as she pushed away her plate.

"What is it?" I asked, stupidly.

She looked up, pinned me with her gaze.

"I can't stand the thought of losing you, Ben." It was almost a whisper.

"Don't worry, you won't. I have no intention of leaving you."

"Don't be so crass!" she said, and her words hurt. "You know what I mean." She shook her head, trying to fight back the tears. "Sometimes I experience a kind of panic. I'm on my own, driving to school or whatever, and I imagine you've been in some accident... and you can't begin to understand how that makes me feel. I don't want to lose you."

"Elisabeth—"

She hit the table with the ham of her right hand. "What if you're in a car crash, or drop dead of a heart attack? What then? You'll be dead, Ben! Dead forever. There'll be no bringing you back." She was crying now. "And I'll be without you *forever*."

"What are the chances of that?" I began.

"Don't be so bloody rational!" she cried. "Don't you see? If you were implanted, then I wouldn't worry. I could love you without the constant, terrible fear of losing you." She paused, and then went on, "And this thing about not being implanted making you appreciate being alive all the more." She shook her head. "I don't believe it for a minute. You're hiding something. You fear the Kéthani or something."

"It's not that."

"Ben, listen to me." Her tone was imploring. "When you're implanted, it invests you with a wonderful feeling of liberation. Of freedom. You really do appreciate being alive all the more. We've been afraid of death for so long, and then the Kéthani came along and gave us the greatest gift, and you spurn it."

We sat in silence for what seemed an age, Elisabeth staring at me, while I stared at the tabletop.

She could have said, then, "If you love me, Ben, you'll have the implant," and I wouldn't have blamed her. But she wasn't the type of person who used the tactics of blackmail to achieve their desires.

At last I said, "My father made my life a misery, Elisabeth. My mother died when I was ten, and from then on he dominated me.

He'd hit me occasionally, but far worse was the psychological torture. You have no idea what it's like to be totally dominated, to have your every move watched, your every word criticised, whatever you do put down and made worthless." I stopped. The silence stretched. I was aware of a pain in my chest, a hollowness. "I've never been able to work out why he was like that. All I know is that, until his illness, I lived in fear of him."

I stopped again, staring at my big, clumsy hands on the tabletop. "His criticism, his snide comments, his lack of love... they made me feel worthless and inadequate. I hated being alive. I'd often fantasise about killing myself, but the only thing that stopped me was the thought that my father would gain some sick satisfaction from my death." I looked up, tears in my eyes, and stared at Elisabeth. "He turned me into a lonely, socially inept wreck. I found it hard to make friends, and the thought of talking to women..."

She reached out, gently, and touched my hand.

I shook my head. "Ten years ago he had his first stroke, and I had to look after him. The bastard had me just where he wanted me, and he made my life even worse. I dreamed of the day he'd die, freeing me..."

"And then the Kéthani came, with their damned gift, and he was implanted, and the thought of my father living forever..." I took a long, deep breath. "I wasn't implanted, Elisabeth, because I wanted to die. As simple as that. I hated being alive, and I was too weak and inadequate to leave and start a life of my own."

"But now?" she asked, squeezing my fingers.

"But now," I said, "he's coming back next week."

We went to bed, and held each other in silence as the white light streaked into the air above the Onward Station.

And Elisabeth whispered, "Don't be afraid any longer, Ben. You have me, now."

* * *

I left the van in the car park and approached the Station. I had never seen it at such close quarters before, and I had to crane my neck in order to see its sparkling summit, five hundred metres overhead.

I felt as cold as the surrounding landscape, my heart frozen. I wanted to get the meeting over as soon as possible, find out what he intended to do.

I passed the letter to a blue-uniformed woman at a reception desk, and another woman led me down a long white corridor. A cold, sourceless light pervaded the place, chilling me even further.

With the fixed smile of an air-hostess, the woman ushered me into a small, white room, furnished with two sofas, and told me that my father would be along in five minutes.

I sat down. Then I stood up quickly and paced the room.

I almost panicked, recalling the sound of his voice, his silent, condemnatory expression. I was sweating, and felt a tightness in my chest.

A door at the far side of the room slid open and a figure in a sky blue overall walked through.

All I could do was stand and stare.

It was a version of my father I recalled from my teenage years. He looked about forty, no longer grey and bent, but strong and upright, with a full head of dark hair.

For so long, in my mind's eye, I had retained an image of my father in his sixties, and had vented my hatred on that persona. Now he was the man who had blighted my early years, and I was the young boy again, abject and fearful.

He stepped forward, and I managed to stand my ground, though inside I was cowering.

He nodded and held out a hand. "Ben," he said.

And the sound of his voice was enough. I had a sudden memory, a vivid flash of an incident from my youth not long after my mother's death: he had discovered me in my bedroom, crying over the faded photograph of her I kept beside my bed. He had stared at me in bitter silence for what seemed like an age, and then, with his big, clumsy hands, he had unbuckled his belt and pulled it from his waist. His first, back-handed strike had laid me out across the bed, and then he had set about me with the belt, laying into me with blows that burned red-hot in time to his words, "You're a man, now, Ben, and men do not cry!"

His beatings had become regular after that; he would find the slightest excuse in my behaviour to use his belt. Later it occurred to me that my beatings were a catharsis that allowed him to vent his own, perverted grief.

But, now, when he stepped forward and held out his hand, I could take no more. I had intended to confront my father, ask him what he intended, and perhaps even tell him that I did not want him to return. Instead, I fled.

I pushed my way from the room and ran down the corridor. I was no longer a man, but the boy who had escaped the house and sprinted onto the moors all those years ago.

I left the Onward Station and stopped in my tracks, as if frozen by the ice-cold night.

I heard a voice. "Ben…" The bastard had followed me.

Without looking round, I hurried over to the van. I fumbled with the keys, my desire to find out his intentions forgotten in the craven need to get away.

"Ben, we need to talk."

Summoning my courage, I turned and stared at him. In the half-light of the stars, he seemed less threatening.

"What do you want?"

"We need to talk, about the future."

"The future?" I said. "Wasn't the past bad enough? If you think you can come back, start again where you left off, spoil the life I've made since you died…" I was amazed that I had managed to say it. I was shaking with rage and fear.

"Ben," my father said. "My own father was no angel, but that's no excuse."

"What do you want?" I cried.

He stared at me, his dark eyes penetrating. "What do *you* want, Ben? I have a place aboard a starship heading for Lyra, if I wish to take it. I'll be back in ten years. Or I can stay here. What do you want me to do...?"

He left the question hanging, and the silence stretched. I stared at him as the cold night invaded my bones. The choice was mine; he was giving me, for the first time in my life, a say in my destiny. It was so unlike my father that I wondered, briefly, if in fact the Kéthani *had* managed to instil in him some small measure of humanity.

"Go," I found myself saying at last, "and in ten years, when you return, maybe then..."

He stared at me for what seemed like ages, but I would not look away, and finally he nodded. "Very well, Ben. I'll do that. I'll go, and in ten years..."

He looked up, at the stars, and then lowered his eyes to me for the last time. "Goodbye, Ben."

He held out his hand, and after a moment's hesitation I took it.

Then he turned and walked back into the Station, and as I watched him go I felt an incredible weight lift from my shoulders, a burden that had punished me for years.

I looked up into the night sky, and found myself crying.

At last I opened the door of the van, climbed inside, and sat for a long time, considering the future.

Much later I looked at my watch and saw that it was seven o'clock. I started the engine, left the car park and drove slowly from the Onward Station. I didn't head for home, but took the road over the moors to Bradley.

* * *

It was nine by the time I arrived at the Fleece.

I had phoned Elisabeth and told her to meet me there, saying that I had a surprise for her. I'd also phoned Jeff Morrow, Richard Lincoln, and the Azzams, to join in the celebration. They sat at a table across the room, smiling to themselves.

Elisabeth entered the bar, and my heart leapt.

She hurried over and sat down opposite me, looking concerned and saying, "How did it go with...?"

I reached across the table and took her hand. "I love you," I said.

She stared at me, tears silvering her eyes. Her lips said my name, but silently.

Then she moved her hand from mine, reached up and, with gentle fingers, traced the outline of the implant at my temple.

INTERLUDE

I renounced my religion soon after my eighteenth birthday and was a committed atheist when the Kéthani came. When I met Zara Zaman she still believed, though she practised a liberal form of Islam which had come about after the East-West troubles in the early part of the century. The coming of the Kéthani sorely tested her faith, as she watched the hard line taken by the imams of Pakistan and Saudi Arabia. Over the years, as a belief in God became untenable with the fact of the Kéthani, I saw her faith erode, to be replaced by a ferocious intellectual quest to understand everything possible about our extraterrestrial benefactors.

That particular Tuesday evening, she reminded me that she wouldn't be coming to the Fleece tonight: her study group was meeting in Bradley and she was giving a presentation.

I tried to hide my irritation, but failed.

She stared at me across the lounge. "I told you, Khal, last week."

"So from now on Tuesday nights at the Fleece are out?"

"For me, yes. No one's stopping you from going."

"You'll be missed. Zara. You could at least come once a month, say."

She shook her head. "I don't think you understand how important this is to me, Khal." She paused, then said, "Or do you resent my doing this? Learning, bettering myself?"

"Of course not!" I said, a little too quickly. I wondered, deep down, if this was the source of my unease: she was learning more and more about areas of Kéthani study which I should have found interesting—especially considering my line of work—but which in my apathy I didn't. Also, she would be meeting other people, other men, and I must admit that this rankled. In retrospect, I admit to being shallow and jealous.

"Khal, you ought to come along."

And miss the company of my friends, I thought. The idea didn't appeal.

She went on, "I'm giving a talk on how the changes have affected international relations. Did you know, for instance, that incidences of espionage have almost ceased since the Kéthani came? And wars—the world is enjoying a period of global peace for the first time in recorded history. Khal, we're studying the reasons for this. It's truly fascinating."

"Well, you can fill me in when you come up with all the answers."

She pulled on her coat. "You cynical bastard!" was her parting shot as she hurried from the house.

I just stood and watched her go, feeling sick.

Something had happened to our relationship over the years. Our mutual passion, our love, had tempered, changed into something that was hard to define, still harder to name. It would be clichéd to say that we had drifted apart, no longer tethered by the tie of mutual interests; our conversations these days centred on day-to-day platitudes. We never discussed real issues. This, I had to admit, was fine by me. I was happy. But Zara, I knew, wanted more. It sickened me to look ahead to the time when she realised that I was no longer the man she had loved, all those years ago.

I found my coat and made my way to the Fleece.

Ben and Elisabeth were already ensconced in the main bar, and were halfway down their first pints. Richard Lincoln was carrying more drinks from the bar, assisted by the new addition to the Tuesday night group. Dan Chester was a ferryman up at the Station, and we'd got to know him soon after his arrival in Oxenworth that summer.

He was a small, dark, thin-faced handsome man in his late thirties. He was divorced and shared the custody of his daughter Lucy with his ex-wife. He'd spoken briefly about his relationship with her—she was a devout Catholic, and considered the Kéthani the minions of Satan.

As we settled ourselves around the table, Richard pulled a copy of today's *Guardian* from the pocket of his tweed jacket and slapped it on the table. It was folded to a page reporting the Pope's recent and unexpected volte-face on the issue of contraception.

"Seen that, Dan?" he asked.

Dan scanned the report. He grunted. "Tell me when the Vatican changes its mind on the Kéthani," he said.

Dan's daughter Lucy was eight years old, and she was not implanted. To say that she was the mainstay of Dan's life would be an understatement. He was devoted to her. He was also, for reasons that were obvious, paranoid about her health and safety.

We chatted for an hour about the medievalism of the Catholic Church.

Dan was quiet. He was going through a difficult period with his wife and Lucy, which I found out about in the most dramatic fashion a few weeks later.

He was a reasonable man caught up in a wholly unreasonable situation.

FOUR

Thursday's Child

I crested the hill, pulled the Range Rover into the side of the lane and stared through the windscreen. There was something about the freezing February landscape, with the westering sun laying a gold leaf patina over the snow-covered farmland in the valley bottom, that struck me as even more beautiful than the same scene in summer.

I took a deep breath and worked to control my anger. It was always the same when I collected Lucy from Marianne. I had to stop somewhere and calm myself.

I was on call for the next hour, but calculated that the chances of being summoned during that time were slight. Marianne would object to my early arrival, but Lucy would be eager to get away. I told myself that I arrived early on these occasions so that I'd have an extra hour with my daughter, but I wondered if, subconsciously, I did it on purpose to spite Marianne.

I started the engine and cruised down the hill. Three minutes later I entered the village of Hockton and pulled up outside a row of cottages, each one quaintly bonneted with a thick mantle of snow.

A light glowed behind the mullioned window of Marianne's front room. Lucy would be watching a DVD of her latest favourite film.

I pressed the horn twice, my signal to Lucy that I was here, and climbed out.

Lucy had hauled the door open before I reached the gate, and only the fact that she was in her stockinged feet prevented her rushing out to meet me.

She was a beautiful skinny kid, eight years old, with a pale elfin face and long black hair. My heart always kicked at the sight of her, after an absence of days.

She seemed a little subdued today: usually she would launch herself into my arms. I stepped inside and picked her up, her long legs around my waist, and kissed her nose, lips, neck in an exaggerated pantomime of affection which made her giggle.

"Love you," I said. "Bag packed?"

"Mmm."

"Where's your mum?"

"I think in the kitchen."

"Get your bag and put some shoes on. I'll just pop through and tell her I'm here."

She skipped into the front room and I moved towards the kitchen, a psychosomatic pain starting in my gut.

Marianne was peeling carrots at the draining board, her back to me. "You're early again, Daniel," she said without turning. She knew I disliked the long form of my name.

I leaned against the jamb of the door. "I was in the area, working."

She turned quickly, knife in her hand. "You mean to say you have a body with you?"

She was a small, pretty woman, an adult version of Lucy. In the early days of our separation, alternating with the anger, I had experienced a soul-destroying sorrow that all the love I'd felt for this woman had turned to hate.

I should have seen what might have happened before we married, extrapolated from her beliefs—but at the time my love for her had allowed no doubt.

Lately she had taken to wearing a big wooden crucifix around her neck. Her left temple was not implanted and neither, thanks to her, was Lucy's.

"Not all my work involves collection," I said. "What time should I bring her back on Thursday?"

"I'm working till five." She turned and resumed her peeling.

I pushed myself away from the door and moved to the lounge. Lucy was sitting on the floor, forcing her feet into a pair of trainers. I picked up her bag and she ran into the kitchen for a goodbye kiss. Marianne, the bitch, didn't even come to the door to wave her off.

I led Lucy to the Range Rover and fastened her into the middle section of the back seat. When I started collecting her, a year ago, she had said that she wanted to sit in the front, next to me. "But why can't I?" she had wailed.

How could I begin to explain my paranoia? "Because it's safer in case of accidents," I'd told her.

I reversed into the drive, then set off along the road back to Oxenworth, ten miles away over the moors.

"Enjoying your holidays?" I asked.

"Bit boring."

I glanced at her in the rear-view mirror. "You okay?"

She hesitated. "Feeling a bit rough," she said, and to illustrate pantomimed a hacking cough into her right fist.

"Did mum take you to the doctor's?"

I saw her nod.

"And?" I asked.

"He gave me some pills."

"Pills?" I said. "What did he say was wrong?"

She looked away, through the window. "I don't know."

"Do you have the pills with you?" Perhaps I'd be able to determine her ailment from the medication.

She shook her head. "Mummy said I didn't need them."

I decided to ring Marianne when we got back, find out what was going on. Or was this yet another manifestation of my paranoia?

We drove on in silence for a while. Cresting the snow-covered moorland, we passed the glittering obelisk of the Onward Station. It never failed to provoke a feeling of awe in me—and I saw the Station every working day. Quite apart from what it represented, it was perhaps aesthetically the most beautiful object I had ever seen.

I wondered if it was the sight of it that prompted Lucy to say, "Daddy, the girls at school have been making fun of me."

I glanced at her in the rear-view mirror. "Why's that?"

"It's because I'm not implanted. They say I'll die."

I shook my head, wondering how to respond. "They're just being silly," I said.

"But if I have an accident," she began.

"Don't worry," I said, marvelling at the fact that she was only eight years old, and yet had worked out the consequences of not being implanted. "You won't have an accident."

Then she asked, "Why aren't I implanted?"

It was the first time she had ever mentioned the fact, and it was a while before I replied. "Because mum doesn't want you to be," I said.

"But *why* doesn't she?"

"I think you'd better ask her that yourself," I said, and left it at that. I changed the subject. "How about a meal at the Fleece when we get back? Would you like that?"

"Mmm," she said, without her usual enthusiasm for the idea, and fell silent.

* * *

We were a couple of miles from home when the onboard mobile rang. I cursed.

"Dan Chester here," I said, hoping the collection would be nearby.

"Dan." It was Masters, the Controller at the Station. "I've just had a call from someone over in Bradley. This is most irregular. They've reported a death."

I slowed down, the better to concentrate. "I don't understand. Was the subject implanted?"

"Apparently so."

"Then why didn't it register with you?"

"Exactly what I was wondering. That's why I want you to investigate. I'm sending a team from the Station straight away, but I thought that as you're in the area..."

I sighed. "Okay. Where is it?"

Masters relayed the address.

"Right. I'll be in touch when I've found out what's going on." I cut the connection.

Bradley was only a mile or two out of my way. I could be there in ten minutes, sort out the problem in the same time, and be at the Fleece with a pint within the half hour.

I glanced back at Lucy. She was asleep, her head nodding with the motion of the Rover.

The Grange, Bradley Lower Road, turned out to be a Georgian house tucked away in a dense copse a mile down a treacherous, rutted track. The Range Rover negotiated the potholes with ease, rocking back and forth like a fairground ride.

Only when the foursquare manse came into view, surrounded by denuded elm and sycamore, did I remember hearing that the Grange had been bought at a knockdown price a few years ago by some kind of New Age eco-community.

A great painted rainbow decorated the façade of the building, together with a collection of smiley faces, peace symbols and anarchist logos.

A motley group of men and women in their thirties had gathered on the steps of the front door, evidently awaiting my arrival. They wore dungarees and oversized cardigans and sweaters; many of them sported dreadlocks.

Lucy was still sleeping. I locked the Rover and hurried over to the waiting group, a briefcase containing release forms and death certificates tucked under my arm.

A stout woman with a positive comet's tail of blonde dreads greeted me. I was pleased to see that she was implanted—as were, so far as a brief glance could tell me, most of the other men and women standing behind her. Some radical groups I'd heard of were opposed to the intervention of the Kéthani, and openly hostile to their representatives.

"Dan Chester," I said. "I'm the ferryman from the Station."

"Dan, I'm Marsha," the woman said. "Welcome to New Haven. I'll show you to…"

The press parted, and Marsha escorted me across a garishly painted hallway and down a corridor.

Marsha was saying, "Sanjay was against the resurrection process, Dan. We were surprised when he decided to be implanted, a couple of weeks ago." She paused outside a door, pushed it open and stood back. I stepped over the threshold and stopped in my tracks.

Sanjay lay on a mattress in the corner of the room. He had opened the vein of his left arm all the way from the wrist to the crook of his elbow. Blood had spurted up the far wall, across the window, and soaked into the mattress around the body.

"Billy found him about thirty minutes ago," Marsha was explaining. "We knew Sanjay was depressed, but we never thought…"

I took in the scene, and knew immediately that there was something not quite right about the corpse. By now the nanomechs released by the implant should have been effecting repairs on the

wound. The body should have the relaxed appearance of someone asleep, not the stone-cold aspect of a corpse.

I hurried over, knelt, and placed my fingertips to the implant
beneath the skin of the young man's left temple.

The implant should have emitted a definite vibration, similar to
the contented purring of a cat. I felt nothing.

I glanced over my shoulder; Marsha and half a dozen others
were watching him from the door. "If I could be left alone for a
minute or two…" I said.

They retreated, closing the door behind them.

I pulled out my mobile and got through to Masters at the
Station.

"Dan here," I said. "I'm with the subject. You're not going to
believe this—he's implanted, but he's dead."

"That's impossible."

"Perhaps… I don't know. I've never heard of a malfunction
before. But there's always a first time."

"No way," Masters said. "They can't go wrong."

"Well, it looks as though this one has." I paused. "What the
hell should I do?"

"The team should be with you any minute. I've called the police
in. They'll take over once they arrive."

I cut the connection, moved to the window, and stared out,
touching my own implant. I avoided another glance at the corpse,
but I knew I would see the man's agonised expression for a long
time to come. He had been implanted, and had taken his own life,
fully expecting to be resurrected…

Five minutes later I watched another Range Rover draw up
beside mine, followed by a police car. Four Station officials, led
by Richard Lincoln, hurried across the snow-covered drive and
up the steps, two constables in their wake.

A minute later Richard appeared at the door, along with the
officials and the police officers.

"What the hell's going on, Dan?" Richard said.

"I wish I knew." I indicated the corpse and went through my findings. The other officials recorded my statement and took video footage of the room.

Richard questioned Marsha and a few of the others, while the police called for forensic back-up.

I followed Richard outside and climbed into the Rover. Lucy was still asleep.

Richard tramped through the snow and I wound down the window. "We'll take the body back to the Station when the police have finished," he said, "try to find out what happened with the implant."

I looked beyond him, to the posse of communards on the steps of the Grange, silent and watchful.

"Has anyone told them?"

Richard shook his head. "I'll come back and explain the situation when we've found out exactly what happened. See you later, Dan."

I fired the engine and headed up the track. The Fleece beckoned. I considered a rich pint of Taylor's Landlord and a hot meal, and tried to forget about what I'd seen back at the Grange.

The Fleece was one of those horse-brass and beams establishments that had resisted the tide of modernisation sweeping the country. Norman, the landlord, had the twin assets of a good publican: friendliness and the ability to keep a good pint. The food wasn't bad, either.

It was seven o'clock by the time we settled ourselves in the main bar, a little too early for the regular Tuesday night crowd. I ordered myself a pint of Landlord and steak and kidney pie with roast potatoes, and for Lucy a fresh orange juice and veggie burger with salad.

The food arrived. Lucy was far from her lively self tonight; she was tired and hardly talked, answered my questions with monosyllabic replies and pushed her food around the plate with a distinct lack of interest.

I put my arm around her shoulders and pulled her towards me. "Home and an early night for you, m'girl."

"Can I watch TV for a bit before I go to bed? *Please.*"

"Okay, seeing as there's no school in the morning."

I was about to suggest we leave when Khalid pushed through the door, a swirl of snow entering with him, and signalled across to me. He mimed downing a pint and pointed at my empty glass. I relented and gave him the thumbs up.

No doubt Lucy would tell Marianne that I'd kept her at the pub way past her bedtime, and I wouldn't hear the last of it the next time I picked her up. Marianne thought alcohol the tipple of the devil, and all who drank it damned.

Khalid ferried two pints from the bar and sat down across the table from me.

"Hi, sleepy-head," he said to Lucy. Her eyelids were fighting a losing battle against sleep.

"Just the man," Khalid said to me. "I hoped you'd be here."

"It's Tuesday night," I said. "What's wrong?"

"The implanted suicide you visited today," he said.

I considered him over my pint. "Masters contacted you?"

Khalid nodded. "They brought the body into the hospital and I inspected the implant."

I voiced what I'd been dreading since discovering the dead man. "It malfunctioned?" I asked, hard though that was to believe.

"Malfunctioned?" Khalid shook his head and accounted for the top two inches of his pint. He sighed with satisfaction. "I'd say that was well nigh impossible."

"So...?"

"This is only the second case I've come across, but I've heard rumours that they're more widespread than we first believed."

He took another mouthful.

"What," I said, unable to stop myself smiling, "is more wide-spread?"

"This is between you and me, okay? Don't tell Masters I said anything. Your people at the Station have yet to come out with an official statement." He saw that I was about to jump in with the obvious question, and raised a hand. "Okay, okay…" He leaned forward, a little melodramatically—only Old Wilf was at the bar, and he was stone deaf. "Some cowboys have started pirating fake implants."

I lowered my pint and stared at him. "Why on earth…?" I began.

"It was only a matter of time," Khalid said. "Think about it. There are thousands of people out there who refuse for whatever reasons to be implanted…" his eyes flickered, almost impercepti-bly, towards Lucy. "They're… what… one in a few hundred thousand? A minority, anyway. And like any minority, they occasionally suffer victimisation. Wouldn't it be easier, they reckon, if they could have something that looks like, but wasn't, an implant? They'd blend in, become one of the crowd. They would no longer stand out."

"It makes a kind of sense," I said. "And so some enterprising back-street surgeon has started offering the service?"

"Doesn't have to be a surgeon. Anyone with a little medical knowledge can perform the operation. A quick slit, insert some-thing the same shape as an implant, and seal the wound with synthiflesh. Thirty minutes later you're back out on the street."

I thought through the implications. "But if these people don't inform friends, loved ones?"

He was nodding. "Exactly. Like today. Sanjay's friends thought he was implanted and fully expected him to be resurrected."

"Christ," I said. "The whole thing's tragic."

"And there are thousands of people going around out there with these fake, useless implants. Masters said something about a law to make them illegal. He's talking to a few politicians tomorrow."

Lucy had stretched out on the seat next to me and was snoring away. Had she been awake and bored, guilt might have driven me homeward. As it was, I owed Khalid a pint, and at that very second Ben Knightly and Elisabeth Carstairs dashed in from the snowstorm that was evidently raging outside. I was off work for a couple of days, and I could treat myself to a lie-in in the morning.

I pointed to Khalid's empty glass. "Another?"

"You've twisted my arm."

I bought another round. Ben and Elisabeth joined us and we stopped talking shop.

It was another hour, and two more pints, before conscience got the better of me. I refused all offers of more beer, eased the still sleeping Lucy into my arms, and carried her from the bar and along the street.

The cold had awoken her by the time I pushed through the front door. I carried her to her room, where she changed into her pyjamas. Five minutes later she was snuggling into my lap before the fire and we were watching a DVD of a French mime act, which apparently was the latest craze in kids' entertainment.

She was asleep ten minutes later, and I turned down the sound and switched over to a news programme. Half awake myself, and cradling my daughter in my arms, I allowed a succession of images to wash over me and considered how lucky I was.

So I might have married the last religious zealot in West Yorkshire, but from that match made in Hell had issued Lucy Katia Chester. And to think that, back in my twenties, I'd vowed never to have children. I sometimes shudder to think of the joy I would have missed had I remained faithful to my bachelor principles.

A newscaster was reporting anti-Kéthani riots in Islamabad, but by then I was fading fast.

I took Lucy to Bolton Abbey the following day. I bundled her up in her chunky pink parka, bobble hat, and mittens against the biting cold, and we walked through the trees along the riverbank. Down below, the river was frozen for the first time in living memory, its usually quicksilver torrent paused in shattered slabs of grey and silver. Later we lobbed snowballs at each other among the stark ruins of the Abbey. It was quiet—no one else had dared to venture out, with the thermometer fifteen below zero—and to hear her laughter echoing in the stillness was a delight. I had quite forgotten to ring Marianne last night, to enquire about Lucy's illness, but she seemed fine today so I decided not to bother.

We had lunch in the Devonshire Arms across the road from the Abbey, and in the afternoon visited Marsworld, a couple of miles north of Skipton. We wandered around the replica rockets that had carried the scientific team to the red planet a couple of years ago, then visited mock-ups of the dozen domes where the explorers were living right at that moment. I had worried that Lucy might find it boring, but she turned out to be fascinated; she'd had lessons about the mission at school, and actually knew more about it than I did.

We drove home through the narrow lanes at four, with dusk rapidly falling. I proceeded with a caution I would not have shown had I been alone: I carried a precious cargo on the back seat... The only time I was truly content, and could rest easy, was when Lucy was with me. At other times, I envisaged, perhaps unfairly, the unthinking neglect with which Marianne might treat her.

"Do you know what would be nice, Daddy?" Lucy said now.

"What?" I asked, glancing at her in the rear-view.

"I would really like it if you and Mummy would live together again."

She had said this before, and always I had experienced a hopeless despair. I would have done anything to secure my daughter's happiness, but this was one thing that I could not contemplate.

"Lucy, we can't do that. We have our separate lives now."

"Don't you love Mummy any more?"

"Not in the same way that I once did," I said.

"But a little bit?" she went on.

I nodded. "A little bit," I said.

She was quiet for a time, and then said, "Why did you move away, Daddy? Was it because of me?"

I slowed and looked at her in the mirror. "Of course not. What made you think—?"

"Mummy said that you stopped loving her because you couldn't agree about me."

I gripped the wheel, anger welling. I might have hated the bitch, but I had kept that animosity to myself. Never once had I attempted to turn Lucy against her mother.

"That's not true, Lucy. We disagreed about a lot of things. What you've got to remember is that we both love you more than anything else, okay?"

We underestimate children's capacity for not being fobbed off with platitudes. Lucy said, "But the biggest thing you disagreed about was me, wasn't it? You wanted me to be implanted, and Mummy didn't."

I sighed. "That was one of the things."

"Mummy says that God doesn't want people to be implanted. If we're implanted, then we don't go to heaven. She says that the aliens are evil—she says that they're in the same football league as the Devil."

I smiled to myself. I just wanted to take Lucy in my arms and hug her to me. I concentrated on that, rather than the anger I felt towards Marianne.

"That isn't true," I said. "God made everyone, even the Kéthani. If you're implanted, then you don't die. Eventually you can visit the stars, which I suppose is a kind of heaven."

She nodded, thinking about this. "But if I die, then I'll go to a different heaven?" she asked at last.

If you die without the implant, I thought, you will remain dead for ever and ever, amen, and no Christian sky-god will effect your resurrection.

"That's what your mum thinks," I said.

She was relentless with her dogged eight-year-old logic. "But what do *you* think, Daddy?"

"I think that in ten years, when you're eighteen, you can make up your own mind. If you want, you can be implanted then." Ten years, I thought: it seemed an eternity.

"Hey," I said, "we're almost home. What do you want for dinner? Will you help me make it?"

"Spaghetti!" she cried, and for the rest of the journey lectured me on the proper way to make Bolognese sauce.

That evening, after we'd prepared spaghetti together and eaten it messily in front of the TV, Lucy slept next to me while I tried to concentrate on a documentary. It was about a non-implanted serial killer in the US, who preyed on implanted victims and claimed, technically, that he wasn't committing murder.

I lost interest and found myself thinking about Marianne.

I had met her ten years ago, when I was thirty. She had been twenty-six, and I suspected that I'd been her very first boyfriend. Her Catholicism had intrigued me at the time, her moral and ethical codes setting her apart in my mind from the hedonism I saw all around. The Kéthani had arrived the year before, and their gift of the implants had changed society for ever: in the early days, many people adopted a devil-may-care attitude towards life—they were implanted, they could not die, so why not live for the day? Others opposed the changes.

I was implanted within a year of the Kéthani's arrival. I was not religious, and had always feared extinction. It had seemed the natural thing to do to accept the gift of immortality, especially after the first returnees arrived back on Earth with the stories of their resurrection.

Not long after my implantation, I trained to become a ferryman—and but for this I might never have met Marianne. Her mother, an atheist and implanted, had died unexpectedly of a cerebral haemorrhage, and I had collected the body.

I had been immediately attracted to Marianne's physicality, and found her worldview—during our many discussions in the weeks that followed our first date—intriguing, if absurd.

She thought the Kéthani evil, the implantation process an abomination in the eyes of the Lord, and looked forward to the day when she would die and join the virtuous in heaven.

She was appalled by my blithe acceptance of what I took to be our alien saviours.

We were married a year after our first meeting.

I was in love, whatever I thought that meant at the time. I loved her so much that I wanted to save her. It was only a matter of time, I thought, before she came to see that my acceptance of the Kéthani was sane and sensible.

She probably thought the reverse: given time, her arguments would bring about my religious salvation.

We had never spoken about what we might do if we had children. She was a successful accountant for a firm in Leeds, and told me that she did not want children. She claimed that Lucy was a mistake, but I'd often wondered since whether she had intended conceiving a child, and whether she had consciously planned what followed.

During the course of her pregnancy, I refrained from raising the subject of implants, but a couple of days after Lucy was born I presented the implantation request form to Marianne for her signature.

She would not sign, and of course, because both our signatures were required, Lucy could not undergo the simple operation to ensure her continual life.

We remained together for another year, and it was without doubt the worst year of my life. We argued; I accused my wife of terrible crimes in the name of her mythical god, while she called me an evil blasphemer. Our positions could not be reconciled. My love for Lucy grew in direct proportion to my hatred of Marianne. We separated at the end of the year, though Marianne, citing her religious principles, would not grant me a divorce.

I saw Lucy for two or three days a week over the course of the next five years, and the love of my daughter sustained me, and at the same time drove me to the edge of sanity, plagued continually by fear and paranoia.

That night, in the early hours, Lucy crept into my bed and snuggled up against me, and I dozed, utterly content.

We slept in late the following morning, had lunch, then went for a long walk. At five we set off for Hockton, Lucy quiet in the back seat.

I led her from the Range Rover to the front door, where I knelt and stroked a tress of hair from her face. I kissed her. "See you next week, poppet. Love you."

She hugged me and, as always, I had to restrain myself from weeping.

She hurried into the house and I left without exchanging a word with Marianne.

I threw myself into my work for the next five days. We were busy; Richard Lincoln was away on holiday, and I took over his workload. I averaged half a dozen collections a day, ranging across the length and breadth of West Yorkshire.

Tuesday night arrived, and not a day too soon; I was due to pick up Lucy in the morning and keep her for the duration of my three-day break. I celebrated with a few pints among congenial company at the Fleece. The regulars were present: Khalid and Zara, Ben and Elisabeth, Jeff Morrow and Richard, the latter just back from the Bahamas with a tan to prove it.

It was midnight by the time I made my way home, and there was a message from Marianne on the answer-phone. Would I ring her immediately about tomorrow?

Six pints to the good, I had no qualms about ringing her when she might be in bed.

In the event, she answered the call with disconcerting alacrity. "Yes?"

"Dan here," I said. "I got the message."

"It's about Lucy. I wouldn't bother coming tomorrow. She came down with something. She'll be in bed for a couple of days."

"What's wrong?" I asked, fear gripping me by the throat.

"It's nothing serious. The doctor came, said something about a virus."

"I'll come anyway," I said. "I want to see her."

"Don't bother," Marianne said. "I really don't want to have you over here if it isn't absolutely necessary."

"I couldn't give a damn about what you want!" I said. "I want to see Lucy. I'm coming over."

But she had slammed down the receiver, leaving me talking to myself.

I considered phoning back, but didn't. It would only show her how angry I was. I'd go over in the morning anyway, whether she liked it or not.

A blizzard began just as I set off, and the road over the moors to Hockton was treacherous. It took me almost an hour to reach the village, and it was after eleven by the time I pulled up outside Marianne's cottage.

I fully expected her not to answer the door, but to my surprise she pulled it open after the first knock. "Oh," she said. "It's you."

I stepped past her. "Where's Lucy?"

She indicated the stairs with a plastic beaker full of juice. I climbed to Lucy's room, Marianne following.

"Daddy!" Lucy called out when I entered. She was sitting up in bed, a colouring book on her lap. She looked thin and pale.

I sat on the bed and took her hand. Marianne passed her the beaker of juice. I looked up at her. "What did the doctor say?"

She shrugged. She was hugging herself, and looked pinched and sour, resentful of my presence. "He just said it was just a virus that's going round. Nothing to worry about."

"What about medication?"

"He suggested Calpol if her temperature rose."

She retreated to the door, watching me. I turned to Lucy and squeezed her hand. "How are you feeling, poppet?"

Her head against the pillow, she smiled bravely. "Bit sick," she said.

I looked up. Marianne was still watching me. "If you'd give us a few minutes alone…"

Reluctantly she withdrew, closing the door behind her.

I winked at Lucy. "You'll be better in no time," I said.

"Will I have to have more tests, Daddy?"

"I don't know. What did the doctor say when he came?"

She shook her head. "He didn't come here. Mummy took me to the hospital."

"*Hospital?*"

She nodded. "A doctor needled me and took some blood."

A hollow sensation opened up in my stomach. I smiled inanely. "What did the doctor say, Lucy? Can you remember what the doctor told Mummy?"

She pulled a face in concentration. "They said something about my blood. It wasn't good enough. I think they said they might have to take it all out and put some new blood in. Then another doctor said something about my bones. I might need an operation on my bones."

My vision swam. My heart hammered.

"Was this at the hospital in Bradley?" I asked her.

She shook her head. "Mummy took me to Leeds."

"Can you remember which hospital?"

She made her concentrating face. "It was a hospital for army people," she said.

I blinked. "What?"

"I think the sign said it was a general hospital."

"Leeds General," I said. "Was that it?"

She nodded. I squeezed her hand. My first impulse was to go downstairs and confront Marianne, find out just what the hell was going on.

Lucy had something wrong with her blood, and might need an operation on her bones... A bone marrow transplant, for Chrissake?

I tried not to jump to the obvious conclusion.

I remained with Lucy a further thirty minutes, read her a book and then chatted about nothing in particular for a while, all the time my mind racing.

By noon, I had decided what to do. I leaned forward and kissed her. "I've got to go now, Lucy. I'll pop in and see you tomorrow, okay?"

I hurried from the room and down the stairs. I paused before the living room door, but didn't trust myself to confront Marianne just yet. I left the cottage and drove home through the snowstorm.

For the next half hour I ransacked the house for the photocopy of Lucy's birth certificate and my passport, for identification purposes. Then I set off again, heading towards Leeds.

It was almost three before I pulled into the bleak car park in the shadow of the tower-block buildings. At reception I explained the situation and requested to see someone in charge. The head registrar examined my documents and spoke in hushed tones to someone in a black suit.

Thirty minutes later I was shown into the waiting room of a Mr. Chandler, and told by his secretary that he would try to fit me in within the hour.

At four-thirty the secretary called my name and, heart thumping, I stepped into the consulting room.

Mr. Chandler was a thin-faced, grey-haired man in his late fifties. The bulge of an implant showed at his left temple.

He was examining a computer flat-screen on his desk, and looked up when I entered. We shook hands.

"Mr. Chester," he said. "According to my secretary, you haven't been informed of your daughter's condition?"

"I'm separated from my wife. We're not exactly on speaking terms."

"This is highly irregular," he muttered to himself.

I resisted the urge to tell him that Marianne was a highly irregular woman. "Can you tell me what's wrong with my daughter, Mr. Chandler?"

He consulted his files, lips pursed.

"Lucy was diagnosed one month ago with leukaemia..." He went on, and I heard him say that the type she was suffering from was pernicious and incurable, but it was as if I had suddenly been plucked from this reality, as if I were experiencing the events in the consulting room at a remove of miles. I seemed to have possession of my body only by remote control.

"Incurable?" I echoed.

"I'm sorry. Of course, if your daughter were implanted..."

I stared at him. "Don't you think I know that?" I said. "Why the hell do you think my damned wife kept her condition quiet?"

He looked away. "I'm sorry."

"Is there nothing you can do? I mean, surely under the Hippocratic oath...?"

He was shaking his head. "Unfortunately I've been in this situation before, Mr. Chester. It requires the consent of *both* legal guardians to allow the implantation process to be undertaken in the case of minors. I'm quite powerless to intervene, as much as I sympathise with your predicament."

I worked to calm myself, regulate my breathing. "How long might Lucy...?" I began.

He said, "As things stand, perhaps one month. You see, since the advent of the Kéthani, the funding once spent on research into terminal diseases has been drastically cut back."

I listened, but heard nothing. Ten minutes later I thanked him and moved from the room in a daze.

I have no recollection whatsoever of leaving the hospital and driving away from Leeds. I recall isolated incidents: a traffic jam on the ring road, passing a nasty accident on the road to Bradley, and almost skidding from the lane myself a mile outside Hockton.

Then I was parked outside Marianne's cottage, gripping the wheel and going over and over the words I would use in an attempt to make her agree to save our daughter's life.

At last I left the Rover and hurried up the path. I had the curious sensation of being an actor on stage, and that, if I fluffed my lines now, the consequences would be dire.

I didn't bother knocking, but opened the front door and moved down the hall.

Marianne was in the living room. She sat in her armchair, legs drawn up beneath her. She was hugging herself as if cold. The TV was on, the sound switched off.

"I've been to the hospital," I said. "I talked with Chandler."

She looked up, showing no surprise.

Heart thumping, I sat in the armchair opposite and stared at her. "We've got to talk about this," I said. "There's more at stake than our principles or beliefs."

She looked away. She was fingering her damned crucifix. "You mean, you want me to sacrifice my principles and beliefs in order to satisfy your own?"

I leaned forward, almost insensible with rage. "I mean," I said, resisting the urge to launch myself at her, "that if we do nothing, then Lucy will be dead. Does that mean anything to you? She'll be bloody well dead!"

"Don't you think I don't know that? This isn't easy for me, you know."

I shook my head. "I don't see how you can have a moment's hesitation. The simple fact is, if you don't agree to the implantation, then Lucy will die. We won't have any second chances. She'll be dead."

"And if I agree, I'll be damning her in the eyes of God."

I closed my eyes and worked to control my breathing. I looked at her. I could not help myself, but I was crying. "Please, Marianne, for Lucy's sake."

She stared at me.

I said, "Listen, let her have the implant. Then, when she's eighteen, she can make up her own mind, have it removed if she wants."

She shook her head. "I don't know… I need time to think about it."

I gave a panicky nod at the thought that she might be relenting. "Chandler said she had a month, but who knows? We need to make a decision pretty damned quickly."

She stared at me, her face ashen. "I need time to think, Dan. You can't pressure me into this."

I wiped away the tears. "Lucy is all we have left, Marianne. We don't have each other any more. Lucy is everything."

This, so far as I recall, was the gist of the exchange; I have a feeling it went on for longer, with clichés from both sides bandied back and forth, to no definite conclusion. The last thing I did before leaving the house was to climb the stairs to Lucy's bedroom, kneel beside the bed and watch my daughter as she slept.

I arrived home around midnight and, unable to sleep, stared at a succession of meaningless images passing before me on the TV screen.

I slept on the settee until ten o'clock the next morning, then showered and tried to eat breakfast. Between ten-thirty and midday I must have phoned Marianne a dozen times. She was either out or not answering.

At one o'clock, the phone rang, startling me. Shaking, I lifted the receiver. "Hello?"

"Daniel?"

"Marianne?"

A silence, then, "Daniel. I have a form you need to sign."

"My God, you mean—?"

"I'll be in all afternoon," she said, and replaced the receiver.

I drove to Hockton, crying all the way. I pulled up before the cottage and dried my eyes, at once grateful for the decision Marianne had come to, and yet resentful that she had made me so pathetically indebted to her.

I hurried up the path, knocked and entered. Marianne was in her usual armchair. A slip of paper sat on the coffee table before her. I sat down and read through the release form. She had already appended her signature on the dotted line at the foot of the page. Fumbling, I pulled a pen from my pocket and signed my name below hers.

I looked up. Marianne was watching me. "You won't regret this, Marianne," I said.

"I've made an appointment for the implant. I'm taking her in at one tomorrow."

I nodded. "I'll drop by to see her after work, okay?"

"Whatever..."

I made my way upstairs. Lucy was sitting up in bed. Intoxicated, I hugged her to me, smothering her in kisses. I stayed an hour, talking, reading to her, laughing...

When I made my way downstairs, Marianne was still in her armchair in the lounge. The room was in darkness.

I said goodbye before I left, but she did not respond.

It was six by the time I arrived home, and I dropped into the Fleece for a celebratory meal and a pint or three.

Khalid was there, along with Richard and Ben, and three pints turned to six as I told them the news: that, first, Lucy was going to be implanted, and second, that she was suffering from a terminal illness. My friends were a little unsure how to respond, then took my line and decided to celebrate.

It was well past one when I staggered home, and I had a raging headache all the next day at work. Fortunately, with Richard back from the Bahamas, the workload was not intense, and I was finished by four.

I returned home, showered and changed, and then made my way over the moors to Hockton.

The cottage door was locked, and I thought at first that perhaps they had not returned. Then it struck me that, perhaps, Marianne had gone back on her word, decided not to take Lucy to the hospital...

The door opened.

"How is she?" I asked, pushing past Marianne and making my way upstairs.

Marianne followed me into Lucy's room. She was lying flat out, staring at the ceiling. She looked exhausted.

She beamed when she saw me. "Daddy, look. Look what I've got!"

Her small fingers traced the implant at her temple. I looked up; Marianne pushed herself away from the door and went downstairs.

I pulled Lucy to me—she seemed no more than a bundle of skin and bone—and could not stop myself from crying. "I love you," I whispered.

"Love you, too," Lucy replied, then said, "Now that I have the implant, Daddy, will God love me as well?"

I lay her down, gently, and smiled. "I'm sure he will, poppet," I said.

Later, as she slept, I stroked her hair and listened to the words of the rhyme in my head: *Monday's child is fair of face, Tuesday's child is full of grace, Wednesday's child is full of woe, Thursday's child has far to go...*

I made my way downstairs. Marianne was in the kitchen, washing dishes.

I leaned against the jamb.

"You've made the right decision, Marianne." I said.

She turned and stared at me. "You don't know how difficult it was, Daniel," she said, without meeting my eyes, and turned back to the dishes.

I said goodbye, left the cottage and drove home.

Lucy went downhill rapidly after that.

The next time she stayed with me, she spent most of the entire three days in bed, listless and apathetic, and too drugged up even to talk much or play games. I told her that she was ill but that in time she would recover, and she gave a brave smile and squeezed my fingers.

During the course of the last two weeks, Marianne and I took time off work and nursed Lucy at home, looking after her for alternating periods of three days.

At one point, Lucy lowered the book she was reading and stared at me from the sofa. "If I die," she said, "will the aliens take me away and make me better again?"

I nodded. "If that happens, you mustn't be frightened, okay? The Kéthani will take good care of you, and in six months you'll come back home to Mum and me."

She smiled to herself. "I wonder what the aliens look like?"

Two days before Lucy died, she was admitted to Bradley General, and I was with her until the end.

She was unconscious, and dosed with painkillers. She had lost a lot of weight and looked pitifully thin beneath the crisp hospital sheets.

I held her hand during the first day and well into the night, falling asleep in my chair and waking at dawn with cramps and multiple aches. Marianne arrived shortly after that and sat with Lucy. I took the opportunity to grab a bite to eat.

On the evening of the second day, Lucy's breathing became uneven. A doctor murmured to Marianne and me that she had only a matter of hours to live.

Marianne sat across the bed from me, gripping her daughter's hand and weeping. After an hour, she could take no more.

She stood and made for the door.

"Marianne…?" I said.

"I'm sorry. This is too much. I'm going."

"This is just the start," I said. "She isn't truly dying, Marianne."

She looked at me. "I'm sorry Dan," she said, and hurried out.

I returned to my vigil. I stared at my daughter, and thought of the time, six months away, when she would be returned to me, remade. Glorious years stretched ahead.

I thought of Marianne, and her inability to see it through to the end. I was struck, then, by an idea so terrible I was ashamed that it had occurred to me.

I told myself that I was being paranoid, that even Marianne could not do such a thing. But once the seed of doubt had been planted, it would not be eradicated.

What if I were right, I asked myself? I had to be sure. I had to know for certain.

Beside myself with panic, I fumbled with my mobile and found Khalid's number.

The dial tone purred for an age. I swore at him to reply, and at last he did.

"Hello?"

"Khalid, thank God! Where are you?"

"Dan? I'm just leaving the hospital."

"Khalid, I need your help." I explained the situation, my fear. "Please, will you come over?"

There was no hesitation. "Of course. I'm on my way." He cut the connection.

He seemed to take aeons to arrive, but only two minutes elapsed before his neat, suited figure appeared around the door. He hurried over, concern etched on his face.

"I need to be sure, Khalid. It might be okay, but I need to know."

He nodded. "Fine. You don't need to explain yourself, Dan. I understand."

He moved around the bed, and I watched in silent desperation. He pulled something from his inside pocket, a device like a miniature mobile phone, and stabbed a code into the keypad.

Then he glanced at me, stepped towards Lucy, and applied the device to the implant at her temple.

He read something from the tiny screen, and shock invaded his expression. He slumped into the seat which minutes before my wife had occupied, and he said something, rapidly, in Urdu.

"Khalid?" I almost wept.

He was shaking his head. "Dan, it's a fake."

I nodded. I felt very cold. I pressed my hands to my cheeks and stared at him. I wanted to throw up, but I hadn't eaten anything for half a day. Bile rose in my throat. I swallowed it with difficulty.

"Khalid," I said. "You've got to help me."

"Dan..." It was a plea to make me understand the impossibility of what I was asking him.

"How long does an implantation take?" I asked. "Thirty minutes? We have time. If you can get an implant, make the cut..." I realised, as I was speaking, that I was weeping, pleading with him through my tears.

"Dan, we need the signatures of both parents. If anyone found out..."

I recalled, then, the consent form that I had signed two weeks ago. My heart skipped at the sudden thought that there had existed a form bearing both our signatures... But for how long, before Marianne had destroyed it?

My mobile rang, and I snatched it from my pocket. "What?"

"Mr. Daniel Chester?"

"What do you want? Who is it?"

The woman gave her name. I cannot recall it now, but she was a police officer. "If you could make your way to Hockton police station..." she was saying.

I laughed at the absurdity of the situation. "Listen, I'm at Bradley Hospital with my daughter. She's dying, and if you think for a second that I'm leaving her—"

"I'm sorry, Mr. Chester. We'll be over right away." She cut the connection. It was evidence of my agitated state that I managed to push the call from my mind.

I sat down and gripped Lucy's hand. I looked up, across the bed at Khalid. I said, "What's more important? Your job or Lucy's life?"

He shook his head, staring at me. "You can't blackmail me, Dan. Marianne doesn't want this. I'm not saying that what she did was right, but you've got to understand that there are laws to obey."

"Sod the fucking laws!" I yelled. "We're talking about the life of my daughter, for Chrissake."

He stared at his clasped hands, his expression set.

I went on, "If this were your daughter, in this situation, what would you do? All it would take is a quick cut. Replace the implant with a genuine one."

He was shaking his head, tears tracking down his cheeks.

"For Chrissake," I hissed. "We're alone. No one would see."

"Dan, I'd need to do paperwork, make a requisition order for an implant. They're all numbered, accounted for. If one went missing…"

I stared at him. I am not proud of what I said then, but I was driven by desperation. "You could replace the genuine implant with this fake," I said, gesturing towards Lucy.

He stared at me in shock, and only then did I realise what I'd asked him to do.

He stood up quickly and strode to the window, staring out into the night.

I sat by the bed, gripping Lucy's hot hand and quietly sobbing. Minutes passed like seconds.

"Mr. Chester?"

The interruption was unwelcome. A small, Asian WPC stood by the door. A constable, who appeared about half my age, accompanied her.

"What the hell?" I began.

"Mr. Chester, it's about your wife, Marianne Chester."

"What?" I said, my stomach turning.

"If you'd care to step this way…"

In a daze I left my seat and accompanied the police officers into the corridor. They escorted me to a side room, where we could be alone.

I sat down, and the WPC sat opposite me. The juvenile constable remained by the door, avoiding my eyes.

"Mr. Chester," the woman said, "I'm sorry to inform you that your wife was found dead a little under one hour ago. A neighbour noticed the front door open. I'm sorry. It appears that she took her own life."

I stared at her. "What?" I said, though I had heard her clearly enough.

I've since learned that police officers are prepared to repeat bad news to people in shock. Patiently, kindly, she told me again.

Marianne was dead. What she had done to my daughter, what she had done to me, had been too much of a burden to bear. She had taken her own life. I understood the words, but not the actuality of what she had done.

I nodded, stood, and crossed the corridor. I returned to Lucy's room. Khalid was still there, seated beside the bed, clutching my daughter's hand and quietly crying.

I sat down and told him what had happened.

One of the joys of being a father is not only the wonder of the moment, the love one feels for one's child every minute of every day, but contemplation of the future. How long had I spent day-dreaming about the girl Lucy would be at the age of thirteen, and then at eighteen, on the verge of womanhood? I saw myself with her when she was twenty, and thirty, sharing her life, loving her. Such pre-emptive 'memories', as it were, are one of the delights of fatherhood.

One hour later, Lucy died.

I was holding her hand, listening to her stertorous breathing and to the regular pulse of the cardiogram. Then her breathing hiccuped, rattled, and a second later the cardiogram flatlined, maintaining an even, continuous note.

I looked across at Khalid, and he nodded.

I reached out and touched the implant at her temple, the implant which Khalid had installed thirty minutes ago when, as Lucy's sole remaining parent, I had signed the consent form. The implant purred beneath my fingertips, restoring my daughter to life.

Presently a ferryman arrived and, between us, we lifted Lucy into the container, which we do not call coffins. Before she was taken away, I kissed her forehead and told her that I would be there to welcome her back in six months. I did not want a farewell ceremony; she would leave for the Kéthani starship tonight.

Later, I left the hospital and drove to Hockton, where I called in at the police station and read the note that Marianne had left. It was sealed in a cellophane folder, and I could not take it away with me.

Dan, I read, *Please forgive me. You will never understand. I know I have done the right thing by saving Lucy from the Kéthani, even though what I have done to you is unforgivable. Also, what I am about to do to myself. It's enough to know that Lucy is saved, even if I am damned by my actions.*

Marianne.

I left the police station and drove onto the moors overlooking the towering obelisk of the Onward Station. It rose in the moonlight like a pinnacle of ice, promising eternity. As I climbed from the Rover and watched, the first of that evening's energy beams pulsed from its summit and arced through the stratosphere. Thus the dead of Earth were transmitted to the Kéthani starship waiting high above.

Thursday's child has far to go...

INTERLUDE

Ten years had elapsed since the arrival of the Kéthani when we met Doug Standish, though he had been friend of Richard Lincoln's long before he became a fixture in the Tuesday night group. He was a big, bluff, slab-faced Yorkshireman, an almost stereotypical copper. He'd worked for the homicide division in Leeds for years before the Kéthani came, and now was stationed in Bradley. I said *almost* stereotypical, because once you got to know him, learned something of the real man beneath the pint-and-pipe exterior, it became apparent that Doug was a shy, sensitive man whose separation from his wife had affected him deeply.

They were in the process of splitting up when we met him. He was investigating a murder—an incredibly rare event these days—in a nearby farmhouse and came into the Fleece with Richard Lincoln to question Ben Knightly, who might have witnessed something germane to the case. A few days later, on Richard's invitation, he joined us again, this time in an unofficial capacity.

I warmed to Doug from the outset. I think, initially, I empathised with what he was going through with his wife.

Things between Zara and myself were tense then.

It was much later—years later, in fact—that Doug told us the story of the murder investigation that winter. The fact was that even he, at the time, was not aware of the larger story being played out behind the smaller, though extraordinary, murder enquiry. He was a pawn in an extraterrestrial game; he was also, perhaps, the first person we had ever met who'd had contact with—albeit unwittingly—a member of the Kéthani race.

A week after the murder investigation was officially closed, Doug and I shared a few pints in a late night lock-in at the Fleece.

"I don't think I've told you about Amanda, have I?"

"Your wife?"

He stared into his fourth pint. "My soon-to-be ex-wife, Khalid."

His words caused me to shift uneasily. "I'm sorry."

"Don't be. It's a disaster..." He took a deep breath and smiled. "But it's nearly over, now. I can look ahead. It's just... when I think about her with this other bloke, and how she deceived me for months..."

He told me the full story.

An hour and three pints later we staggered from the Fleece. I made my way home, let myself in through the front door—after a few futile attempts—and climbed to the bedroom.

As I'd expected, Zara was still out. The bed was empty. I sat on the edge of the duvet and tried not to weep. It was one in the morning. Zara would be back, soon, and would slide quietly into bed in an attempt not to wake me. Over breakfast she'd make the excuse that the study group had run on late and they'd continued the discussion back at a friend's house in Bradley. And I would smile and try not to show my suspicions, and then we would part and go to our respective jobs, and I would be sick with jealousy for the rest of the day.

But... less about my problems, at this juncture. The next episode concerns Doug Standish and the strange events that occurred that winter.

FIVE

The Touch of Angels

The sun was going down on another clear, sharp January day when Standish received the call. He'd left the station at the end of his shift and was driving over the snow-covered moors towards home and another cheerless evening with Amanda. As he reached the cross-roads, he decided to stop at the Dog and Gun for a couple beforehand; let a few pints take the edge off his perceptions so that Amanda's barbs might not bite so deep tonight.

His mobile rang. It was Kathy at control. "Doug. Where are you?"

"On my way home. Just passing the Onward Station." The alien edifice was a five hundred metre-tall spire like an inverted icicle on the nearby hillside.

"Something's just come up."

Standish groaned. Another farmer reporting stolen heifers, no doubt.

"A ferryman just rang. There's been a murder in the area. I've called in a scene-of-crime team."

He almost drove off the road. "A murder?"

131

She gave him the address of a secluded farmhouse a couple of miles away, then rang off.

He turned off the B-road and slowed, easing his Renault down a narrow lane between snow-topped dry-stone walls. The tyres cracked the panes of frozen puddles in a series of crunching reports. On either hand, for as far as the eye could see, the rolling moorland was covered in a pristine mantle of snow.

Murder…

Ten years ago Standish had worked as a detective inspector with the homicide division in Leeds. He had enjoyed the job. He'd been part of a good team and their detection and conviction rate had been high. He viewed his work as necessary in not only bringing law and order to an increasingly crime-ridden city, but also, in some metaphorical way, bringing a measure of order to what he saw as a disordered and chaotic universe. He had no doubt that every time he righted a wrong he was, on some deep subconscious level, putting right his own inability to cope with the hectic modern world he was finding less and less to his taste.

And then the Kéthani came along…

Within months, crime figures had dropped dramatically. Within a year, murders had fallen by almost eighty per cent. Why kill someone when, six months later, they would be resurrected and returned to Earth? In the early days, of course, murderers thought they could outwit the gift of the Kéthani. They killed their victims in hideous ways, ensuring that no trace of the body remained, and attempted to conceal or destroy the implant devices. But the nanotech implants were indestructible, and emitted a signal that alerted the local Onward Station to their whereabouts. Each implant contained a sample of DNA and a record of the victim's personality. Within a day of discovery, the device would be ferried to the Kéthani home planet, and the individual successfully brought back to life. And then they would return to Earth and assist with investigations…

Two years after the coming of the Kéthani, the Leeds homicide division had been disbanded, and Standish shunted sideways into the routine investigation of car thefts and burglaries.

Like most people he knew, he had rejoiced at the arrival of the aliens and the gift they gave to humanity. He had been implanted within a month and tried to adjust his mind to the fact that he was no longer haunted by the spectre of death.

Shortly before the arrival of the Kéthani, Standish married Amanda Evans, the manageress of an optician's franchise in Bradley. For a while, everything had been wonderful: love and life everlasting. But the years had passed, and his marriage to Amanda had undergone a subtle and inexplicable process of deterioration and he had gradually become aware that he was, somewhere within himself, deeply dissatisfied with life.

And he had no idea who or what to blame, other than himself.

The farmhouse was no longer the centre of a working farm but, like so many properties in the area, had been converted into an expensive holiday home. It sat on a hill with a spectacular view over the surrounding moorland.

Standish turned a corner in the lane and found his way blocked by the Range Rover belonging to one of the local ferrymen. He braked and climbed out into the teeth of a bitter wind. He turned up the collar of his coat and hurried across to the vehicle.

The ferryman sat in his cab, an indistinct blur seen through the misted side window. When Standish rapped on the glass and opened the door, he saw Richard Lincoln warming his hands on a mug of coffee from a Thermos.

"Doug, that was quick. Didn't expect you people out here for a while yet."

"I was passing. What happened?"

He'd got to know Lincoln over the course of a few tea-time sessions at the Dog and Gun a year ago, both men coming off-duty at the same time and needing the refreshment and therapy of good beer and conversation.

Lincoln was a big, silver-haired man in his sixties, and unfailingly cheerful. He wore tweeds, which gave him a look of innate conservatism belied by his liberal nature. His bonhomie had pulled Standish from the doldrums on more than one occasion.

Lincoln finished his coffee. "Bloody strange, Doug. I was at the Station, on the vid-link with Sarah Roberts, a colleague. She was at home." He pointed to the converted farmhouse. "We were going over a few details about a couple of returnees when she said she'd be back in a second—there was someone at the door. She disappeared from sight and came back a little later. She was talking to someone, obviously someone she knew. She was turning to the screen to address me when there was a loud... I don't quite know how to describe it. A crack. A report."

"A gunshot?"

Lincoln nodded. "Anyway, she cried out and fell away from the screen. I ran to the control room and sure enough... We were being signalled by her implant. She was dead. Look."

Lincoln reached out and touched the controls of a screen embedded in the dashboard. An image flickered into life, and Standish made out the shot of a well-furnished front room, with a woman's body sprawled across the floor, a bloody wound in her upper chest.

Absently, Lincoln fingered the implant at his temple. "I contacted you people and drove straight over."

"Did you pass any other vehicles on the way here?"

Lincoln shook his head. "No. And I was on the lookout, of course. The strangest thing is... Well, come and see for yourself."

Lincoln climbed from the cab and Standish joined him. They moved towards the wrought-iron gate that barred their way. It was locked.

"Look," Lincoln said. He indicated the driveway and lawns of the farmhouse. A thick covering of snow gave the scene the aspect of a traditional Christmas card.

Standish could see no tracks or footprints.

"Follow me." Lincoln walked along the side of the wall that encircled the property. Standish followed, wading through the foot of snow that covered the springy heather. They climbed a small rise and halted, looking down on the farmhouse from the elevated vantage point.

Lincoln pointed to the rear of the building. "Same again," he said, looking at Standish.

"There's not a single damned footprint to be seen," Standish said.

"Nothing. No footprints, tyre-marks, tracks of any kind. The snow stopped falling around midday, so there's no way a new fall could have covered any tracks. Anyway, the killer came to the house forty-five minutes ago."

"But how? If he didn't leave tracks…" Standish examined the ground, searching for the smallest imprint. He looked at Lincoln. "There is one explanation, of course."

"There is?"

"The killer was always in the house, concealed somewhere. He came before the snow fell and hid himself. Then he emerged, crept through the house to the door, stepped outside and knocked."

"But that'd mean…"

Standish nodded. "If I'm right, then he's still in there."

"What do you think?" Lincoln asked. "Should we go in?"

In the old days, before the Kéthani, he would not have risked it. Now, with death no longer the threat it used to be, he didn't think twice.

"Let's go," he said.

They returned to the front gate and climbed over. Standish led the way, high-stepping through the deep snow.

He had the sudden feeling of being involved in one of those Golden Age whodunits he'd devoured as a teenager, stories of ingenious murders carried out with devious cunning and improbable devices.

The front door was unlocked. Taking a handkerchief from his pocket, Standish carefully turned the handle and pushed open the door. He led the way to the lounge.

Sarah Roberts lay on her back before the flickering vid-screen. The earlier image of her, Standish thought, had done nothing to convey her beauty. She was slim and blonde, her face ethereally beautiful. Like an angel, he thought.

They moved into the big, terracotta-tiled kitchen and checked the room thoroughly. They found the entrance to a small cellar and descended cautiously. The cellar was empty. Next they returned to the kitchen and moved into the adjacent dining room, but again found nothing.

"Upstairs?" Lincoln said.

Standish nodded. He led the way, climbing the wide staircase in silence. There were three bedrooms on the second floor, two bare and unoccupied, the third furnished with a single bed. They went through them from top to bottom. He was aware of the steady pounding of his heart as Standish pulled aside curtains and opened wardrobes. Last of all they checked the converted attic, spartanly furnished like the rest of the bedrooms, and just as free of lurking gunmen.

"Clean as a whistle," Lincoln said as they made their way downstairs.

"I wish we'd found the killer," Standish muttered. "I don't like the alternative." What was the alternative, he wondered? An eerie, impossible murder in a house surrounded by snow...

They entered the lounge. Lincoln knelt beside the body, reached out, and touched the woman's implant.

Years ago, before the Kéthani, Standish had seen any number of bodies during the course of a working week, and he had never really become accustomed, or desensitised, to the fact that these once living people had been robbed of existence.

Now, when he did occasionally come across a corpse in the line of duty, he was immediately struck by the same feeling of futile waste and tragedy—only to be brought up short with the realisation that now, thanks to the Kéthani, the dead would be granted new life.

Lincoln looked up at him, his expression stricken. "Christ, Doug. This isn't right."

Standish felt his stomach turn. "What?"

Lincoln slumped back against the wall. Standish could see that he was sweating. "Her implant's dead."

"But I thought you said... you received the signal at the Station, right?"

Lincoln nodded. "It was the initial signal indicating that the subject had died."

"So it should still be working?"

"Of course. It should be emitting a constant pulse." He shook his head. "Look, this has never happened before. It's unknown. These things just don't pack up. They're Kéthani technology."

"Maybe it was one of those false implants? Don't people with objections to the Kéthani sometimes have them?"

Lincoln waved. "Sarah worked for the Kéthani, Doug. And anyway, it *was* working. I saw the signal myself. Now the damned thing's dead."

Standish stared down at the woman, a wave of nausea overcoming him. He was struck once more by her attenuated Nordic beauty, and he was sickened by the thought that she would never live again... Amanda would have called him a sexist bastard: as if the tragedy were any the greater for the woman being beautiful.

"Can't something be done?"

Lincoln lifted his shoulders in a hopeless shrug. "I don't honestly know. The device needs to be active in the minutes immediately after the subject's death, in order to begin the resurrection process. Maybe the techs at the Station might be able to do something. Like I said, this has never happened before."

The room was hot, suffocatingly so. Standish moved to a window at the back of the room and was about to open it when he saw something through the glass.

He stepped from the lounge and into the kitchen. The back door was open a few inches. He crossed to it and, with his handkerchief, eased it open a little further and peered out.

The snow on the path directly outside the door had been melted in a circle perhaps a couple of metres across, revealing a stone-flagged path and a margin of lawn. The snow began again immediately beyond the melt, but there was no sign of footprints or any other tracks.

He returned to the lounge. Lincoln was on his mobile, evidently talking to someone at the Onward Station. "And there's nothing at your end, either? Okay. Look, get a tech down here, fast."

Standish crossed the room and stood before the big picture window, staring out at the darkening land with his back to the corpse. He really had no wish to look upon the remains of Sarah Roberts. Her reflection, in the glass, struck him as unbearably poignant, even more angelic as it seemed to float, ghost-like and evanescent, above the floor.

Lincoln joined him. "They're sending someone down to look at the implant."

Standish nodded. "The scene-of-crime team should be here any minute." He glanced at the ferryman. "You didn't hear her visitor's voice when she returned from answering the door?"

"Nothing. I was aware that there was someone in the room by Sarah's attitude. She seemed eager to end the call. But I saw or heard no one else."

"Have you any idea which door she answered, front or back?"

Lincoln turned and looked at the vid-screen. "Let's see, she was facing the screen, and she moved off to the left—so she must have answered the back door."

That would fit with the door being ajar—but what of the melted patch?

"What kind of person was she? Popular? Boyfriend, husband?"

Lincoln shrugged. "I didn't really know her. Station gossip was that she was a bit of a cold fish. Remote. Kept herself to herself. Didn't make friends. She wasn't married, and as far as I know she didn't have a partner."

"What was her job at the Station?"

"Well, she was designated a liaison officer, but to be honest I don't exactly know what that entailed. I kept her up to date with the dead I delivered and the returnees, but I don't know what she did with the information. She worked with Masters, the Station Director. He'd know more than me."

"How long had she been at the Station?"

"Two or three months. But before that she'd worked at others up and down the country, so I heard."

Standish nodded. "I'm just going to take another look around. I'll be down when the scene-of-crime people turn up."

He left the lounge and climbed the stairs again. He stood in the doorway of the only furnished bedroom and took in the bed—a single bed, which struck him as odd—and the bedside table with nothing upon it.

He moved to the bathroom and scanned the contents: a big shower stall, a Jacuzzi in the corner, plush white carpet... He stared around the room, trying to fathom precisely why he had the subtle feeling that something was not quite right. It was more a vague sensation than anything definite.

He heard the muffled groan of a labouring engine and rejoined Lincoln in the lounge.

Two minutes later Kendrick, the scene-of-crime team chief, appeared at the door with three other officers, and Standish and Lincoln went over their findings.

The tech from the Station turned up shortly after that and knelt over the corpse, examining the woman's implant with the aid of a case full of equipment, scanners and a softscreen, and other implements Standish didn't recognise.

Kendrick drew Standish to one side. "They're bringing in a chap from Manchester, inspector. I know technically this is your territory, but the commissioner's decided he wants the big boys in."

Standish opened his mouth to complain, then thought better of it. Kendrick was merely the messenger; it would achieve nothing to vent his frustration on the scene-of-crime chief.

Twenty minutes later Lincoln clapped him on the shoulder. "Heading past the Dog and Gun? Fancy a quick one?"

"You're a mind-reader, Richard. Lead the way."

They retreated with their pints of Old Peculier to the table beside the fire. The barroom of the Dog and Gun was empty but for themselves and half a dozen youngsters at the far end of the bar. The kids wore the latest silvered fashions—uncomfortably dazzling to the eye—and talked too loudly amongst themselves. As if we really want to hear their inane views of life in the twenty-first century, Standish thought.

"What is it, Doug?" Lincoln asked, reducing the measure of his pint by half in one appreciative mouthful.

"What's happened to society over the past ten years, Richard?"

Lincoln smiled. "You mean since the coming of the Kéthani? Don't you think things have got better?"

Standish shrugged. "I suppose so, yes." How could he express his dissatisfaction without sounding sorry for himself? "But... Okay, so we don't die. We don't have that fear. But what about the quality of the life we have now?"

Lincoln laughed. "You've been reading Cockburn, right?"

"Never heard of him."

"A Cambridge philosopher who claims that humankind has lost some innate spark since the arrival of the Kéthani."

"I wouldn't know about that," Standish said. He took a long swallow of rich, creamy ale. "It's just that... perhaps it's me. I lived so long with the certainties of the old way of life. I knew where I belonged. I had a job that I liked and thought useful..."

At the far end of the bar, one of the kids—a girl, Standish saw—threw her lager in the face of a friend, who didn't seem to mind. They laughed uproariously and barged their way from the pub. Seconds later he saw them mount their motorcycles and roar off, yelling, into the night.

"All the old values have gone," he said.

"The world's changing," Lincoln said. "Now that we no longer fear death, we're liberated."

Standish smiled and shook his head. "Liberated from what—what freedom have we found? The freedom to live shallow, superficial lives? Perhaps it's my fault," he went on. "Perhaps I was an old fart before the aliens came, and now I'm too set in my ways to change." That was a glib analysis, he thought, but it hinted at some deeper, psychological truth.

Lincoln was watching him. "Don't you think about the future, and feel grateful for what we've got?"

Standish considered this. "I don't know. Sometimes I'm struck by the greater uncertainty of things. Before we had the certainty of death—oblivion, if you had no faith. Now we come back to life and go among the stars... and that seems almost as terrifying."

Lincoln contemplated his empty glass for a second or two, then said, "Another pint?"

"You've twisted my arm."

Lincoln returned, sat down, and regarded Standish in silence for a while. "How's things with Amanda?" The question was asked with the casual precision of a psychiatrist getting to the heart of his patient's problem.

Standish shrugged. "About the same. It's been bad for a year or so now." Longer, if he were to be honest with himself. It was just that he'd begun to notice it over the course of the past year.

"Have you considered counselling?"

"Thought about it," he said. Which was a lie. Their relationship was too far gone to bother trying to save. Amanda felt nothing for him any more, and had said as much.

He shrugged and said, "There's really not much to say about it, Richard. It's as good as over." He buried his head in his drink and willed the ferryman to change the subject.

It was over, he knew, but something deep within him, that innate conservatism again, that fear of change, was loath to be the one to admit as much. It was as if he lived in hope that things might change between them, become miraculously better.

But in lieu of improvement, he held onto what he had got for fear of finding himself with nothing at all.

Lincoln said, "Doug, perhaps you'd feel better about life in general if you could sort things out with Amanda, one way or another."

Standish finished his pint, and said, too quickly, obviously trying to silence the ferryman, "One for the road?"

Lincoln looked at his watch. "Better not. I've an early start in the morning." He stood. "Keep in touch, okay? How about coming over to the Fleece one night? There's a great crowd there, and the beer's excellent."

Standish smiled. "I'll do that," he said, knowing full well that he would do nothing of the sort.

He sat for a while after Lincoln had left, contemplating his empty glass, then went to the bar for a refill. The room was empty, save for himself. He'd have a couple more after this one, then go home. Amanda would no doubt comment on the reek of alcohol and make some barbed remark about driving while over the limit, but by that time Standish would be past caring.

He thought about Sarah Roberts and the impossibility of her murder. The image of the woman, ethereally angelic, floated into his vision. The tech from the Onward Station had been unable to ascertain if Roberts could be saved, and seemed nonplussed at the dysfunction of her implant.

The entire affair had an air of insoluble mystery that made Standish uncomfortable. The unmarked snow, the circular melt, the failure of her implant... Perhaps it was as well that he wouldn't be working on the case.

His mobile rang, surprising him. "Doug?"

"Amanda?" he said.

"I thought you said you'd be back by six?" Her clipped Welsh tone sounded peremptory, accusing.

"Something came up. I'm working late."

"Well, I have to go out. Kath's babysitter's let her down at the last minute. I'll be back around midnight. Your dinner's in the microwave."

"Fine. Bye—"

But she had cut the connection.

Five minutes later he finished his drink and was about to go to the bar for another when, through the window, he saw a small blue VW Electro halt at the crossroads, signal right, and then turn carefully on the gritted surface.

On impulse he stood and hurried from the bar. He was over the limit, but he gave it no thought as he slipped in behind the wheel of the Renault and set off in pursuit of the VW.

Amanda's best friend, Kath, lived in Bradley, five miles in the opposite direction to where Amanda was heading now.

Seconds later, through the darkness, he made out a set of rear lights. The VW was crawling along at jogging pace. Amanda always had been too cautious a driver. He slowed so as not to catch her up, and only then wondered why he was following her.

Did he really want to know?

He wondered if Richard Lincoln's last pearl of wisdom had provoked him into action. *"Doug, perhaps you'd feel better about life in general if you could sort things out with Amanda, one way or another."*

Perhaps he'd had long enough of feeling powerless. Who had said that knowledge was power? He shook his head. The alcohol was fuddling his thinking. He really should turn around and go home, leave Amanda to whatever petty adultery she was committing.

He hunched over the wheel and concentrated on the road ahead.

Five minutes later they entered the village of Hockton and the VW slowed to a crawl and pulled into the kerb beside a row of stone-built cottages. Standish drove on, overtook the parked car, and came to a halt twenty metres further along the road.

He turned in his seat and watched as Amanda climbed out and hurried through the slush. A light came on in the porch of the cottage where she'd parked, and the figure of a man appeared in the doorway.

Amanda ran into his embrace, then slipped into the house. The light in the porch went out. The door closed. He imagined his wife in the arms of the stranger and then whatever else they might get up to in the hours before midnight.

The strange thing was that he felt no anger. No anger at all. Instead, he experienced a dull ache in his chest, like an incipient coronary, and a strange sense of disappointment.

Now he knew, and nothing could ever be the same again.

He turned his car and drove back past the house, noting the number. He would check on its occupant later, when he had thought through the implications of Amanda's actions.

He drove home, considered stopping at the Dog and Gun for a few more, but vetoed the idea. Once home, he tried to eat the meal Amanda had left for him, managed half of it and threw the rest.

He went to bed, but not in the main bedroom. He slept in the guest room and wondered why he hadn't had the guts to do so before now.

He was still awake well after midnight when Amanda got back. He heard her key in the front door and minutes later the sound of her soft footsteps on the stairs. He imagined her entering the bedroom and not finding him there, and the thought gave him a frisson of juvenile satisfaction.

A minute later she appeared in the doorway, silhouetted in the landing light behind her. "Doug? Are you okay?"

She was a small woman, dark-haired and voluptuous. He recalled the first time he had seen her naked.

He wanted to ask her why, but that would be to initiate a conflict in which he could only finish second best. He knew why. She no longer loved him. It was as simple as that.

She waited a second, then said, "Pissed again, are you? Well, stay there, then."

She pushed herself away from the jamb, and Standish said, "Don't worry, I fully intend to."

She hesitated, considering a rejoinder, but thought better of it and moved back to the main bedroom, turning off the landing light and filling the house with darkness.

Later, in the early hours, Standish awoke suddenly, startled by the burst of white light as the Onward Station beamed its freight of dead humans to the orbiting Kéthani starship.

That night he dreamed of angels.

He awoke early next morning and left the house before Amanda got up. It was another crystal clear, dazzlingly bright day. A fierce frost had sealed the snow overnight and the roads into Bradley were treacherous.

The desk-sergeant apprehended Standish before he reached his office and handed him a printout.

Detective Inspector Singh wanted to see him about the Roberts case.

"He's here?" Standish asked.

The sergeant shook his head. "Up at the farmhouse with a forensic team."

He drove from Bradley and over the moors, taking his time. He crested a rise and, before him, the spun-crystal pinnacle of the Onward Station came into view. It looked at its best in a setting of snow, he thought: it belonged. He wondered at the homeworld of the Kéthani, and whether it was a place of snow and ice.

How little we know of our benefactors, he thought as he arrived at the farmhouse.

A fall of snow during the night had filled in the footsteps made by Standish, Lincoln, and the others the evening before, but a new trail of prints led up the drive from two police cars parked outside the gate, now unlocked. He climbed from his car and hurried over to the house.

Detective Inspector R.J. Singh stood in the front room, arms folded across his massive stomach. He was a big man in a dark suit and a white turban, and when he spoke Standish detected a marked Lancastrian accent. "Inspector Standish. Glad you could make it. Good to have you aboard."

"I hope I can help." They shook hands, and Standish looked down at where, yesterday, the body of Sarah Roberts had sprawled.

Today, a series of holographic projectors recreated the image. It was the first time Standish had witnessed the technology at work, and he had to admit that it was impressive. But for the presence of the three small tripod-mounted projectors, he might have believed that the body was still *in situ*.

Even though he knew it was not the real thing, he still found it hard to look upon the ethereal beauty of the spectral image.

A couple of forensic scientists knelt in the corner of the room, minutely inspecting the carpet with portable microscopes.

Singh questioned him about the discovery of the body, and Standish recounted his impressions.

They moved across the room, to where a series of photographs had been spread out across the table. They showed the farmhouse and the surrounding snow-covered grounds from every angle.

"Not a clue," Singh said, gesturing at the photographs. "Nothing. The killer came and went without leaving a trace. We've thought of everything. I don't suppose you've come up with anything?"

He told Singh about his theory that the killer might have concealed himself somewhere in the house.

"Thought of that," Singh said. "We went through the place with a fine-tooth comb."

Standish shook his head. "I don't know what else to suggest. I just can't see how the killer did it."

"I've studied the recordings of Roberts on the vid to the ferryman, Richard Lincoln," Singh said. "No clues there, either. One minute she's talking to Lincoln, and the next she goes to answer the door, comes back and... bang."

Standish moved to the window and looked out. The melted circle that he had noted yesterday was filled now with the night's snowfall.

"Did you see...?" he began.

Singh nodded. "One of the photos picked it up. I'm checking things like underground pipes. I don't think it's anything significant." He looked around the room. "She certainly kept a tidy house."

He had noticed that yesterday, Standish thought now, though then he'd hardly registered the fact. The place was as unlived in as a show-house.

"I've been looking into Sarah Roberts's past," Singh said. "You might be interested in what I've discovered."

Standish nodded. "Anything that might shed light—?"

Singh interrupted. "Nothing." He smiled at Standish's puzzlement. "The records go back three years, during her time with over half a dozen Onward Stations up and down the country. Before that, Sarah Roberts didn't exist, officially, that is."

"So 'Sarah Roberts' was an alias?"

"Something like that. We're checking with the Ministry of Kéthani Affairs. Chances are that the whole thing will be taken away from us and declared classified. If she was important enough to work for the Ministry in some hush-hush capacity, then the killing might be deemed too sensitive a matter for us mere workaday coppers."

"And you think the killing might have been linked to her work?"

"Impossible to tell. Between you and me, I don't think we'll ever find out."

Standish let his gaze stray again to the projected image of Sarah Roberts. "Have the techs come up with any reason for the dysfunction of her implant?"

"They're mystified. I wondered if it could have been linked to the killing—if the killer had in some way disabled it—but they simply couldn't tell me. They've never come across anything like it."

"And she's... I mean, there's no way they can save her?"

Singh pulled an exaggeratedly doleful face. "I'm afraid not. Sarah Roberts is dead."

Standish averted his gaze from the ghost of the woman lying on the carpet, and asked, "Is it okay if I take another look around?"

"Be my guest. Forensic have almost finished."

Standish climbed the stairs and inspected the bedrooms again. He was struck by the improbability of a woman in her mid-twenties choosing to sleep in a single bed. He looked around the room. It was remarkable only for the lack of personality stamped upon the room during the three months that Sarah Roberts had lived there: a brush and comb sat on a dresser, next to a closed make-up box. They looked like they had been placed there by stagehands, to give spurious authenticity to a set.

He moved to the bathroom, where yesterday he had been aware of something not quite right. Now he realised what he'd missed: the room was bare, no toothpaste, shampoo, conditioner, hair-gels, hand creams, or toiletries of any kind.

Another damned mystery to add to all the others.

He returned downstairs and found the detective inspector in the kitchen, peering into the fridge.

"Strange," Singh said when he saw Standish. "Empty. Nothing, not even a pint of milk."

Standish told him about the empty bathroom.

"Curiouser and curiouser," Singh said to himself.

"I might go over to the Onward Station and talk to the Director," Standish said. "If you don't mind my trespassing on your territory, that is?"

"Let's share anything we come up with, okay?" Singh said. "God knows, I need all the help I can get."

Standish took his leave of the farmhouse and motored across the moors to the looming monument of the alien Station. A new fall of snow had started, sifting down from a slate-grey sky. He found himself trailing a gritter for half a mile, delaying his arrival.

He thought about Sarah Roberts, her existence as pristine as the surrounding snow, and wondered if he would learn anything more from the Director.

Five minutes later he parked in the shadow of the Station and stepped through the sliding glass doors. The décor of the interior matched the arctic tone of the landscape outside. He'd only ever visited the Station once before, for the returning ceremony of a fellow policeman, and now he recalled the unearthly atmosphere of the place, the cool, quiet otherness of the white corridors and the spacious, minimally furnished rooms.

He showed his identification to a blue-uniformed receptionist and he was kept waiting for almost thirty minutes before the Director consented to see him.

The receptionist escorted him down a long white corridor, carpeted in pale blue, and left him in front of a white door. It slid open to reveal a stark room with a desk like an ice-table standing at the far end, before a floor-to-ceiling window that looked out over the frozen landscape.

The room seemed hardly more hospitable than the terrain outside.

A tall, attenuated man rose from behind the desk and gestured Standish to enter. Director Masters was in his fifties, severely thin and formal, as if his humanity had been leached by his involvement with such otherworldly matters as the resurrection of the dead.

They shook hands and Standish explained the reason for his visit.

"Ah," Masters said. "The Roberts case. Terrible thing."

"If it's all right with you, I'd like to ask a few questions about Ms Roberts."

"By all means. I'll assist in any way possible."

Standish began by asking what had been Sarah Roberts's function at the Station.

Masters nodded. "She was the Station's liaison officer."

"Which means?"

"She was the official who liaised between myself and my immediate superiors in Whitehall."

"So technically she worked for the government?"

"That is so."

"I presume you had daily contact with her?"

"I did."

"And how did you find her? I mean, what kind of person would you say she was?"

Masters eased himself back in his seat. "To be honest, I found Ms. Roberts a hard person to get to know. There was the age difference, of course. But even so, she was very withdrawn and reserved. Other members of my staff thought the same."

"She didn't socialise with anyone from the Station?"

Masters smiled. "She wasn't the kind of person to, ah... socialise."

"University educated?"

"Oxford."

Standish nodded. He was forming a picture of Roberts that in all likelihood was nothing like the person she had been. No doubt somewhere there was a mother and father, perhaps even a lover.

"Were you aware of anyone who might harbour a grudge or resentment against Ms. Roberts?"

"Absolutely not. She hardly interacted with anyone in any way that might have caused resentment or suchlike."

"Do you by any chance have a personnel dossier on Ms. Roberts?"

Masters hesitated, then nodded. He leaned towards a microphone. "Danielle, could you bring in the Sarah Roberts file, please?"

Two minutes later Standish was leafing through a brief, very brief, document which listed Roberts's other postings at Onward Stations around the country, and little else. There was no mention of her work before she joined the Ministry of Kéthani Affairs, nothing about her background or education.

But there was a photograph. It showed a fey, fair, beautiful woman in her early twenties, and Standish found it haunting.

He pulled the picture from its clip and asked Masters, "I don't suppose I could keep this?"

"I'll get Danielle to make a copy," Masters said, and called his secretary again.

For the next ten minutes, before Director Masters rather unsubtly glanced at his watch to suggest that time was pressing, Standish questioned the Director about Roberts's work. He learned that she collected data about the day-to-day running of the Station, the processing of the dead from the area, and passed the information on to a government department in London. Masters could tell him no more than that, or was unwilling to do so.

Standish thanked the director and left the Station. He sat in his Renault for ten minutes in contemplative silence, staring at the stark magnificence of the alien architecture, before starting the car and driving into Bradley.

He spent the afternoon in his office, processing what in the old days would have been called paperwork. He took time out to look up the identity of his wife's lover, then finished his shift at six.

That night he ate a steak and kidney pie in the Dog and Gun, drank more than was healthy, and at closing time was sitting by himself next to the open fire and staring at the photograph of the dead woman.

She reminded him of... what was the name of the Elf Queen from that old film, *The Lord of the Rings*? Anyway, she looked like the Elf Queen.

Serene and fey and... innocent?

He replaced the photograph in his breast pocket and left the pub. Electing to leave the car, he walked unsteadily along a lane made treacherous by black ice. It was after midnight when he arrived home. Thankfully Amanda was already in bed.

He slept in the guest room again, and awoke only when the bright white light from the Onward Station reminded him of his destiny, and the dead woman who would never live again.

The following morning he slipped from the house before Amanda got up, drove into Bradley and began work. Around eleven, R.J. Singh looked into the office and they discussed the case. Standish recounted his meeting with Director Masters and both men agreed that they were getting nowhere fast.

He had a quick sandwich in the staff canteen and after lunch returned to the routine admin work. By four, his eyes were sore from staring at the computer screen. He was considering going down to the canteen for a coffee when his mobile rang.

It was Richard Lincoln.

"Richard, how can I help?"

"It's about the Roberts affair," Lincoln said. "It might not amount to much, but a friend thought he saw something in the area on the afternoon of the murder."

"Where can I contact him?"

"Well, we're meeting in the Fleece in Oxenworth tonight, around seven. Why don't you come along?"

"I'll do that. See you then. Thanks, Richard."

He refuelled himself with that promised coffee and worked for a further couple of hours. Just after six he left the station and drove over the moors to Oxenworth, a tiny village of a dozen houses, two converted mills, a local store-cum-post office and a public house.

He arrived early and ordered scampi and chips from the bar menu. He was on his second pint when Richard Lincoln pushed through the swing door from the hallway, followed by a man and a woman in their forties.

Lincoln introduced the couple as Ben and Elisabeth Knightly; Ben was a dry-stone waller, Elisabeth a teacher at Bradley comprehensive. They had the appearance of newly-weds, Standish thought: they found each other's hands beneath the table when they assumed no one was looking and established eye contact with each other with charming regularity.

It reminded him of the early days with Amanda... Christ, was it really twenty years ago, now?

Ben Knightly said, "I read about the murder in this morning's paper..."

Standish nodded. "We've got no further with the investigation, to be honest. We need all the help we can get. Richard mentioned you saw something."

Ben Knightly was a big man with massive, outdoor hands. When he wasn't holding his wife's hand beneath the table, he clutched his pint, as if nervous. "I was working in the Patterson's top field," he said hesitantly. "I was just across the valley. It was around four, maybe a bit later."

"How far were you from the Roberts' farmhouse?" Standish asked, wondering exactly how far away "just across the valley" might be.

"Oh, about a mile, maybe a little bit less."

Standish halted his pint before his lips. "And you say you saw something. From that distance?"

Knightly glanced at his wife, then said, "Well, it wasn't hard to miss..."

A helicopter, Standish thought, his imagination getting the better of him. A hot-air balloon?

"At first I thought it was a shooting star," Knightly said. "I see them all the time, but not quite that early. But this star just went on and on, dropping towards the earth. I thought at first it was a beam bringing the returnees home, but it wasn't heading for the Station."

Standish nodded, wondering where this was leading. "Where did it fall?"

Ben Knightly shrugged his big shoulders. "It went down behind the trees next to the Roberts' house."

Standish looked at Lincoln. "A meteorite? I'm not very up on these things."

"Meteorites usually come in at an acute angle," the ferryman said, "not straight down."

"I thought I was seeing things," Knightly said. "But when I read about the murder..."

Standish shook his head. "I really don't see how..." Then he recalled the melted patch outside the back door of the farmhouse.

The conversation moved on to other things, after that. A little later they were joined by more people, friends of Lincoln. Standish recognised an implant doctor from Bradley General, Khalid Azzam, and Jeffrey Morrow and Dan Chester, another ferryman.

They were pleasant people, Standish thought. They went out of their way to make him feel part of the group. He bought a round and settled in for the evening. The ferrymen talked about why they had chosen their profession, and perhaps inevitably the topic of conversation soon moved round to the Kéthani.

"Come on, you two," Elisabeth said to Richard and Dan, playfully. "You come into contact with returnees every day. They must say something about the Kéthani homeworld?"

Lincoln smiled. "It's strange, but they don't. They say very little. They talk about the rehabilitation process in the domes, conducted by humans, and then what they call 'instructions', lessons in Zen-like contemplation, again taught by humans."

Dan Chester said, "They don't meet any Kéthani, or leave the domes. The view through the domes is one of rolling hills and vales—probably not what the planet looks like at all."

Standish looked around the group. They were all implanted. "Have you ever," he said, marshalling his thoughts, "had any doubts about the motives of the Kéthani?"

A silence developed, while each of the people around the table considered whether to answer truthfully.

At last Elisabeth said, "I don't think there's a single person on the planet who hasn't wondered, at some point. Remember the paranoia to begin with?"

That was before the returnees had returned to Earth, miraculously restored to life, with stories of the Edenic alien homeworld. These people seemed cured not only in body, but also in mind, assured and centred and *calm*... How could the Kéthani be anything other than a force for good?

Standish said, "I sometimes think about what's happened to us, and... well, I'm overcome by just how much we don't know about the universe and our place in it."

He shut up. He was drunk and rambling.

Not long after that the bell rang for last orders, and it was well after midnight before they stepped from the warmth of the bar into the sub-zero chill of the street. Standish made his farewells, promising he'd drop in again but knowing that, in all likelihood, in future he would do his drinking alone at the Dog and Gun.

He contemplated taking a taxi home, but decided he was fit enough to drive. He negotiated the five miles back to his village at a snail's pace, grateful for the gritted roads.

It was well after one o'clock by the time he drew up outside the house. The hall light was blazing, and the light in the kitchen, too. Was Amanda still up, waiting for him? Had she planned another row, a detailed inventory of his faults and psychological flaws?

He unlocked the front door, stepped inside, and stopped.

Three big suitcases filled the hallway.

He found Amanda in the kitchen.

She was sitting at the scrubbed-pine table, a glass of Scotch in her hand. She stared at him as he appeared in the doorway.

"I thought I'd better wait until you got back," she said.

"You're leaving?" He pulled out a chair and slumped into it. What did he feel? Relief, that at last someone in this benighted relationship had been strong enough to make a decision? Yes, but at the same time, too, a core of real regret.

"Who is she?" Amanda asked, surprising him.

He blinked at her. "Who's who?"

She reached across the table and took a photograph from where it was propped against the fruit bowl.

"I found it in the hall this morning. Who is she?"

It was the snap of Sarah Roberts he'd taken from the Station yesterday. Instinctively he reached for his breast pocket. The photograph must have slipped out last night when he'd tried to hang his jacket up.

"Well?" She was staring at him, something very much like hatred in her eyes.

A part of him wanted to take her to task over her hypocrisy, but another part was too tired and beaten to bother.

"It has nothing to do with you," he said.

"I'm going!" she said, standing.

He watched her hurry to the kitchen door, then said, "Staying with... what's his name? Jeremy Croft, in Hockton?"

She stopped in the doorway, turned, and stared at him. He almost felt sorry for her when she said, "I met him last year, Doug, when things were getting impossible here. I wanted someone to love me, someone I could love."

"I'm sorry you couldn't find that with me."

She shook her head. "Sometimes these things just don't work, no matter how hard you try. You know that." She hesitated, then said, "I hope you find what you want with..." She gestured to the snap of Sarah Roberts on the kitchen table, then hurried into the hall.

He opened his mouth to say something, but thought better of trying to correct her.

He heard her open the door and struggle out with the cases. He pushed himself upright and moved into the hall.

He pulled open the door and stepped outside. Amanda was driving away.

Strangely, he no longer felt the cold. In the silence of the night, he walked from the house and stood in the lane, staring up at the massed and scintillating stars.

Then he saw a shooting star—denoting a death, somewhere— and then he knew. It was as if he had known all along, but the sight of the shooting star had released something within him, allowing him the insight.

It made sense. Sarah Roberts, a woman without a past, living in a pristine house, empty of all the trivial products of the modern world. It made perfect sense. Perhaps, after all, she was an angel.

Laughing to himself, he staggered back inside and shut the door behind him. He moved to the lounge, collapsed on the sofa, and slept.

That night, not even the pulsing light from the Onward Station could wake him from his dreams.

He woke late the following morning, dragged from sleep by something indefinable working at the edge of his consciousness. He lay on his back and blinked up at the ceiling, recalling the events of the night before and sensing the start of a debilitating depression.

Then he became aware of what had awoken him: his phone, purring in the pocket of his jacket where he'd dropped it last night.

He pulled his jacket towards him and fumbled with the phone. "Standish here."

"Inspector Standish? Director Masters at the Station. I wonder if you could spare me a little of your time?"

"Concerning Roberts...?"

"Not over the phone, inspector."

"Very well. I'll be right over."

The Director thanked him and rang off.

He splashed his face with cold water, brushed his teeth and then made his way out to the car, his head throbbing from too many beers in the Fleece last night.

It was another sunny morning. He wondered what Amanda was doing now. As he drove through the quiet lanes and over the moors, towards the Onward Station, he imagined her in the arms of her lover.

At the sight of the rearing obelisk, he recalled what had come to him in the early hours, as he stood staring up at the spread of stars.

It seemed, in the harsh light of day, highly improbable.

He left his Renault in the parking lot and stepped through the sliding door. Director Masters himself was on hand to greet him.

"If you'd care to step this way."

He led Standish along a white corridor. They came at last to a sliding door, but not that of Masters's office.

The door eased open without a sound, and the director gestured Standish through.

He stepped into a small, white room, furnished only with a white, centrally located settee. He heard the door click shut behind him, and when he turned to question Masters he realised that the director had left him alone in the room.

A minute elapsed, and then two. Vaguely uneasy, without quite knowing why, he sat on the settee and waited.

Almost immediately a concealed sliding door opposite him opened quickly, and he jumped to his feet.

Someone stepped through the opening, backed by effulgent white light, and it was a second before his vision adjusted.

When it did, he could only stare in disbelief.

A slim, blonde woman stood before him. She was dressed in a white one-piece suit. Her expression, as she stared at him, was neutral.

It was Sarah Roberts.

He opened his mouth, but no words came. Then he looked more closely at the woman before him. It was almost Roberts, but not quite; there was a slight difference in the features, but enough of a similarity for the woman and Roberts to be sisters.

Standish managed, "Who are you?"

She smiled. "I think you know that, Doug." It was the familiarity of her using his first name that shocked him, as much as what she had said.

"I was right? Roberts was...?"

She inclined her head. "This soma-form, and variations upon it, is how we show ourselves on Earth."

His vision blurred. He thought he was going to pass out.

Was he one of the few people ever to knowingly set eyes on a member of the Kéthani race?

"Why? I mean—"

"We need to come among you from time to time, to monitor the progress of our work."

"But this..." He gestured at her. "This isn't how you appear in reality?"

She almost laughed. "Of course not, Doug."

"What do you look like?"

She regarded him, then said, gently, "You would be unable to apprehend our true selves, or make sense of what you saw."

He nodded. "Okay..." He took a breath. His head was pounding, with more than just the effects of the hangover. "Okay, so... what do you want with me? Why did you summon me here? Is it about—?"

She smiled. "The killing of the woman you knew as Sarah Roberts."

"The light from the sky," he said, "the patch of melted snow outside the farmhouse..." He shook his head. "Who killed her?"

"There is so much you don't know about the Kéthani," the woman said, "so much you have to learn. Like you, we have enemies. There are races out there who do not agree with what we are doing. Sometimes, these races act against us. Two nights ago, three enemy agents came to various locations on Earth to assassinate our envoys. They escaped before we could apprehend them."

He nodded; let the seconds elapse. "Why do they object to what you're doing?"

She smiled. "In time, Doug, in time. You will die, be reborn, and eventually go among the stars. Then you will learn more than you can possibly imagine."

"Why have you told me this?"

"We want you to solve the crime," she replied. "You will return to the farmhouse and search it. You will find a concealed space behind a bookcase in the main bedroom. You will assume that the killer hid there, emerged, and killed Sarah Roberts, stole her jewellery box, then escaped a day later using the cover of the tracks in the snow made by you and your colleagues."

It was his turn to smile. "But I *know* what really happened," he began.

"You do now," she said, "but when you leave the Station you will remember nothing of our meeting."

He was overcome, then, with some intimation of the awesome power of the Kéthani, and his people's ignorance.

"You are a good person, Doug." The woman smiled at him, with something like compassion in her eyes. "Let what has happened to you of late be the start of a new life, not the end."

He was suddenly aware of his pulse. "How do you know?"

"We know everything about you," the alien said. She stepped forward and reached up.

Her fingers touched the implant at his temple, and he felt a sudden dizziness, followed by an inexplicable, heady surge of optimism.

"The implants allow us access to your very humanity," she said. "Goodbye, Doug. Be happy."

She stepped through the sliding door, and seconds later the door to the corridor opened and Standish passed through. Masters's secretary escorted him towards the exit.

By the time he left the Station, Standish could only vaguely recall his meeting with Director Masters. He blamed the effects of the alcohol he'd consumed last night, and headed towards his car.

It came to him that he should check the farmhouse again. There had to be a rational explanation of what had happened there the other day. Murderers simply did not appear out of the blue and vanish again just as inexplicably.

He paused and gazed over the snow-covered landscape, marvelling at its beauty. He recalled Amanda's leaving last night and it came to him that it wasn't so much the end of his old life, but the beginning of a new phase of existence. He experienced a sudden, overwhelming wave of optimism. He recalled the invitation from Lincoln and the others to join them at the Fleece again, and knew in future that he would.

Smiling to himself, without really knowing why, Standish started the engine and drove slowly away from the Onward Station.

INTERLUDE

That Tuesday, Zara came home in a good mood. That in itself was reason enough for me to be suspicious. These days she was usually quiet, uncommunicative. I'd ask her what was wrong, and she'd reply that she was tired, or stressed out at work. For a long time now we'd lived what amounted to separate lives, going about our own interests and concerns without involving each other. From time to time I'd make the effort, attempt to rekindle the spark of our early relationship; but her rebuffs left me feeling hollowed and isolated. Often my enquiries escalated into full-blown rows, as if she resented the fact that I was questioning the state of our relationship. Perhaps she was feeling guilty.

So that evening when she breezed in and smiled at me, I wondered what was wrong. She had left the front door wide open, and before I could ask why, two overalled delivery men shuffled in carrying something heavy shrouded in bubble-wrap. They deposited it in the lounge and departed, and I asked, "What is it?"

She was still smiling. Without replying, she knelt and tore off the bubble-wrap, revealing a sculpture in dark wood. It was a half life-sized representation of a man and a woman, entwined in the act of making love.

She dragged it over to the corner of the room. "What do you think, Khalid?"

I didn't look at her. "It reminds me of something," I said. "Let me think... Ah, that's it. It reminds me of the time when we used to make love... How long ago was that, Zara?"

She just stared at me. "And whose fault is that?"

"Well," I said, working to maintain my temper, "it certainly isn't mine. I'm game, any time. How about tonight? Tell you what. I won't go to the pub. We'll go to bed now, if you like."

She looked away. "You know it's my study group night."

"So miss it for once. Make love to me, instead."

She approached the sculpture, knelt and examined it.

She said, "It's beautiful, isn't it?"

I wondered if she were taunting me. She went on, "I managed to secure it for half its sale price. I know the artist. He comes to the study group."

I tried to sound casual. "Oh? Who is he?"

"Simon Robbins. He's quite famous. You might have heard of him..." As she said this, she reached out and caressed the sleek buttock of the male figure.

The name did ring a bell. "Wasn't he the artist who was jailed for murder... what, twenty years ago?"

She nodded, abstracted. "He served his time, came out, and when the Kéthani came he killed himself. He... he didn't like the person he was. He thought the Kéthani might *cure* him."

I hesitated, then said, "And did they?"

She smiled. "Yes, Khalid, they did. He came back from Kéthan a changed man, became an artist. He's a good person." Her fingertips rested on the sculpture, and her eyes had a far away look.

I crossed to her, touched her luxuriant hair. "Zara..." I was close to tears, for reasons I couldn't quite work out.

She pulled away, stood hurriedly, and moved to the stairs. "Must rush. Can't be late for the study group."

She disappeared, and I fixed myself something to eat as she changed and left the house.

That night I arrived early at the Fleece and had downed three pints by nine o'clock before the others arrived.

"Khal," Doug Standish laughed when he saw me. "Are you living here?"

I attempted a smile. "Feels like it sometimes."

Elisabeth sat beside me and gave me a hug. "You okay?"

"I'm fine," I said. "Long day at the ward."

Dan Chester and Richard Lincoln blew in and Dan bought a round. They were talking shop. Apparently, Dan had been reading some paper put out by the government department that oversaw the running of the Onward Stations in England.

He took a long pull on his pint and said, "Interesting fact." He looked around the table. "Okay, here's a little quiz for you. How many returnees come back to Earth and commit crimes?"

The question brought to mind what Zara had told me about Simon Robbins.

Doug Standish frowned. "You mean, per thousand? What percentage?"

Dan shook his head. "No, I mean how many individuals?"

Elisabeth laughed. "In Britain, Europe, worldwide?"

"Worldwide."

Jeff Morrow placed his pint precisely on its mat and said, "Well, it's obviously low. So I'd say... God, I don't know. How many returnees are there every year, worldwide?"

"In the region of a million," Richard Lincoln said, helpfully.

"In that case," Jeff said, "I'd guess around twenty, thirty thousand..."

Dan smiled and said, "Lis?"

"I don't know, around the same figure."

It went on like this, until all eyes rested on me. I said, meaning to be dismissive, "How about ten, Dan?" and hid behind my pint.

Dan slapped the table. "Well, Khalid's the closest."

Expostulations sounded around the table.

Ben said, "What kind of crimes are we talking about, here? Murders?"

"All crimes," Dan said. He paused dramatically, then said, "The actual figure is precisely zero."

Elisabeth laughed, incredulous.

Before anyone could demur, Dan pulled a pamphlet from his coat pocket and slid it across the table.

Elisabeth picked it up and read through it quickly.

Dan was saying, "The UN conducted a study recently. If you look on page ten, second paragraph, Lis," he directed. "It's an incontrovertible fact. Returnees do not commit crimes, of any kind."

Jeff looked across at Doug Standish. "Can you confirm this, Doug? Have you arrested any returnees recently?"

Doug looked up from his pint. "The odd thing is... and this isn't official police policy... but when I'm considering suspects, I tend almost always to discount those we know are returnees. I'm not even sure it's a conscious thing." He shrugged. "But I don't doubt the report," he finished.

For the rest of the evening we discussed what the Kéthani were doing to us, out there.

It is a paradox: it took an alien race to invest us with humanity...

I absented myself from proceedings before closing time, attracting a few worried glances at this untoward behaviour, and made my way down the main street. Instead of letting myself into the house, which would be cold and empty at this late hour, I slipped into my car and sat in the driving seat, considering what I was going to do next.

I was drunk, and hardly capable of driving safely, but to be honest this was the least of my worries.

I started the engine and drove from the village, then turned onto the bypass and headed towards Bradley. I drove slowly. It was a fine summer's night, and a full moon illuminated the countryside, but even at this late hour there was other traffic on the road. In retrospect I'm amazed that I managed to drive the seven miles into Bradley without killing myself or some other hapless driver.

I parked across the road from where Zara and her study group met every Tuesday evening. It was a big Georgian terrace house, with a stained glass door and a flashy silver Porsche sitting by the kerb.

There were no lights on in the downstairs windows. But upstairs, in the main bedroom, an orange light burned.

I was filled with sufficient anger to fuel my rage: part of me wanted to charge in and confront Zara there and then. But that intemperate action would have robbed me of my ultimate act of revenge.

One hour later, the bedroom light went out. I steeled myself. The light in the hallway came on, and a minute later the front door opened.

I saw Zara, and the man behind her. I wondered if this were the celebrated artist, Simon Robbins—the man the Kéthani had turned into a paragon.

I looked away. I didn't want to see them say goodbye... I started the car and drove off at speed, so that I would arrive home before Zara.

I feigned sleep when she arrived a little later. In reality I lay awake, planning what I should do...

I find it impossible to write about what happened over the course of the next few weeks, even after all these years. Richard Lincoln was there at the beginning, and at the end, and I've talked to him about it over many a beer since then. So let Richard tell my sorry story...

SIX

The Wisdom of the Dead

I was in the main bar of the Fleece when Khalid announced that his wife was leaving him, and I was in the lounge of his converted coach-house a year later when he explained to me the circumstances of his death.

That night I finished a long shift making deliveries to the Onward Station high on the moors, and I was in need of a pint or two in the company of the usual Tuesday night crowd.

It was a balmy summer's evening, and the clientele of the Fleece were making the most of the weather and drinking in the lane. The main bar was almost empty, but for the regulars: Ben and Elisabeth, Jeff Morrow, Dan Chester my colleague, Doug Standish, and Khalid.

I carried my pint over to their table, sat down, and stared around at my friends. They were quiet. "You look as though you've just got back from a funeral," I said.

They said nothing, and I thought for a second that I'd committed terrible social gaff, and they *had* been to a funeral.

Jeff just shrugged, uneasy. Ben and Elisabeth looked away. I smiled. "What's wrong?"

Khalid said, "I think it's my fault, Richard," and fell silent.

Jeff said, "You can tell us, Khal. We're friends, you know?"

Elisabeth caught my gaze and pulled a worried face.

Khalid was sitting at the end of the table, his pint untouched before him. He was usually immaculately turned out, clean-shaven and dapper. Tonight he was unshaven, his hair dishevelled. His gaze was remote.

From time to time he fingered the implant at his temple, absent-ly.

He looked up at each of us in turn.

Only then did I think to myself: *I'm not going to like this one bit...*

He cleared his throat and said, "Zara's leaving me." He looked at his watch. "In fact, she's probably left already."

Doug Standish said, "My God."

Elisabeth took Khalid's hand.

I murmured something along the lines that I was sorry. More than that, I was shocked. I liked Zara. She taught English at Jeff's school in Bradley, an attractive, intelligent woman in her early forties. She and Khalid had always struck me as a loving and devoted couple.

Khalid stared at his pint. "Things haven't been going well for a while. We haven't been communicating. She was... cold, remote. I thought it was..." He shrugged and looked helpless. "I don't know what I thought. Then last week I... I confronted her. She admitted she was seeing someone and... and she decided to move out."

We sympathised, with all the useless old platitudes that come to play in these situations.

Khalid fell silent, obviously not wanting to say anything more, and we changed the subject. Conversation was forced for the rest of the evening. Khalid downed his pint, and I bought him another, then a third and a fourth.

At eleven-thirty the others made their farewells and left.

Khalid finished his pint and looked at me. "How about a drink back at my place, Richard? I have some bottled Landlord."

Khalid lived in a coach-house a few doors down from the Fleece. It was a big place, with a front door that opened straight onto the pavement. Khalid, key in hand, paused before the door, and took a deep breath.

We stepped into the cold house and I settled myself in a sofa while Khalid fetched the beer. It was a large, comfortable room, with white walls, ancient black beams and a big brass-cowled fireplace.

Then I noticed the sculpture.

Khalid entered the room and stopped. He stared at the sculpture, his expression folding. I thought he was about to weep.

The carving, in dark, polished wood, showed two figures, a man and a woman, entwined in an intimate embrace.

A Post-it note was affixed to the woman's out-thrust buttock. Before Khalid snatched it up, I read: *Khal, I couldn't fit this in the car. I'll be back for it later. Zara.*

He looked at me. "We think we know people, don't we?"

I smiled sympathetically and took a long swallow of ale.

Khalid slumped into an armchair. "I was happy with Zara in the early years. She was perfect. We fitted. I always thought I wanted to spend the rest of my life with this woman." He shrugged, regarding the bottle in his hand. "I assumed she thought the same. Then things started going wrong. A couple of years ago... I sensed a shift in things, how we related. She was keeping something back. I thought it was a phase."

I shook my head. His words released unpleasant memories. Six months after the coming of the Kéthani my wife, Barbara, had left me in acrimonious circumstances. Even though our relationship hadn't been working for years, and the split was inevitable, it was still painful. I could imagine the anguish Khalid was suffering.

He looked up. "When I confronted her, she said she'd met someone at the study group she went to on Tuesdays, and intended to live with him. He's an artist. A sculptor."

I glanced at the entwined figures without making it obvious: of course, now that I looked closely, the naked female figure in the arms of the male was Zara.

Khalid saw my gaze and laughed. "She bought this about six months ago. She put it in the bedroom. I mean, Richard, how bloody cruel can you get?"

The silence stretched. I wanted to say something, but nothing seemed appropriate.

He went on, "I tried asking, again and again, what I'd done wrong, what was wrong with our relationship. The frustrating thing was, she refused to talk. She simply said that she was sorry, that she'd fallen out of love with me, as simple as that. She said we had nothing in common any more, we didn't communicate. And then she met... Simon, he's called." He wept, pressing the back of his hand to his mouth in a bid to stem the sobs.

Then, quickly, he apologised, and I smiled and shook my head and told him how it had been with Barbara, all those years ago. It was the early hours before I dragged myself home.

But I recall the last thing he said to me before I left. "Richard, I never realised that love could turn to so much hatred."

Life continued.

We met in the Fleece every Tuesday. Khalid was there in body, but not in spirit. He seemed to inhabit some far-off realm. Usually eager to take part in any discussion, these days he was silent, unwilling to be drawn on any topic. He would nurse his pint and stare into space, emanating an almost palpable air of misery.

I called around one day to find him slumped in an armchair, staring into the empty hearth.

"It's only me," I called from the hall on finding the front door open. "I've brought this back." I indicated the hammer I'd borrowed weeks earlier.

"I won't stay," I went on, seeing him in the chair. But he protested.

"No, stay a while. Coffee?" He seemed eager for company.

"The hell of it is," he said a little later, "that everything reminds me of Zara. This house, the village."

"Have you thought of moving? Selling this place, I mean?"

He shook his head. "To be honest I've been so low that I can't shift myself to do anything. I've thought about selling up, but that'd be as good as admitting defeat. I keep thinking that the pain will stop, in time. But if anything it only gets worse."

I indicated the place beside the hearth where the sculpture had stood. "I see she's taken it away."

"She hasn't been back here," he said, bitter. "I had to take it round to Simon's place. I never really realised how easy it would be to murder someone and think nothing of it." He looked up at me. "You're shocked, I can see. I went round to his studio and told him I wouldn't be needing the sculpture, thanks. He was so damned reasonable about things that I wanted to hit him over the head with it. The terrible thing is, Richard, that I feel I could be violent towards Zara, too."

I nodded. "Have you seen her since...?"

"Once, by accident."

"Don't you think it'd make things easier if you could still be friends?"

"I don't know. Sometimes I think that, and at others I think I never want to see her again."

* * *

A few weeks later I was in the supermarket in Bradley when I heard a familiar voice behind me.

"Richard?" Her tone was diffident, unsure.

I turned. "Zara. Nice to see you."

She looked radiant. She had that demure, elegant poise possessed by some Anglo-Pakistani women in their forties; she was tall, slim, raven-haired and wore subtle purple eye-shadow that complemented her mocha skin.

"Richard..." She waited until an old woman was out of earshot, then went on in a low voice, "I hope you don't hate me for what happened between me and—"

I blustered. "These things happen."

She laid a hand on my arm. "I just had to get out, Richard. The relationship was just too oppressive."

I nodded, at a loss to know how to respond.

"Khal comes from a very traditional Bradford family," she went on. "He was domineering. Do you know, he didn't really like my teaching?"

I made some murmured comment along the lines that I never realised...

"Life was getting oppressive. Towards the end I really hated him. And then I met Simon, and I knew that I'd made a big mistake in marrying Khal."

I nodded again, and said, "Sometimes these realisations hit you, Zara. And you're happy now?"

She hesitated. "Simon and I want to get married, but Khal—"

"He won't grant a divorce?" I didn't know whether to be disappointed at Khalid's pettiness or amazed at Zara's bourgeois desire to marry. Once bitten, I wanted to tell her...

"How cruel can you get, Richard? I spoke to him on the phone the other day, and the hatred..."

"Have you talked with him about why you left? Have you tried telling your side of the story?"

She almost laughed at that. "You don't know him!" she said. "He wouldn't listen to a word I said. He's in the right, always. Richard, as far as he's concerned, I'm just a woman."

I said goodbye a little later, saying that we must keep in touch.

I recall driving home through the autumn twilight and wondering who was right, who wrong, and if objective truth was a valid concept.

I called on Khalid that evening, to see if he wanted to join me in a pint. He opened the front door and blinked at me. Even in the shadow of the hallway, I noticed his black eye.

"Argument with the door?" I asked.

He didn't see the humour in my observation. "With Simon Robbins," he said. "Zara was on the phone this morning, telling me that she wants a divorce. Simon wants to marry her."

I almost said that he'd gain nothing from refusing Zara's request.

"I snapped. I went round to his studio earlier and did what I should have done months ago."

I winced. "That wouldn't endear Zara to you—"

"You don't think I give a fuck about what she thinks any more, do you?" he said. He looked at his knuckles; they were bruised and bloodied, and I felt a quick stab of sympathy for the victim of his anger.

I asked him if he'd care for a drink, but he just smiled and said he wasn't feeling up to socialising.

Over the course of the next few months, Khalid rarely showed up at the Fleece for our Tuesday night sessions. I called round a few times, but he was sullen and uncommunicative.

At one point he seemed so low that I said, "Khal, look... Don't do anything stupid, okay?"

He stared at me, then laughed. "What, like kill myself? The Kéthani have taken away that option, haven't they?" He tapped his implant. "Though I could always have this taken out, I suppose." Something in his bitter tone, his intense stare as I left him, alarmed me.

Winter arrived. Snow fell with a vengeance. The village was cut off for two days, lending a siege mentality to the place. We made the best of it and inhabited the main bar of the Fleece, as you do in emergencies. Lucy and the other kids made snowmen and sledged until frostbite threatened.

A week before Christmas, with snow still falling and more on the way, Khalid called around. It was a fortnight since I'd last seen him, and I took his visit as a hopeful sign. He seemed a little brighter.

He was going away for the holiday period, visiting student friends in Norfolk, and wanted to borrow the elasticated rope I used to secure luggage on my roof-rack.

We chatted desultorily over coffee; not once did he mention Zara, which I took as another good sign.

Christmas Eve came around yet again, and I was due to meet everyone at the Fleece for our traditional festive get-together. This year Ben and Elisabeth had invited Jeff Morrow and myself—lone sheep at this time of the year—along with Dan Chester and Lucy, round to their place for Christmas day. I was looking forward to the occasion. I usually make lame excuses and stay at home, or put my name down on the work roster, but for some unaccountable reason this time I'd succumbed to pressure and agreed to forgo my usual seasonal humbug. Perhaps the thought of watching Lucy, opening her presents, stirred memories of my own daughter doing the same, many years ago.

She was in Canada now, married with a child. I kept meaning to visit, but apathy always won out. I've noticed that with the advance of the years we find our safe routines and resist all opportunities to deviate.

I heard the sound around eight. I had never before heard a gun-shot, and I had no idea, then, that it was such. It sounded too dull and muffled—reminiscent of the bangers we let off in the confined space of the gents' loo when we were kids.

I thought nothing more of it, until five minutes later when I heard a hammering on the front door.

It sounded frantic.

I hurried into the hall and pulled open the door.

"Zara," I began.

She clutched my arm. "Richard, you've got to come! It's Khal…"

She was shaking and looked shocked: that vacant, dead expression the face assumes when the brain cannot assimilate the fact of tragedy.

I found my shoes, dragged on a coat, and followed her along the snow-covered pavement.

Khal's front door was open. Zara was explaining, "He asked me to come round. He said he had a present. I said I could only stay for a few minutes…" She broke down.

I hurried into the house.

The lounge was in disarray. An armchair had been overturned, a lamp-stand knocked over. A magazine rack had toppled, sending its glossy contents avalanching across the carpet.

I did not immediately see Khalid—perhaps my eyes saw him, but my brain refused to accept the image.

Only when I had taken in the state of the room did I notice the body.

He was lying before the hearth, on his back. In the centre of his chest—gaudy crimson on his white shirt—was a bloodstain. His eyes were open, staring glassily at the ceiling.

I was overcome with a fleeting dizziness. In my line of work I deal with bodies everyday, but I had never before witnessed a victim of violence.

Then I recalled what Khalid had said, in jest, a few weeks back about having his implant removed. I knelt, reached out, and touched his implant. It vibrated quickly beneath my fingertips.

I looked up. Zara was standing by the door, fingers to her lips, sobbing.

I moved to her and took her in my arms. "It's okay," I soothed. "The team at the Onward Station will know of his death. They'll send out a ferryman and notify the police."

The room was cold. There was no fire lit in the hearth, and the door was still open. I closed it.

"When did you get here?" I asked.

"Just minutes ago. I came straight in, and when I saw... I came straight to you."

I recalled hearing the gunshot, perhaps ten minutes ago. I opened the door and looked out, but the snow on the pavement was a churned and slushy mess, bearing no obliging record of the killer's footprints.

I returned to Zara. She stared at me. "Who'd do such a thing?" she asked. "It doesn't make sense."

It didn't make any sense at all. It was hard to think who might have hated Khalid enough to kill him—but in this day and age it was almost impossible to work out why anyone might be drawn to homicide, other than in the heat of the moment. Why kill someone when they would be brought back to life to incriminate their killer? Of course, murder was still committed—crimes of passion, incidents of hatred when the killer was barely conscious of the act...

There was a knock at the door. I opened it, expecting a ferryman or the police, or both. Instead, a tall, balding stranger stood on the front step, stamping his feet in the cold.

Zara hurried over to him. "Simon," she said.

I looked mystified. Zara explained, "Simon dropped me off and went to park at the Fleece."

Simon nodded to me and stepped inside. "What's the delay—?" he began and then saw the body. He went white, then slid down the wall and slumped into a sitting position.

Zara sat next to him, quietly crying on his shoulder.

Five minutes later Dan Chester arrived, accompanied by the local constable. While the policeman called in his superiors over at Bradley, I took Dan to one side and explained the situation.

He stared down at the body. "Christ, who'd do such a thing...?" He glanced across at Zara.

"No way!" I hissed. "She came straight round to my place when she found him. She was distraught. And anyway, why would she do something so stupid when Khalid would incriminate her when he returned?"

He shrugged. "Okay, but what if she came here without intending to kill him? They argued, struggled. The place is a mess. What if Khal threatened her?"

"And she just happened to be carrying a gun? Highly bloody unlikely!"

"What about her new bloke? What if they argued?"

I recalled what Khalid had told me a while back, about the bust-up he'd had with Simon. Had Simon harboured a resentment?

"Okay," I said, "but the same question applies. Why kill when you'll be found out in six months? You just wouldn't do it—not even in the heat of the moment."

Minutes later the CID from Bradley arrived, along with a forensic team and a scene-of-crime squad.

While the forensic scientists photographed the body, a detective inspector took preliminary statements from Zara, Simon, and myself.

Later we were driven in separate cars to Bradley police station and questioned there at length.

It was almost ten by the time I returned home, changed, and made my way to the Fleece.

Ben and Elisabeth were in the main bar, with Jeff Morrow. They looked concerned when they saw me.

"Richard," Jeff said, "what's happening? We saw the police cars outside Khal's. Where's Khal?"

Before saying anything, I bought myself a drink—a double whisky—and suggested we occupy a table beside the fire.

"What?" Elisabeth asked.

I told them what had happened that evening, from my hearing the gunshot, and Zara's arrival, to finding Khal's body.

"But who the hell would kill Khalid?" Ben asked, a question that I'd heard enough already and was to hear countless times again over the course of the next few weeks.

I told them about Dan's errant speculation that Zara or Simon had pulled the trigger. "But it just doesn't make sense," I said, and outlined my objections again.

"You said that Khal beat up this Simon character a bit back?" Ben asked.

I nodded. "But I hardly think that's a motive enough to kill someone."

"You don't know what this Simon's like."

"But, again, why would he kill Khal when, in six months Khal will return to point the finger? It's absurd."

Jeff said, "Perhaps Simon didn't pull the trigger, as it were. He hired a hit-man to do it, someone Khal wouldn't know from Adam."

I almost laughed at that. "This is sounding more like an old episode of *Morse* by the second. Look, the explanation will be very simple. Khal disturbed someone burgling the house. He picked up a poker to fight off the intruder. Intruder pulls a gun and without considering the consequences—in self-defence, he might claim—fires. End of story."

Or so I wanted to think. But my friends' suspicions had sown seeds of doubt in my mind.

It was a sombre Christmas. Okay, so thanks to the Kéthani Khalid would be resurrected by summer, but that didn't remove the fact that a nasty crime had been committed on our doorstep and that the killer was still at large.

In the slow, dead period immediately after Christmas, Khalid's murder made the national news. Reporters—the scum of the Earth, in my opinion—doorstepped Khalid's every acquaintance in the village. They wrote lurid stories of his break-up with Zara and his affair—wholly apocryphal—with a young nurse at his hospital. I ignored every one of the skulking bastards, but did come close to punching a particularly obnoxious hack who offered me 25,000 euros for my exclusive story.

I was called into Bradley police station again to give another account of my actions on the night of the murder, and from local gossip learned that Zara and Simon had made frequent visits to the station, where they were questioned. The case was put on hold until the time of Khalid's return in June, and gradually media interest faded away.

Life returned to normal. After the Christmas break I resumed my four-day-on, three-day-off stint delivering the dead to the Onward Station. Late at night, after a long shift, I would often look up at the winter darkness and wonder where Barbara, my wife, might be among the massed stars. I thought of Khalid, too, his resurrection and eventual return to Earth for questioning about his death.

The topic of conversation every Tuesday night for a long while was of course the murder. Doug Standish, the latest recruit to the Tuesday night crowd, and a detective inspector over at Bradley, told us that Khalid had been shot at close range, no more than half a metre away, by a single bullet from a 0.2 automatic, not that this information meant much to the rest of us. The police were no nearer apprehending his killer; if truth be known, they weren't even working on the case, as in all likelihood it would be solved on Khal's return.

One Tuesday in March, Jeff Morrow fuelled speculation. He joined us with his pint, took an appreciative mouthful, and said, "You recall we were kicking around the idea that Zara or Simon might have done the deed."

"*You* were kicking the idea around," I reminded him.

He nodded. "Okay, so concede for a second that one of them might have pulled the trigger. In June, when Khalid returns, the game will be up. They'll be exposed."

"If," I pointed out, "they had anything to do with it."

"And if they had, do you think they'd stay around to be incriminated?"

Elisabeth said, "Obviously not, but like Richard I don't think—"

Jeff said, "Zara left school on Friday and hasn't been seen since. Simon likewise. Police called round his house on Sunday and found it empty. They've done a bunk."

I stared at him. "So they've gone away for a while, a short break. They'll be back."

Dan said, "They weren't under any kind of restraint to remain in the area, Jeff. As long as they notify the police of their whereabouts every week, as far as I understand it..."

The weeks passed. There was no sign of Zara or Simon, and local gossip was rife. We tried to find out from Doug Standish if indeed the couple were in contact with the authorities, but if Doug knew he was saying nothing.

June came, and the day of Khalid's return.

I'd made the last delivery of an early shift around four o'clock that afternoon, and I hung around until five hoping to see Khalid, maybe even snatch a word or two with him. In the event he was met by two plainclothes officers who whisked him away in an unmarked police car, presumably to Bradley for questioning.

Around seven that evening I received a phone call.

"Richard?"

"Khalid! Where are you?"

"I'm at home. I was wondering... could you call round?"

"Of course. I'm on my way."

Two minutes later I stepped into the lounge where, six months earlier, I had seen Khalid sprawled dead, a bullet hole in his chest.

Now he stood in the middle of the room, as large as life. He was wearing a crisp white shirt, identical to the one I had seen saturated in blood; it seemed a lifetime ago, now.

We live life with a mere abstract understanding of what the implants—the symbol of our immortality—mean to us. The concept of continued life is just too vast a notion for our puny human brains to grasp. I found it hard to believe, as I stared at him across the room, that Khalid had died and been returned.

I stepped forward and hugged him. "It's great to have you back, Khal."

He smiled, his eyes filmed with tears. "You don't know how good it is to be back."

He fixed me a coffee, and we sat before the empty hearth while I brought him up to date with what had been happening in the village in his absence.

We seemed to be playing around the edges of what we really wanted to talk about. I had the burning desire to ask him, firstly, what it had been like on the home planet of the Kéthani. Returnees rarely talk of their experiences on Kéthan, and then only in the most abstract of terms. It's as if the desire to expound on the circumstances of their resurrections had been programmed out of them by their alien benefactors. The first returnees had been besieged by the media with offers of riches for their stories. They all refused.

Then, of course, I wanted to ask him about what had happened on the evening of his death.

After a period of silence, Khalid stared into the empty fire. He played with his coffee cup. "I had a lot of time to think about life while I was up there," he said.

I nodded. "It must have been a profound experience."

"We never saw the Kéthani, you know. We were schooled by human instructors, who oddly enough seemed alien themselves. Calm, centred, all knowing."

"What was it like?"

He shook his head. "We were housed in vast domes, looking out over idyllic pastures." This was the stock line the returnees came out with. "I suspect the landscape wasn't what Kéthan was like at all, just some virtual scene manufactured to soothe us. I met many people. We meditated a lot, were instructed in what I can only call Kéthani-Zen." He laughed. "And me, a good ex-Muslim!"

He paused, then continued, "I looked into myself, Richard. I saw what a shallow, self-centred person I was, before. The way I treated Zara, for instance."

I looked away, embarrassed.

He went on, "It might have looked like the perfect marriage from the outside, but I wasn't the perfect husband." He smiled to himself. "In retrospect, it's little wonder she left me for someone else."

I shifted in my seat, uncomfortable. To change the subject, I said, "The night you... you died. Zara found you and came round." I shrugged. "Everyone thought you'd interrupted an intruder. There was a scuffle..."

He stared at me, his gaze uncomfortably penetrating. "I've just told the police that I came from upstairs to find a masked man in the lounge. I picked up the first thing to hand—a poker," he indicated the implement, standing innocently in its holder, "and went for him. The man drew a gun and fired before I could react. I told the police that I had no hope of recognising him."

"So the killer's still out there somewhere," I said.

Khalid lifted his gaze and stared at me. "Except, Richard, that isn't what happened."

My stomach turned. I recalled meeting Zara in the super-market, tall and elegant and quite beautiful. I wondered how she could have brought herself to kill—or cause to have killed—her husband, no matter how domineering he might have been.

Despite my objections to Dan Chester's theory in the pub all those months ago, I knew what was coming.

"You mean," I found my voice at last, "it was Zara or Simon?"

He smiled. "No," he said, "but at first that's what I'd planned."

I stared at him. "I'm sorry? You've lost me."

"I was consumed by so much rage and hatred in the months after Zara left me," he said. "I never thought I could feel such anger towards anyone. And then I had that run-in with Simon. All I wanted was revenge. Life seemed pointless. Then it came to me, how I could kill two birds with one stone, as it were."

I felt a growing emptiness inside me. "I'm not sure I follow…"

"I planned to come back and incriminate either Zara or Simon. I wasn't sure which. Maybe both of them. I'd come back and tell the police that they'd entered the house, we'd argued, then they'd pulled a gun, and bang… But I learned a lot up there, Richard. I learned that I shouldn't blame others, but look into myself and seek the causes there."

The silence stretched. "You killed yourself," I murmured at last. "But how on Earth…? I mean, they never found the gun—"

He silenced me by reaching behind a cushion on the sofa and handing me a torch. I stared at it. For a second I thought that this was the murder weapon, ingeniously disguised.

Eric Brown

But Khalid was indicating the open hearth. "Look up the chimney, Richard. It's okay, it's clean."

I stared at him, switched on the torch, then manoeuvred myself into the roomy fireplace. Khalid had removed the grate, and I crouched and shone the torch upwards, illuminating draughty brickwork.

"I don't see anything," I said.

"Reach up, behind that projecting stone."

I did as instructed, and my hand touched something icy cold. I pulled, but was met with resistance. "It isn't coming," I said, and I knew why, then.

I pulled harder, and the icy object appeared around the brickwork. It reflected the light of the torch.

The pistol was affixed to the elasticated rope I had given Khalid the week before his death.

I ducked from the hearth, pulling the pistol after me. The rope reached the limit of its elasticity, about a metre from the fireplace.

"It's okay," he said, noticing my distaste as I stared at the weapon. "It was loaded with a single bullet."

I looked at him. "You messed up the room, made it look as if there'd been a struggle. Then, when Zara was due..." I lifted the pistol to my chest. "Bang," I said and released my grip on the weapon.

It crashed against the brass cowling and rattled up the chimney-breast. "Ingenious," I said.

"It was a measure of my anger, my immaturity, my jealousy," Khalid said. "I've come to realise that now. We live and learn." He smiled. "Or rather, in my case, we die and learn."

I hesitated. "What now?" I said.

"I had to tell someone," Khalid said. "Now it's up to you. You can tell the authorities, and they'll charge me for wasting valuable police time. I'd understand—"

I stopped him. "You've come to see what a mistake you made," I said. "Nothing else matters."

He released a long, pent-up breath. "I could kill a pint, Richard."

We stepped from the house, turned, and hurried along the lane. Then we stopped and stared into the night sky.

High over the moors, arching into the darkness, was a bolt of pure white energy, the latest consignment of dead to be beamed from the Onward Station towards the waiting Kéthani starship.

I looked at Khalid. "Have you decided what you're going to do?"

"I considered going among the stars," he said, "an ambassador for the Kéthani. Maybe I'll go later, Richard. I have all the time in the universe, after all."

I smiled.

"I'll remain on Earth," Khalid said, "working at the hospital. The implantation process is important. I feel as if I'm doing some good in the world. There are a lot of people out there who refuse the implants. Perhaps I can tell them something of the wonder and enlightenment I experienced up there."

And as the dead illuminated us on their journey heavenwards, we made our way to the Fleece.

INTERLUDE

I met Stuart Kingsley a couple of years after my resurrection. A lecturer in medieval French at Leeds University, he moved into the village that summer and began drinking at the Fleece, where he soon gravitated into the orbit of the Tuesday night crowd. He was a quiet, thoughtful man who got on well with everyone. Stuart had his serious side—he was a highly respected academic with a string of weighty tomes to his name—but I like to think that our friendship brought out the fun-loving side of his personality. When drunk, he liked nothing more than telling long, convoluted, and hilarious stories about his experiences in life.

On one particular Tuesday night in the main bar, talk turned to the resurrection process, and what actually went on in the domes of the Kéthani home planet. It was a topic of conversation that we never exhausted.

As I was the only returnee in the group, it was natural that Stuart should elicit my opinion. "What happened, Khal?" he asked in his soft Devon burr.

I shrugged and gave a vague description of what I recalled of the resurrection dome.

I found it hard to speak of my time on Kéthan, as if the desire to do so had been edited from my mind. Some people cite the fact that returnees find it hard to talk about the experience as further evidence of Kéthani duplicity: why not allow us to speak openly about what happens within the domes?

I said as much now. "But I have a theory."

Jeff Morrow smiled. "Let's hear it then, Khalid."

"I think that we're not allowed a true memory of what happens there because the resurrection process, and the tuition that follows, is too... too alien for our minds to grasp. I don't mean that it's too horrific, merely that it is totally *alien* and ungraspable to the human mind." I paused, then went on, "In place of the truth, the Kéthani fill us with a version of what happens: we recall human instructors, pacific and Zen-like, and views from the domes of Eden-like tranquillity."

"But," Stuart said, "the reality is unknowable to the human mind."

I shrugged. "Something like that," I said.

"But whatever happens," Elisabeth said, "returnees are changed on some fundamental level. I mean, look at Khalid here." She gripped my hand. "Sorry, Khal."

I smiled. "I readily admit that I'm a changed man," I said and left it at that.

Elisabeth turned to Dan Chester. "What about Lucy? Have you noticed a change in her since she returned?"

Dan regarded his pint, considering the question. Lucy was a teenager now, living with Dan in the village. I saw her from time to time, a slim, dark thirteen-year-old who always had time for a chat. On these occasions I had always thought her more mature than her contemporaries.

Dan smiled. "It's hard to say... but I think perhaps she was a little more... thoughtful, reflective, after her return."

The conversation switched to other topics.

It was a couple of weeks later when I noticed that Stuart was taking a lot of interest in the barmaid, Sam. She was in her mid-twenties, at a guess, blonde and exhibitionist and a little loud, but friendly and always ready with a smile. Not to sound too patronising about it, she was the type of person I thought perfectly suited to a vocation pulling pints.

That Stuart Kingsley should find her attractive was, frankly, bizarre; that he should not only find her attractive but, a month later—after a whirlwind affair—should propose marriage, we found not only odd but alarming.

Richard Lincoln didn't lose an opportunity to rib Stuart mercilessly about his choice of partner, and behind Stuart's back he gave the marriage six months, at most. The truth to tell, we agreed with him.

A year later, our doubts were dispelled. Stuart and Sam were living proof that opposites not only attract, but complement each other. Sam became a vital part of the group and brought even more humour and vitality from the university lecturer.

One week before Stuart's death, we were in the Fleece and talk again turned to the resurrection domes. I cannot recall that much about the conversation—it was late, and I was five pints the worse—but I do remember that Sam was almost... well, *frightened* at the prospect of life after death.

And I recall her saying she feared that, if either she or Stuart died, the Kéthani would drive them apart.

SEVEN

A Heritage of Stars

I had never really given much thought to my death, or what might follow. Perhaps this was a reaction to the fact that in my youth, before the arrival of the Kéthani, I had been obsessed with the idea of my mortality, the overwhelming thought that one day I would be dead.

Then the Kéthani descended like guardian angels, and my fear of the Grim Reaper faded. In time I became a happy man and lived life to the full.

That night, though, it was as if I had an intimation of what was about to happen. I was driving home from the university, taking the treacherous, ice-bound road over the moors to Oxenworth. I passed the towering obelisk of the Onward Station, icy and eerie in the starlight. As I did so, a great actinic pulse of light lanced from its summit, arcing into the heavens towards the awaiting Kéthani starship. Although I knew intellectually that the laser pulse contained the demolecularised remains of perhaps a dozen dead human beings, I found the fact hard to credit.

For a few seconds, as I stared up at the light, I wondered at the life that awaited me when I shuffled off this mortal coil.

Ironic that this idle thought should have brought about the accident. My attention still on the streaking parabola, I saw the oncoming truck too late.

I didn't stand a chance.

Perhaps a week before I died, I arrived home to find Samantha in tears.

We had been married for just over a year, and I was still at that paranoid stage in the relationship when I feared that things would crumble. Our marriage had been so perfect I assumed that it could only end in tears. I knew my feelings for Sam, but what if she failed to reciprocate?

When I stepped into the living room and found her curled up on the sofa, sobbing like a child, my stomach flipped with fear. Perhaps this was it. She had discovered her true feelings; she had made a mistake in declaring her love for me. She wanted out.

She had a book open beside her. I saw that it was a copy of my third monograph, a study of gender and matriarchy in the medieval French epic.

"Sam, what the hell...?"

She looked up at me, eyes soaked in tears. "Stuart, I don't understand..." She fingered the Kéthani implant at her temple, nervously.

I hurried across to her and took her in my arms. "What?"

She sobbed against my shoulder. "Anything," she managed at last. "I don't understand a bloody thing!"

My friends at the Fleece, the Tuesday night crowd including Richard and Khalid and Jeff and the rest, had mocked me mercilessly when I started going out with Samantha. To them she represented the archetype of the dumb-blonde barmaid. "I'm sure you'll find lots to talk about when the pleasures of the flesh wear thin," Richard had jibed one night.

Attraction is a peculiar phenomenon. Sam was ten years my junior, a full-figured twenty-five-year-old high-school drop-out who worked in the local Co-op and made ends meet with occasional bar-work. Or that was how the others perceived her. To me she was an exceptionally sensitive human being who found me attractive and funny. We hit it off from the start and were married within three months.

She pulled away from me and stared into my eyes. She looked deranged. "Stuart, why the hell do you love me?"

"Where do you want me to begin?"

She wailed. "I just don't understand!"

She picked up my book, opened it at random, and began reading, holding it high before her like a mad preacher.

"... as Sinclair so perceptively states in *Milk and Blood*: 'The writing and the page exist in a symbiotic relation that serves to mark the feminine "page" as originally blank and devoid of signification...' a dichotomy that stands as a radical antithesis to Cixous's notion of writing the body."

She shook her head and stared at me. "Stuart, what the hell does it all mean?" She sobbed. "I'm so bloody stupid—what do you see in me?"

I snatched the book from her and flung it across the room, a gesture symbolising my contempt for theory at that moment.

I eased her back onto the sofa and sat beside her. "Sam, listen to me. A Frenchman comes to England. He speaks no English—"

She snorted and tried to pull away. I held onto her. "Hear me out, Sam. So, Pierre is in England. He never learned to speak our language, so he doesn't understand when someone asks him the time. That doesn't make him stupid, does it?"

She stared at me, angry. "What do you mean?"

I gestured to the book. "All that... that academic-speak, is something I learned at university. It's a language we use amongst ourselves because we understand it. It's overwritten and convoluted and ninety-nine people out of a hundred wouldn't have a clue what we we're going on about. That doesn't make them stupid."

"No," she retorted, "just uneducated."

She had often derided herself for her lack of education. How many times had I tried to reassure her that I loved her because she was who she was, university degree or not?

That night, in bed, I held her close and said, "Tell me, what's really the matter? What's upsetting you?"

She was silent. The bedroom looked out over the moors, and I always left the curtains open so that I could stare across the valley to the Onward Station. Tonight, as we lay belly-to-back, my arms around her, I watched a spear of white light lance towards the orbiting starship.

She whispered, "Sometimes I wonder why you love me. I try to read your books, try to make sense of them. I wonder what you see in me, why you don't go for one of those high-flying women in your department."

"They aren't you."

She went on, ignoring me, "Sometimes I think about what you do, what you write about, and... I don't know... it symbolises what I can't understand about everything."

"There," I joked, "you're beginning to sound like me."

She elbowed me in the belly. "You see, Stuart, everything is just too much to understand."

"Einstein said that we don't know one millionth of one per cent of anything," I said.

"You know a lot."

"It's all relative. You know more than Tina, say."

"I want to know as much as you."

I laughed. "And I could say I want to know as much as Derrida knew." I squeezed her. "Listen to me. We all want to know more. One of the secrets of being happy is knowing that we'll never know as much as we want to know. It doesn't matter. I love you, sugar plum."

She was silent for a long while after that. Then she said, "Stuart, I'm frightened."

I sighed, squeezed her. The last time she'd said that, she confessed that she was frightened I would leave her. "Sam, I love you. There I was, an unhappy bachelor, never thinking I'd marry. And then the perfect woman comes along..."

"It's not that. I'm frightened of the Kéthani."

"Sam... There's absolutely nothing to be frightened of. You've heard what the returnees say."

"I don't mean the Kéthani, really. I mean... I mean, what happens to us after we die. Listen, what if you die, and when you come back from the stars... I don't know, what if you've seen more—more than there is here? What if you realise that I can't give you what's out there, among the stars?"

I kissed her neck. "You mean more to me than all the stars in the universe. And anyway, I don't intend to die just yet."

Silence, again. Then a whisper, "Stuart, you're right. We don't know anything, do we? I mean, look at the stars. Just look at them. Aren't they beautiful?"

I stared at the million twinkling points of light spread across the ice-cold heavens.

"Each one is a sun," she said, like an awe-struck child, "and millions of them have planets and people... well, aliens. Just think of it, Stuart, just think of everything that's out there that we can't even begin to dream about."

I hugged her to me. "You're a poet and a philosopher, Samantha Gardner," I whispered. "And I love you."

A couple of days later we attended the returning ceremony of Graham Leicester, a friend who'd died of a heart attack six months earlier.

I'd never before entered the Onward Station, and I was unsure what to expect. We left the car in the snow-covered parking lot and shuffled across the slush behind the file of fellow celebrants. Samantha gripped my hand and shivered. "C-cold," she brrr'd.

A blue-uniformed official, with the fixed smile and plastic good looks of an air hostess, ushered us into a reception lounge. It was a big, white-walled room with a sky blue carpet. Abstract murals hung on the walls, swirls of pastel colour. I wondered if this was Kéthani artwork.

A long table stood before a window overlooking the white, undulating moorland. A buffet was laid out, tiny sandwiches and canapés, and red and white wine.

Graham's friends, his neighbours and the regulars from the Fleece, were already tucking in. Sam brought me a glass of red wine and we stood talking to Richard Lincoln.

"I wonder if he'll be the same old happy-go-lucky Graham as before?" Sam asked.

Richard smiled. "I don't see why not," he said.

"But he'll be changed, won't he?" Sam persisted. "I mean, not just physically?"

Richard shrugged. "He'll appear a little younger, fitter. And who knows how the experience will have changed him psychologically."

"But don't the aliens—" Sam began.

Richard was saved the need to reply. A door at the far end of the room opened and the Station Director, Masters, stepped into the reception lounge and cleared his throat.

"First of all, I'd like to welcome you all to the Onward Station." He gave a little speech extolling the service to humankind bestowed by the Kéthani and then explained that Graham Leicester was with close family members right at this moment, his wife and children, and would join us presently.

I must admit that I was more than a little curious as to how the experience of dying, being resurrected, and returning to Earth after six months had affected Graham. I'd heard rumours about the post-resurrection period on Kéthan: humans were brought back to life and 'instructed', informed about the universe, the other life-forms that existed out there, the various tenets and philosophies they held. But I wanted to hear first-hand from Graham exactly what he'd undergone.

I expected to be disappointed. I'd read many a time that returnees rarely spoke of their experiences on Kéthan: that either they were reluctant to do so or were somehow inhibited by their alien saviours.

Five minutes later Graham stepped through the sliding door, followed by his wife and two teenage daughters.

I suppose the reaction to his appearance could be described as a muted gasp—an indrawn breath of mixed delight and amazement.

Graham had run the local hardware store, a big, affable, over-weight fifty-something, with a drinker's nose and a rapidly balding head.

Enter a revamped Graham Leicester. He looked twenty years younger, leaner and fitter; gone was the rubicund, veined face, the beer-belly. Even his hair had grown back.

He circulated, moving from group to group, shaking hands and hugging his delighted friends.

He saw us and hurried over, gave Sam a great bear hug and winked at me over her shoulder. I embraced him. "Great to see you back, Graham."

"Good to be back."

His wife was beside him. "We're having a little do down at the Fleece, if you'd like to come along."

Graham said, "A pint of Landlord after the strange watery stuff I had out there…" He smiled at the thought.

Thirty minutes later we were sitting around a table in the main bar of our local, about ten of us. Oddly enough, talk was all about what had happened in the village during the six months that Graham had been away. He led the conversation, wanting to know all the gossip. I wondered how much this was due to a reluctance to divulge his experiences on Kéthan.

I watched him as he sipped his first pint back on Earth.

Was it my imagination, or did he seem quieter, a little more reflective than the Graham of old? He didn't gulp his beer, but took small sips. At one point I asked him, nodding at his half-filled glass. "Worth waiting for? Can I get you another?"

He smiled. "It's not as I remembered it, Stuart. No, I'm okay for now."

I glanced across the table. Sam was deep in conversation with Graham's wife, Marjorie. Sam looked concerned. I said to Graham, "I've read that other returnees have trouble recalling their experiences out there."

He looked at me. "I know what they mean. It's strange, but although I can remember lots..." He shook his head. "When I try to talk about it..." He looked bewildered. "I mean, I know what happened in the dome, but I can't begin to express it."

I nodded, feigning comprehension.

"Have you decided what you're going to do now?"

His gaze seemed to slip into neutral. "I don't know. I recall something from the domes. We were shown the universe, the vastness, the races and planets... The Kéthani want us to go out there, Stuart, work with them in bringing the word of the Kéthani to all the other races. I was offered so many positions out there..."

I had to repress a smile at the thought of Graham Leicester, ex-Oxenworth hardware store owner, as an ambassador to the stars.

"Have you decided what you're going to do?" I asked.

He stared into his half-drunk pint. "No," he said at last. "No, I haven't." He looked up at me. "I never thought the stars would be so attractive," he murmured.

Graham and his wife left at nine, and the drinking continued. Around midnight Sam and I wended our way home, holding onto each other as we negotiated the snowdrifts.

She was very quiet, and at home took me in a fierce embrace. "Stuart," she whispered, "rip all my clothes off and make love to me."

Sometimes the act of sex can transcend the mere familiar mechanics that often, after a year of marriage, become rote. That night, for some reason, we were imbued with a passion that recalled our earlier times together. Later we sprawled on the bed, sweating and breathless. I was overcome with an inexpressible surge of love for the woman who was my wife.

"Stuart," she whispered.

I stroked her thigh. "Mmm?"

"I was talking to Marjorie. She says Graham's changed. He isn't the man he was. She's afraid."

I held her. "Sam, he's undergone an incredible experience. Of course he's changed a little, but he's still the same old Graham underneath. It'll just take time for him to readjust."

She was quiet for a few seconds, before saying, "Perhaps, Stuart, they take our humanity away?"

"Nonsense!" I said. "If anything, they give us a greater humanity. You've heard all those stories about dictators and cynical businessmen who return full of compassion and charity."

She didn't reply. Perhaps five minutes later she said, "Perhaps the Kéthani take away our ability to love."

Troubled, I pulled Sam to me and held her tight.

A few days later I arrived home with a book for Samantha. It was Farmer's critically acclaimed account of the arrival of the Kéthani and its radical social consequences.

I left it on the kitchen table and over dinner said, "I found this in the library. Fascinating stuff. Perhaps you'd like to read it."

She picked up the book and leafed through it, sniffed, with that small, disdainful wrinkle of her nose I found so attractive.

"Wouldn't understand it if I did," she said.

After dinner she poured two glasses of red wine and joined me in the living room. She curled next to me on the sofa.

"Stuart..." She began.

She often did this—said my name and then failed to qualify it. The habit at first drove me crazy, but soon became just another of her idiosyncrasies that I came to love.

"Do you know something?" she began again. "Once upon a time there were certainties, weren't there?" She fingered her implant, perhaps unaware that she was doing so.

I stared at her. "Such as?"

"Death," she said. "And, like, if you loved someone so much, then you were certain that it would last forever."

"Well, I suppose so."

"But not any more."

"Well, death's been banished."

She looked up at me, her gaze intense. "When I met you and fell in love, Stuart, it was like nothing I'd experienced before. You were the one, kind and gentle and caring. You loved me—"

"I still do."

She squeezed my hand. "I know you do, but..."

"But what?"

"But with the coming of the Kéthani, how long will that last? Once, true love lasted forever—until death—or it could if it really *was* true. But now, when we live forever, on and on, for centuries..." She shook her head at the enormity of that concept. "Then how can our love last so long?"

And she began crying, copiously and inconsolably.

Even later, when I awoke in the early hours and watched a beam of light pulse high into the dark sky, Sam was still sobbing beside me.

I reached out and pulled her to me. "I love you so much," I said.

They were the last words I ever spoke to her, in this incarnation.

She was still asleep early the following morning when I dressed and left the house. I spent an average day at the faculty, conducting a couple of seminars on chivalry in the French medieval epic. And from time to time, unbidden but welcome, visions of my wife flooded my consciousness with joy.

That night, driving past the Onward Station, I stared in wonder at the pulsing light.

I saw the oncoming truck, its blinding headlights bearing down, but too late. I swerved to avoid the vehicle, but not fast enough to avert the shattering impact.

I died instantly, apparently. Various pieces of the truck's cab sheared through the car, decapitating me and cutting me in half, just below the ribs. Much later, over a pint in the Fleece, Richard Lincoln laughingly reported that I'd been the messiest corpse he'd ever dealt with.

The last thing I recalled was the light—and, upon awakening, the first thing I beheld was another light, just as bright.

I remember a face hovering over me, telling me that the resurrection was complete, and that I could begin the lessons when I next awoke.

At least, I think the word was "lessons". Perhaps I'm wrong. There is so much about that period that I cannot fully recall, or, if I do recall, do so vaguely. I know I was on the Kéthani home planet for exactly six months, though in retrospect it seems like as many weeks.

As with every other resurrectee, I was housed in a dome with five other humans. There were perhaps as many teachers as resurrectees, though whether they were humans or Kéthani wearing human forms I cannot say. Beyond the wall of the dome was a pastoral vista of rolling green glades and meadows, which must surely have been some virtual image designed to sedate us with the familiar.

I wore a body I recalled from perhaps ten years ago, leaner than my recent form, healthier. My face was unlined. I felt physically wonderful, with no after-effects of the accident that had killed me.

The resurrectees in my dome did not socialise. None were British, and none so far as I recall spoke English. We had our lessons, one to one with our instructors, and then returned to our separate rooms to eat and sleep.

The lessons consisted of meditation classes, in which we were instructed simply to empty our minds of *everything*. We were given "poems" to read, pieces that reminded me of haiku and koan, which although bearing much resemblance to Zen, were subtly other, alien.

After a while we were allowed access to what were called the library files. These consisted of needle-like devices that could be fed into a wallscreen, upon which materialised the texts of every book ever printed on Earth. They even had every one of my own dozen volumes.

But more. I soon discovered that there were other texts available, those not of Earth but penned by poets and philosophers and storytellers from many of the far-flung races of the universe. All were translated into English, and some were comprehensible and some so obscure as to be unfathomable. I struggled over texts too profound for my intellect, and then found others that expanded my awareness of being with the same heady rush of knowledge I experienced in my late teens when reading Freud and Lacan for the very first time.

I recall too—but this is vague, and I suspect our Kéthani over-seers of having somehow edited it from my consciousness—being visited by other teachers, not those who usually instructed us. At the time I knew there was something odd about them. They did not speak to us, I seem to recall, but reached out, touched our brows, and later I would wake to find myself bequeathed knowl-edge new to me.

I became voracious, questing after all that was new in the uni-verse. Perhaps I had become jaded on Earth, my mind dulled by the repetitive nature of my job, stressed by having to fit my orig-inal research into my spare time and study breaks. On Kéthan, it was as if my mind had been made suddenly a hundred per cent more receptive. I discovered alien writers and philosophers whose wisdom superseded the tired tenets of Earth's finest thinkers.

I became aware, by degrees—surely a process carefully moni-tored by the Kéthani, so as not to overload our minds with too much information too soon—of the vast cornucopia of otherness existing Out There, of the million teeming worlds and ways of thinking that awaited my inspection.

I recalled what Sam had said that night, which seemed like a lifetime ago, *"Just think of it, Stuart, just think of everything that's out there that we can't even begin to dream about."*

And Sam? Was she in my thoughts? Did I miss her as I had, dur-ing the first months of our marriage, when research had taken me to Paris for three painful weeks?

I thought of her often during my first days there, and then, I must admit, not so frequently. Soon she was supplanted in my thoughts by the sheer wonder of what surrounded me, the possi-bilities suddenly open to my experience, the amazing inheritance that death and resurrection was offering.

At first I felt guilty, and then less so. Perhaps, even then, some survival mechanism was kicking in: I was forcing myself to realise that our love was doomed, a short-term thing, a mayfly liaison that could not hope to compete with the eternal allure of the stars.

She would understand, one day.

What had she said, so wisely? *"But now, when we live forever, on and on, for centuries... Then how can our love last so long?"*

At night I would lie awake and stare through the dome, marvelling at the spread of stars high overhead, the vast and magnificent drifts and nebulae. Their attraction was irresistible.

Towards the end of my stay on Kéthan, an instructor gave me a needle containing an almost endless list of vacancies open for my consideration. Teachers were required on primitive worlds in the Nilakantha Stardrift; tutors aboard vessels called quark-harvesters plying routes at the very periphery of the universe; ethnographers on planets newly discovered; sociologists on ancient worlds with complex rites and abstruse rituals...

I wept when I thought about the future, the wonder of discovery that awaited me, and the thought of telling Sam of my decision.

Six months to the day after my death, I was returned to Earth and the Onward Station high on the Yorkshire moors.

I came awake in a small room within the Onward Station. Director Masters was there to greet me. "Welcome back, Mr. Kingsley," he said. "Your friends are in the reception lounge, but perhaps you'd care for a few minutes alone?"

I agreed, and he slipped from the room.

A china pot of tea, a cup and saucer, stood on a small table, all ridiculously English and twee.

I thought of Graham Leicester's reception a while ago and recalled that he had spent time with his family before greeting his friends in the lounge. I had expected Sam to be the first person to welcome me home, and her absence relieved me.

I wondered if she was wary of the person I had become—the being remade by the Kéthani. What had she said, the night before my death? *"Perhaps the Kéthani take away our ability to love."*

No fool, Samantha...

I stepped from the small room and entered the lounge. There were half a dozen familiar faces awaiting me—I had expected more and was instantly put out, and then troubled by the expression on their faces.

Richard Lincoln stepped forward and gripped my arm. "Stuart, Sam isn't here."

"What—?" I began.

"Two days after your accident," Richard said, "she took her own life. She left a note, saying she wanted to be resurrected with you."

I nodded, trying to work out where that left us, now. She had never read anything about the Kéthani. How could she have known that the Kéthani never conducted the rebirth of loved ones together in the same dome, for whatever reasons?

I contemplated her return in two days' time and joined my friends in the Fleece for a quiet pint.

In the two days I was on my own, in the house we had shared for a year, I thought of the woman who was my wife and what she had done because she loved me.

I moved from room to room, the place empty now without Sam's presence to fill it, to give it life and vitality. Each room was haunted by so many memories. I tried to avoid the bedroom where she had slit her wrists, and slept in the lounge instead.

And, amazingly, something human stirred within me, something very like the first blossoming of love I had felt for Samantha Gardner. It came to me that knowledge and learning was all very well, but was nothing beside the miracle that is the love and compassion we can feel for another human being.

I faced the prospect of Sam's return with a strange mixture of ecstasy and dread.

The Station seemed even more alien today, rearing like an inverted icicle from the moorland. I left my car in the snow and hurried inside. Director Masters ushered me into the private reception room, where I paced like something caged and contemplated the future.

It all depended, really, on Sam, on her reaction to what she had undergone on the home planet of the Kéthani.

Long minutes later the sliding door sighed open and she stepped through, smiling tentatively at me.

My heart gave a kick.

She came into my arms, crying.

"Sam?" I said, and I had never feared her words so much as now.

"We have a lot to talk about," she said. "I learned so much out there."

I nodded, at a loss for words. At last I said, "Have you decided...?"

She stared into my eyes, shook her head. "Let's get this over with," she said and, taking my arm, led me into the reception lounge before I could protest.

I endured the following hour with Sam's family and mutual friends, and then we made our excuses and left the Onward Station. It was a short drive home across the moors, fraught with silence. More than once I almost asked whether she would remain with me on Earth.

But it was Sam who broke the silence. "Do you understand why I did it, Stuart? Why I..."

I glanced at her as I turned into the driveway. "You feared losing me?"

She nodded. "I was desperate. I... I thought that perhaps if I experienced what you were going through, then it might bring us closer together when we got back."

I braked. "And has it?"

She stared at me without replying, and said, "What about you, Stuart? Do you still love me?"

"More than ever."

Quickly she opened the door and hurried from the car.

The house was warm. I fixed coffee and we sat in the lounge, staring out through the picture window at the vast spread of the snow-covered moorland. The sun was going down, laying gorgeous tangerine strata across the horizon. In the distance, the Onward Station scintillated in the dying light.

Sam said, "I became a different person on Kéthan."

I nodded. "So did I."

"The small concerns of being human, of life on Earth, seem less important now."

I wanted to ask her if her love for me was a small concern, but was too afraid to pose the question.

"Could you remain here on Earth?" I asked.

She stood and paced to the window, hugging herself, staring out. "I don't know. I don't think so. Not after what I've learned about what's out there. What about you?"

I was silent for a time. "Do you remember what you said all those months ago, about the Kéthani taking away our ability to feel love?"

She looked at me, nodded minimally.

"Well, do you think it's true for you?" I asked.

"I... I don't know. What I feel for you has changed."

I wanted to ask her if I could compete with the allure of the stars. Instead I said, "I have an idea, Sam. There are plenty of vacancies for couples out there. We could explore the stars together."

Without warning she hurried from the room, alarming me.

"Sam?"

"I need time to think!" she cried from the hall. I heard the front door slam.

A minute later I saw her, bundled up in her parka and moon-boots, tramping across the snow before the house, a tiny figure lost in the daunting winter wilderness.

She stopped and gazed up into the night sky.

I looked up, too, and stared in wonder.

Then, slowly, I dropped my gaze to the woman I loved. She was struggling through the deep snow, running back towards the house and waving at me.

My heart hammering, I rushed from the house to meet her.

Overhead the night was clear, and the stars were appearing in their teeming millions, a vast spread of brilliant luminosity promising the universe.

INTERLUDE

"In the first five years after the coming of the Kéthani," Stuart Kingsley was saying, "the population of Earth did inevitably increase."

We were sitting in the beer garden of the Fleece and watching the sun going down over the moors in great orange and red banners; it was high summer, and the day had been blistering.

Andy Souter, the latest member of the Tuesday night group, had initiated this line of conversation by asking what the present population of the world might be. He wanted to know if any more resurrectees were staying out there to do the work of the Kéthani.

Stuart went on, "Now, thirteen years later, I'd say things have reached an equilibrium. The same number come back as stay out there."

Richard Lincoln laughed. "What Stuart's getting round to saying is that the world's population stands at around five billion, give or take a few."

Andy said, "But that wasn't always the case, was it?" He shrugged and mopped a strand of ginger curls from his perspiring forehead. "I mean, in the early days how did we cope with the population explosion?"

Dan Chester pointed at him. "We had help."

"Help?"

"Think about it. How could we have coped with a population growing by ten per cent every few months? How could we house these people, let alone feed them? We had help."

Andy said, "The Kéthani?"

Richard nodded. "Didn't you notice the fleet of white juggernauts coming to and going from the Onward Station all night long for years? The Kéthani beamed down all the provisions we'd ever need to supply a burgeoning population."

"And now?"

"No longer necessary," Richard said.

"In fact," Stuart said, "the world's population is undergoing a gradual decline. In a few years the place will be depopulated as citizens take to the stars..."

We sat and thought about this for a while, and then Sam asked if anyone had seen the latest computer-animated Bogart movie.

I turned to Stuart and asked if he'd thought any more about leaving Earth. After his and Sam's resurrection, they had seriously considered the option.

He stared into his pint, then said, "It's strange, but we had more or less decided that that's what we were going to do. We still contemplate it, from time to time... Then," he smiled sheepishly, "then we slip back into the old routine: work, the village, friends. I don't know, maybe one day..."

Later, I chatted to Andy Souter about his music. He was a professional cornet player with various brass bands in the area, and in demand as a session musician. He was a shy, hesitant man in his mid-thirties and had recently moved to the village to look after his ailing mother.

He was implanted, but I received the impression that, even so, he held a deep distrust of the Kéthani.

That night, I remember, we chatted about how the aliens' presence on Earth—or rather how what they had done to transform the planet—had come little by little to be accepted.

We noted how even religious opposition to the gift of the Kéthani mellowed over the years, as theocratic doctrine—as is the way—sought to accommodate itself to the exigencies of the modern world... or to compromise its principles.

I was to recall this conversation when, a few months later, as the scorching summer gave way to a compensatory winter of gales and snowstorms, we gained another—albeit temporary—member of the Tuesday night group. He was Father Matthew Renbourn, a Catholic priest convinced that his God still occupied His throne on high, and that the Kéthani were but part of His overall grand plan...

Andy Souter came to know Matthew very well, and is the best person to relate the priest's remarkable—some might even say unbelievable—story.

EIGHT

Matthew's Passion

I first met Matthew Renbourn in the public bar of the Fleece. He was sitting at the table beside the open fire with the rest of the Tuesday night crowd, a pint of Landlord in his hand. He was laughing at a joke that Elisabeth had just told. Okay, it wasn't that funny a joke, but he had such a deep, appreciative laugh that everyone else was laughing too. I didn't catch on to his true identity at first. This wasn't surprising: he was, in his own words, undercover. Besides, he was implanted.

It was my first Tuesday night at the Fleece for a while, and in my absence Matt had made himself a regular in the group. Now Khalid formally introduced us.

"Andy Souter. Andy plays the cornet," Khalid said. "Front row for Brighouse and Rastrick, among others. Been round the world as a session man, too. Maybe you should ask him if he'll help you out with the orchestra."

I shrivelled inside at this introduction; but I shouldn't have worried. Matthew was a likeable man. Maybe I should say an exceptional man.

People have a funny way of acting when they meet someone who has made a success of one of their own particular interests. Matthew was a keen amateur musician; nonetheless, he didn't turn to me in a show of bravado or excess bonhomie as many do when they approach me in my professional capacity. Nor did he make a pretence of false modesty and engage me in sycophantic conversation. He smiled his wide, genuine smile, leaned across the table and shook my hand. "Delighted to meet you," he said.

Khalid went on, "Matthew is the priest at St. Luke's."

Matt laughed. "I'm here undercover," and he slipped two fingers into his shirt pocket and pulled out a strip of white plastic. It took me a moment to realise what I was looking at. A dog collar.

I stared at the implant at his temple.

He smiled. "No," he said. "It's real. Not one of those fakes you hear about."

He could see I was surprised; he was expecting it, almost looking forward to my reaction.

I don't believe in first impressions: I think the time to make your mind up about someone is never, and although Matt Renbourn thought the same, he knew other people would disagree. He realised that he was always on show, and so he lived up to it. He liked to make an impression.

Later he told me about his "orchestra".

"Well," he smiled. "We used to have a band to accompany the Sunday service. You know, couple of guitars, violinist, kids playing flutes and clarinets. But then we found ourselves an organist, and suddenly the band felt themselves a bit surplus to requirements. My fault, I suppose, but I think you need an organ for the Gloria and so on."

I said nothing. Call me a snob, but I've often thought that if there is a hell for musicians, their punishment will be to spend eternity sitting in a band such as the one Matthew just described playing, "Shine, Jesus Shine".

"Anyway," he said, sipping from his pint, "the band didn't want to just drift along doing nothing, so we continued to meet and practice. Once you removed the 'church' association, others wanted to join in. Things have grown from there."

"Novel," I said. "Oxenworth has never had an orchestra before."

"It's not really an orchestra," he said, but you could hear the pride in his voice. "More a show tunes sort of band. I'm trying to arrange a series of concerts to help with the restoration fund. I'm going to schedule one for next month. Give the band something to work towards."

"Still no luck with the pianist?" Khalid asked him. He can be such a stirrer.

"Good pianists are thin on the ground," Matt said, equably.

I was tempted to volunteer. Earlier, I'd heard Khalid whisper to Matt that I was pretty handy on the piano as well as the cornet, but he didn't presume upon me. That was one of the many nice things about Matt, I came to discover. The *truly* religious are hardly ever pushy.

The evening wore on. I had a couple more than my usual two pints, and the more I talked to Matt, the more I warmed to him. He came over as humane and genuine, and more than willing to listen to the other person's argument.

Towards the end of the evening I asked him, "This orchestra. When are the rehearsals?"

"Every Wednesday evening." He looked at me.

"And what nights are you planning the concerts for?"

"Sundays," Matt said, face still impassive.

I nodded. "Well, I have nothing much on those days. Okay if I come along and help out?"

He gave a wide grin. "More than okay, Andrew! Welcome aboard."

If the truth be told, the orchestra was not very good, but what they lacked in talent, they made up for in Matthew Renbourn. It turned out that he was actually a fairly competent pianist himself, but that wasn't his real strength.

There are some bandleaders who can take a group of musicians and make them play better than they have ever done before. They have a feeling for the music and a way of communicating their enthusiasm that lifts the band to a higher level.

I know, I've worked with people like that; and I say without any modesty, I've worked with the best. And although these people may have been significantly better *musicians*, none of them came close to Matthew in his ability as a leader of men and women.

The more I played with him, the better friends we became. And the more I began to have an inkling of what his congregation must feel each Sunday as he preached from the pulpit. When Matthew lifted the band in music, he was lifting us closer to his God.

It was this insight that threw his emerging mysterious side into harsh relief.

I remember one particularly cold Tuesday night in February. The usual crowd had made it to the Fleece through the snowstorm, and there was an atmosphere around the table of bonhomie that often unites people against the elements.

Matt, oddly, was quiet that night. He was not at all unfriendly, heaven forbid. (Heaven forbid? Listen to me! That's Matt's influence.) He didn't have an unfriendly bone in his body, but he was distant, as if preoccupied with his own thoughts. He was certainly not his usual gregarious self.

When it was his round, he took people's orders and moved to the bar. I gave it a couple of minutes and went to help him with the drinks. While we were alone at the bar, I said, "Is everything okay, Matt? You're quiet."

He smiled. "It's that obvious?"

"You're usually the life of the party."

He looked at me, biting his lip. "Well, to tell the truth, I think I'm being followed," he said, and then returned to the table bearing three pints.

I stared after him, then resumed my seat.

Later that night, more to draw Matt into the conversation, I asked him, "How's the congregation looking these days?"

Most of Matthew's flock were implanted, which I found bizarre. They seemed to see no contradiction in worshipping at St. Luke's and throwing in their lot with the Kéthani: hedging one's bets, I think it's called.

Matthew waggled a palm above the table.

"We stay the same. We stay the same. But, the important thing is, we're no longer falling in numbers." He looked around the table. "I tell you, the turn around is beginning. The Kéthani offer compassion, but it's a cold and mechanistic thing. Nobody who has not been reborn really understands it. We view the returnees from the home planet with suspicion."

I exchanged a smile with Khalid.

"Nobody who has not been reborn?" I said. "You're mangling the English language, Matthew. Besides, aren't you paraphrasing a line from the Bible?"

He nodded. "Well done. Still, the Kéthani gift has fallen too easily to us. Anything that is worth having has to be worked for."

"Many would disagree, Matthew," Khalid said. I nodded, feeling mellow, halfway through my second pint in the warm bar. Through the leaded window, the sight of the snow sifting down only added to my sense of well-being.

"Many would, indeed," Matt said. "But I wonder if they still feel that truth in their hearts? People used to toil in the fields to stay alive. Now their daily bread is handed to them on a plate," he smiled, "quite literally! And so they grow fat. Some exercise to burn that off, but others look for the quick fix: liposuction to suck the fat from their bodies and low calorie meals so they can commit their acts of gluttony and not feel the consequences."

He nodded his head slowly. "Now, as we seek to expand our sugar-free life, where we taste the pleasures and forgo the pain, we are told that we can be resurrected without any sacrifice on our own part."

I laughed. I knew Matthew that well by then, I knew when I could speak without causing offence. "There's a strong puritan streak runs through you, Father Renbourn. Are you saying that man must sacrifice his pleasure in this life to achieve happiness in the next?"

He laughed loudly at that and shifted in his chair in an exaggerated fashion.

"This horsehair underwear prickles the backside," he said, and laughed again. He took another drink and then settled back with a reflective smile.

"Ah, you have a point, Andy. You have a point."

Khalid bought a round.

"But don't underestimate the human need for balance," Matt went on, smiling his thanks at Khalid. "The conscious mind goes for the quick fix, but the subconscious knows that everything has a price."

He held up his pint. "I was talking about diet. We now face the prospect of eternal life, but still the need for healthy eating exists in our society. The doctors say a little alcohol is good for the body, but how many heed the call and drink a glass of good red wine each day? The Hollywood stars that act as our new messiahs preach self-denial: they prefer the truth of lettuce and low sodium diets to the gospel of Timothy Taylor."

He folded his hands as in prayer and looked to the ceiling and I started to laugh. Despite the relatively small quantities consumed, I think we were both farther along the road to drunkenness than we suspected.

"Maybe you have something there," I said. "I feel guilty if I don't devote at least an hour a day to practice." I patted my battered cornet case, tucked safely on the seat next to me. "It's not just that my embouchure suffers."

"Puritanism is hardwired into the brain," said Matthew. "Resurrection is not enough. Don't underestimate the Church's ability to adapt and absorb, Andy. We took the winter festivals and made them Christmas, we brought the marriage vows from the doorstep to the altar, we took the rite of the funeral pyre and made it into cremation."

Khalid looked up from his pint and winked at me. "So how are you going to make the Kéthani your own, Matt?" he asked.

"The Kéthani are but tools to achieve God's purpose," Matthew said. "As are we all."

I was stunned.

"Surely that's not the papal line?" I said.

Matthew smiled. "Not yet," he said.

Last orders were called, and conversation turned to a different topic.

The following evening I tramped through the snow to the draughty village hall. My way was lighted, once, by the shaft of light from the Onward Station as it beamed the remains of that day's dead to the orbiting starship.

I had intended to have a word with Matt about what he'd told me at the bar the night before, that he thought he was being followed. That had to wait: as I arrived he was mediating a dispute between the band and Katherine Emmett. Davey, her mentally handicapped son, wanted to play the triangle in the orchestra, but the rest of the band was not happy about this. Naturally, all sorts of reasons were being given, except for the real one: we don't want the dummy in the band.

"He keeps putting me off," said Kelly Wrigley, resting her flute on her knees.

"He hits it too hard, especially in the pianissimo sections."

"He doesn't always keep time," said Graham Leicester.

A lesser man would have pointed out that Graham didn't always keep time either. But not Matthew. He gazed mildly at Graham and the noise of the complaints just drained away. When he was sure he had everyone's attention, he spoke quietly.

"Graham, why are you in this band?"

Graham looked confused.

"To help raise money for the restoration fund."

"Why else?"

A pause.

"I enjoy playing," he said eventually. He was blushing.

Matthew stared at the band, the uncomfortable silence lengthening.

"Why are you here, then, Matthew?" asked Graham, gaining courage.

"For the same reasons as you, Graham, but I also play to the glory of God." This reminded me of something Matt had once told me after a few pints: "You know Andy, Benjamin Britten said of J.S. Bach that to truly understand his music one must realise that it was all written to the glory of God."

Now Graham gave a clever smile. "Shouldn't the music sound good then, if it's to the glory of God?"

Some of the other band members nodded their heads. Graham had scored a point.

"Of course," said Matthew, and something in his tone meant that the nodding suddenly ceased. He spoke in his softest voice. "But even without Davey, will the music we make be perfect?"

Graham dropped his eyes and shook his head.

"Then let him play."

The music resumed. Davey, thirty years old and like his mother not implanted, sat on a plastic chair at the back of the hall, enthusiastically, if ineptly, bashing away at big steel triangle.

Oh, and just in case I am giving the impression that Matthew is some sort of saint, let me point out that I saw him wince, just as painfully as the rest of us, every time Davey tapped off the beat.

By nine o'clock, the time we usually packed up, Matt was on a roll.

"That was good. That was very good…" He looked around us all. "But it could be better! Guitars, we need more energy. Stab out the chords. Keep them short! Dit! Dit Dit! Not der-der-der."

It was a piece without piano accompaniment, and I sat out, leafing through the local paper and looking forward to a pint at the Fleece after the rehearsal.

The orchestra started up, and seconds later the music stuttered into silence as first one instrument and then another gave up the ghost.

I looked up. Matt seemed frozen, the pencil he was using as a baton poised in the air. He was staring over the heads of the orchestra towards the door to the kitchen and toilets. He looked shocked, shaken, and I turned in my seat to see what he was staring at.

"Andy," he said, "would you mind terribly if I handed you the reins for a minute?" And so saying he dropped the pencil in my lap and hurried over to the door. He peered within, circumspectly, then stepped through.

I took my place before the bemused villagers. "Okay," I said. "Bar forty-six, I'll count three in…"

They played, and seconds later Matt reappeared. He entered the hall and looked around, then strode past us and moved to the front door. He was gone for about five minutes. I wondered if he'd seen an intruder and was about to call a halt and see if he needed assistance when he hurried back into the hall, thanked me and took up the baton. His hand, as I passed it to him, was shaking.

Ten minutes later he brought the rehearsal to a close.

I packed up, then caught Matt's eye while he was in conversation with Mrs. Emmett. He seemed distracted, not himself, and he kept darting glances towards the kitchen door. I mimed downing a pint, and received his affirmative nod. While the others were packing up, I left the hall and hurried through the village, more than a little perplexed at Matthew's odd behaviour.

The Fleece was a haven of warmth and inviting firelight.

Of the usual Tuesday night crowd, only Khalid and Doug Standish were present. Doug was a big, almost stereotypically burly, gruff police type, whose initial morose manner had mellowed, as we'd come to know him, to reveal a sensitive character with a dry sense of humour.

I secured a pint of Landlord and joined them by the fire.

A minute later the door blew open admitting a cascade of confetti-like snow and the red-faced figure of Father Matthew Renbourn.

Khalid waved him over. "Ah, 'tis the Father, bejesus, and you'll be having yourself a pint of the usual, I'll be bound?" This hardly raised a smile from Matt.

Khalid went on, serious now, "Are you okay?"

Matt sat down before the fire. I gestured to Sam at the bar to pull Matt a pint.

"What is it?" I asked.

Matt looked from Doug to Khalid, and then at me. "You know I mentioned yesterday that I thought I was being followed?"

I nodded, guessing what was coming.

"Followed?" Doug said, his professional interest aroused.

"For about a month or so now," Matt said, "I've been seeing... well, I don't know if you'll understand..."

"Try us," Khalid said.

"Well, I've been seeing bright, white figures lurking at the edge of my vision, which mysteriously disappear when I try to look closer..."

I said, "And you saw another figure tonight, right?"

Matt took a long draft of creamy ale and nodded. He explained to Khalid and Doug, "In the hall, towards the end of the rehearsal. I saw something… a figure… near the door to the kitchen and cloakroom, but when I went to have a look… Nothing. It'd vanished."

Doug said, "Tell us more about these figures."

"There isn't much more to tell," Matt said. "I've seen about half a dozen of them now, approximately once a week. Tall, glowing figures, watching me—or that's what I feel they're doing. And when I investigate, they're gone in a flash of light."

Something about the expression on Doug's big, jowly face prompted me to ask, "What?"

"It's strange," he said, staring into the remains of his pint with a distant expression, "but remember the murder of Sarah Roberts a few years ago?"

Khalid said, "Wasn't she something to do with the Onward Station?"

Doug nodded. "A liaison officer. Anyway, I investigated the case. Very mysterious." He gave a gruff laugh. "Like something out of an Agatha Christie novel. Roberts was found dead in a house surrounded by snow—no footprints leading to or from the place. Also," he looked up at me, "Ben Knightly reported seeing a great beam of light, almost like a meteorite's tail, fall into the valley where the farmhouse was, on the night she was killed."

Matt stared at him. "And? Was the case ever solved?"

"It's odd, but I always thought there was something strange about the affair. As if certain aspects of it were hushed up. Oh, officially it was *explained*—we found that the killer had probably stowed himself in the house before the snow fell, and then escaped later when the snow on the path to the house had been thoroughly churned. But it was never solved. The killer was never found. And do you know something, I've always had a strange feeling about that case—as if there was more involved than met the eye."

"Like what?" Khalid wanted to know.

"Well, I heard rumours much later that Sarah Roberts wasn't human at all, but a Kéthani emissary, keeping an eye on things on Earth."

"But why would anyone want her dead?" I asked, amazed.

Doug shrugged his big, bison-like shoulders. "I honestly don't know. It's almost as if, when I think about it, I'm prevented from recollecting the events with any clarity."

Khalid hummed the signature tune from an old sci-fi TV show. "Creepy. And you think that Matt's mysterious figure and white light might be linked?"

Doug looked at the priest. "Do you have you any idea what they might be, Matt? Any theories?"

Matt stared into the leaping flames of the log fire, as if contemplating whether to tell us what he was thinking. He looked up, at each of us in turn. "I don't expect you to share my conviction, gentlemen, but it occurred to me that they just might be angels."

He drained his pint, excused himself on the grounds of a sick parishioner, and left the three of us staring at each other in wonderment.

On Thursday evening I finished practising around nine and decided to pop into the Fleece for a quick one.

Khalid and Doug, Ben and Elisabeth, along with Richard Lincoln and Dan Chester, the local ferrymen, were encamped around the table beside the fire. The topic of conversation, not surprisingly, was Matt and his angels.

"Do you think he's going off his rocker?" Elisabeth asked.

"You know these religious types," Dan said. He'd been married to a Catholic who'd refused to have their daughter, Lucy, implanted. He viewed all religions that were opposed to the Kéthani with suspicion, and it had taken him a while to welcome Matt into the fold.

"I'm concerned," Khalid said. "Matt doesn't seem to be himself these days."

"Well, neither would you if you were seeing angels!" Elisabeth said.

"I think the hallucinations are manifestations of... I don't know... stress, overwork." Khalid looked at me. "What do you think, Andy? You know him well. He always seems hale and hearty, but what is he like when he isn't..." he smiled and said, "performing?"

I laughed. "Do you know something? I think he always is performing."

"Even when alone?" Elisabeth asked.

"Is a man who believes, as Matt does," I speculated, "ever alone?"

"You mean he's performing before his God?" Dan said, sarcastically. "Nice one."

Elisabeth stared into her Belgian lager. "What do you expect from a religion that doesn't allow its clergy to express their sexual desires? It's a wonder he isn't hallucinating *Playboy* centrefolds."

"Anyway," I said, in an attempt to bring the conversation back into line. "I don't mind saying that I'm worried for Matt. Let's keep an eye on him, okay?"

We all nodded and agreed.

Towards closing time, I noticed that Khalid was looking somewhat pensive.

"A penny for them," I said.

"Oh, I was just remembering something. You recall a while back, Matt said something along the lines that the Kéthani are in the power of God?"

I nodded. "It struck me as bizarre, too."

"Well... What he said just doesn't sit with what I experienced on Kéthan, with what I learned."

"Go on." Conversation around the table had ceased, and all eyes were on Khalid.

"The odd thing is, when I look back on my experience of resurrection on Kéthan, to be honest I can't actually recall exactly what happened." He smiled. "I learned a lot about myself. I became a better human being. And I know I absorbed philosophies, too. Anyway, the abiding impression I gained is that the Kéthani don't believe in a spiritual afterlife. I gathered that they think the foundation of the universe is purely materialistic. That's why they go about the universe, bestowing immortality upon 'lesser' races..." He shrugged. "I think Matt's deluding himself."

Elisabeth said, "But you said yourself that you don't have a perfect recollection of what happened."

He nodded. "I know. And perhaps I'm wrong. But that doesn't make me any the less worried for Matt, though."

As we were leaving the pub that evening, Elisabeth caught up with me and said, "About Matt, Andy—you're seriously concerned?"

I said reassuringly, "I'm sure it's nothing to worry about, Elisabeth."

Three days later, though, I had cause to revise that opinion.

I was driving home from a job in Leeds, taking the treacherous moor road towards Bradley. The roads had been gritted the night before, but were still icy in patches, and the undulating countryside on either hand was resplendent with snow in the light of the setting sun.

I was a couple of miles from Oxenworth when I saw the old Micra.

It had veered off the lane and into the ditch, and the driver's door was flung open. I slowed as I approached. There was no sign of the driver or any other occupant.

I braked and only then realised that I recognised the vehicle. It was Matt's. The mental alarm bells started ringing.

I jumped from my car and strode over to the little red car, half expecting to find Matt collapsed in the ditch.

He wasn't, but what I found was perhaps even more worrying. A set of footprints led away from the abandoned vehicle, up the snow-covered grass verge towards a stile. On the other side, I made out the footsteps disappearing off up the rise of a field.

I set off in pursuit, wondering what on earth might have provoked Matt into leaving the car, climbing the wall, and haring off over a snow-covered field at sunset.

I clambered over the stile and sank into the snow up to my knees. I plodded up the incline, panting with the unaccustomed exercise. It was hard going, as I had to lift my feet high to clear the snow with each step.

I followed the trail left by Matt up the rise of the field to its high crown. The evidence of the snow showed that he'd stumbled from time to time, creating churned areas of dark shadow in the blindingly white mantle.

I wondered how long he'd been out here and hoped that I wouldn't find him unconscious after hours of exposure.

In the event I found him fully conscious, though that hardly came as a relief.

I crested the crown of the hill and peered down the other side. I made out a dark figure, reduced in the distance. It gave the odd impression of being that of a dwarf, at first, until I realised that Matt was kneeling in the snow so that only his upper body showed.

I yelled his name and clumsily galumphed down the hillside.

"Matt! What the hell—"

I drew near. He was kneeling in prayer, his red hands clasped beneath his chin, and his body was shaking with sobs.

"Matt!" I cried again, falling beside him and putting my arm around his shoulders.

He seemed barely aware of my presence. He was staring into the distance, his expression at once amazed and terrified.

"Matt!"

He turned and stared at me. "Andrew?"

"Come on," I said, attempting to haul him to his feet. The cold was getting to me, and I could only assume that Matt was half-frozen. "Back to my car."

"Andrew," he went on, "if only you could have seen them! They were... beautiful and at the same time terrible. The light... But what can they mean, Andrew? What portent? Am I damned or exalted? *What do they mean?*"

It was his words, more than the fact of his sequestration in the middle of a frozen field, that alarmed me then. Initially I had been worried for his physical health; now I worried about his mental stability.

"They were at the side of the road," he said, "watching me. I stopped and climbed out. They moved, flew towards the sunset, creatures of such beauty and grace, Andrew." He stared at me as I hauled him to his feet and walked him slowly back to the car. "But what can they want with me?"

Somehow I managed to get him over the stile and safely ensconced in the passenger seat of my car. I found his keys and locked his Micra, then drove the remaining mile into the village.

He sat beside me, hunched, occasionally wiping his eyes with a big handkerchief. He said nothing, and I found it impossible to initiate any meaningful conversation. At one point he broke down again, sobbed briefly, and then pulled himself together—actually squared his shoulders and sat upright, as if chastising himself for such a lapse.

I drove him to his house beside the church. "I'll see you inside, Matt," I said.

I helped him from the car and walked him down the drive. He gave me the keys and I opened the door and ushered him into the lounge. He sat on the sofa, fingering his rosary, while I fixed a couple of stiff scotches from a well-stocked bar in the corner of the room.

He gripped the glass and smiled at me. "I needed this, Andrew. Thanks."

"If there's anything else I can do...?" I said lamely.

He shook his head. "I'm fine. It's just... well, it isn't every day that one is pursued by angels, is it? I cannot help but wonder what it is they want with me."

I smiled and looked away from his penetrating gaze.

"Do you know, Andrew, sometimes, I can't work out whether I am blessed, or damned..."

I considered what Khalid had told me last night, about his experience on Kéthan, and wondered whether to broach the subject with Matt. I decided against it, however: he was confident in his belief; one might almost say his passion. Who was I to gainsay that?

A little later, after assuring him that I'd fetch his car, and his reassuring me that he was feeling much better now, I took my leave and repaired to the Fleece.

It was after nine by this time, and the table by the fire was crowded. Khalid, Ben, and Elisabeth budged up to make room for me. Dan said, "I was just telling the others, Andy. On the way over from Bradley I saw a car abandoned in the ditch. I'm sure it was Matt's. You know? That little red one he has?"

I nodded. "I know. I saw it too—then I found Matt."

I gave them the story.

Everyone was silent when I finished. I looked around the table, and the similar expressions of concern on the faces was in an odd way reassuring. It confirmed what I'd thought for a while: these men and women, my friends for over a year since I moved to the village, were good people.

"So," I said into the silence. "What do we do?"

Dan said, "Is there much we can do, Andy? Be there for him…"

"Perhaps," Elisabeth said, "the Catholic Church has some kind of… I don't know… helpline for distressed clergy."

"Maybe we should contact his bishop," Ben suggested.

"I'm not too sure he'd appreciate our going behind his back like that," I said.

Khalid said, "I'll look into it at hospital, talk to a shrink and see if there's anything they might suggest."

We all nodded, impotent in the light of our friend's religious hallucinations.

The topic of conversation changed, and I enjoyed a few more pints, but I could not help but contrast the Matt I had known over the weeks and the figure I had seen collapsed in manic prayer earlier that evening.

The following night I arrived at rehearsal five minutes late, and the players were already tuning up. Old Mrs. Emmett gestured me over. "Matthew just phoned," she said. "He's at the church, in a meeting. He said he'd be here at eight."

I suggested that we run through a few numbers for thirty minutes until he arrived, and I conducted the Oxenworth Community Orchestra through an arrangement of the theme tune to *Raiders of the Lost Ark*. It sounded strangely flat and lifeless without Matthew in charge. Eight o'clock came and went, with no sign of our conductor. At eight-thirty, Mrs. Emmett said, "You don't suppose anything's happened to him? Surely he would have phoned to tell us if he couldn't make it?"

I remembered last night, and part of me feared for Matt. I volunteered to pop along to see what was keeping him.

The snow had not let up in the last week, and it was a foot deep in the little-used lane that connected the church to the village hall. I hurried through a fresh fall, shoulders hunched, came to the church and pushed through the heavy timber doors.

The place was warm and silent. I hurried down the aisle, looking for Matt. I peered into the vestry, but he wasn't there, and so I tried his little office next door.

It was there that I found him.

He was sitting in a swivel chair behind his vast oak desk. The chair was not facing the desk, but turned away, as if he had been addressing someone standing in front of the roaring fire.

He was smiling, his posture slightly slumped, and something about the glassy immobility of his stare told me that he was dead.

I hurried around the desk and felt for his pulse. There was none. I touched the implant at his temple: the small, square device thrummed beneath my fingertips. Even now, the nano-machines would be coursing through Matt's system, working their miracle, and bringing him back to life.

Already, the Onward Station would know about his death; a ferryman would be on his way.

I phoned the police at Bradley, and then let Mrs. Emmett know that Matt wouldn't be in that night. I left it at that; for some reason I couldn't bring myself to say that my friend was dead.

I found a chair and sat down, considering that a few years ago, before the coming of the Kéthani, Matt would have been dead forever. Like my mother and father, and my brother...

Ten minutes later the police arrived, and minutes after that Dan Chester. I could see the sadness in their eyes as they took in the corpse: despite the fact of our resurrection, evidence of our erstwhile mortality still has a powerful effect on us. Dan and his assistant removed Matt's body from the office; I gave a statement to the police and fifteen minutes later returned to the village hall to relay the news to a shocked orchestra.

After that, there was nowhere else to go but the Fleece, for a session of liquid therapy.

Khalid was there, propping up the bar, and I told him about the evening's events.

An hour later, Doug Standish joined us. "Thought you two might be here, somehow. The usual?"

When he returned from the bar, he said, "I was down at the station when I heard about Matt. Apparently he had a massive heart attack."

For the rest of the evening we reminisced about Matt, telling stories of our friend, and smiling at the memories. As we left the Fleece around midnight, we were halted in our tracks by a blinding bolt of light from the distant Onward Station as it beamed the demolecularised remains of the dead up to the Kéthani starship.

Khalid stared up, his brown face made pale by the light. "There he goes," he whispered.

"I wonder what kind of Matt he'll be on his return?" I wondered.

I took charge of the rehearsals at the village hall, and in spring we staged the first and what would turn out to be the last of the concerts in the church itself. It went down well, but something was missing—Matthew. The orchestra was a dying thing. In six months, I guessed, it would be gone, with no hope of resurrection, Kéthani or otherwise. Only when life became eternal did I truly appreciate the fact that nothing ever lasts forever.

Matt was missing from our Tuesday night sessions, too; our gatherings just weren't the same without him.

The day of his return came about, and there was a big crowd of locals in the reception lounge of the Onward Station that afternoon: his parishioners were out in force, ninety-nine per cent of them implanted; a gaggle of clergy was present, too. His Tuesday night friends formed a small knot among the crowd.

At three on the dot, the head of operations at the Station, Director Masters, made a short speech, and Matt stepped through the sliding doors and greeted us.

Matthew, in his late forties when he died, now looked a good ten years younger, his waistline slimmed down, the fat of his face pared—even the distinguished grey at his temples was gone. He looked leaner, fitter, somehow more full of energy, if that were possible.

He made the rounds, shaking hands, hugging, slapping backs; many of his flock were in tears.

I wondered if it was significant that he was no longer wearing his dog collar, or if he was undercover here, too.

"The beer brigade!" he greeted the Tuesday nighters. "God, I've missed a pint where I was…" We laughed.

One hour later, Matt was driven away by the officials of his Church.

As I watched him go, I thought over what he had said all those months ago about the Kéthani and their place in the scheme of things, and I wondered if Father Matthew Renbourn would slip quietly back into his old way of life in the village. I should have known the answer to that, of course.

That evening, just as I was about to call it a day, pack up my cornet, and slip out for a quick one at the Fleece, the phone rang.

It was Matt.

I couldn't conceal my surprise. "Matt, great to hear you. Look, do you fancy a pint? We're meeting at the Fleece at nine."

He made an excuse—he had a lot of work on. But, he said, he would like to see me.

I evinced my surprise yet again. "Well, of course. Great. Where?"

"Could you pop along to the church in ten minutes?"

It was high summer and a magnificently balmy evening. Not that I appreciated the sunset and the birdsong as I made my way down the lane to St. Luke's. My head was full of my imminent meeting with Matt.

I found him in his office, seated behind his desk in the very same chair I'd found him in six months earlier.

He smiled at me. "Andy, sit down. I'd like to thank you for your work with the orchestra."

"You're welcome. It's not the same without you... But that isn't why you wanted to see me, is it?"

He grinned disarmingly. "Of course not. Doug told me that it was you who discovered the... my body."

I nodded. "It was something of a shock," I said.

"I can well imagine." He paused and thought about what he was going to say next. "I think I owe you an explanation," he continued.

I stared at him, not understanding. "About what?"

"About my death," he murmured, "what else?"

I made a feeble gesture. "But what is there to explain?" I said. "You died of a massive coronary."

"Officially, Andrew, I died of a massive coronary."

I tried a smile. "And unofficially?"

"I'm not at all sure you'd believe me."

"Try me."

Matt leaned back in his chair and arranged his fingers in a fair imitation of a church steeple. "There is a lot we don't know about, Andy. A lot happening in the big, wide universe out there that we, with our limited perceptions, cannot even guess at." He paused, looked at his hands. "Do you recall those figures—the figures of light? I mentioned they were following me."

"How can I forget?"

He nodded. "That night, six months ago, one came to see me, came here, into this very office. That night. Orchestra night."

"What happened?" I asked, my voice far from steady. "What did it say?"

"It said nothing," he told me. "It merely sent me on the next stage of my journey."

I was suddenly aware of how loud my heartbeat was. "It killed you?" I murmured.

"It reached out," he said, "and touched my chest, just here," he lay his fingertips on his sternum, "and I felt a sudden and ineffable sense of joy, of affirmation, and I knew that my true quest had begun."

I shook my head. "I don't think I understand," I began.

"When I was resurrected on Kéthan, I was instructed. I learned many things about the universe, the various races out there, the many philosophies. I was given the option of returning to Earth, or going among the stars. They showed me a vast starship, due to explore what we call the Lesser Magellanic Cloud. They want me to be aboard it when it sails."

I hardly heard myself say, "In what capacity?"

He beamed at me. "To spread the word," he said.

"The Kéthani..." I whispered. "You said, a while ago, that they were but tools to achieve God's purpose."

He nodded. "And I think they know that, too, my friend."

A little later he showed me to the door of the church and shook my hand.

"Goodbye, Andrew," Matt said, and turned and walked up the aisle towards the altar and the figure of Jesus on the cross. I watched him kneel and bow his head in prayer.

That was the last time I saw Father Matthew Renbourn. In the morning he slipped quietly from the village, leaving behind him the mystery of his death and the even greater mystery of his mission among the stars.

That night, I left Matt praying to his God and made my slow way to the Fleece. There, I informed the others what Matt had told me, and we speculated long into the night whether our friend was blessed... or deluded.

INTERLUDE

Fifteen years had passed since the coming of the Kéthani, and I often looked back and marvelled that so short a time had elapsed since that momentous day on the moors when I beheld the arrival of the Onward Station. I looked back, too, and found it hard to imagine life before the Kéthani. The world had been a vastly different place, then; but more, the human race had been very different. In the centuries and millennia BK, as we came to know it, humanity had schemed and grabbed and fought and killed on a global level, playing out imperatives that had their roots in individual neuroses: we were the descendants of animals, and within us was the conditioning of the jungle. We had feared death, and in consequence perhaps we had also feared life.

And now, a decade and a half later?

I'll employ a cliché: humanity was more humane. I witnessed more small acts of charity in my day-to-day dealings with people, more gestures of care and kindness. I saw less cruelty, less hatred. We were, perhaps, leaving behind the animal within us and evolving into something else.

So much change in fifteen years...

All this is a preliminary to the scene I'm about to relate, which happened unsurprisingly in the main bar of the Fleece.

It was a few days before Christmas, the fire was roaring, and the usual faces were gathered about the table. Conversation was good.

Then I looked up as the door opened, admitting a swirl of wind and a beautiful woman.

She was dressed in high boots and a black coat buttoned up to her chin, and the face I stared at was pale and elfin, with a midnight fall of jet-black hair.

She stamped her feet and brrr'd her lips, then looked over to our group, smiled and lifted gloved fingers in a little wave—and only then did I realise, with a start, who it was.

Dan Chester stood, crossed the room, and embraced his daughter, Lucy.

She hugged us one by one, saying how good it was to be back home. "Khal," she said. "It's great to see you!"

She sat down and sipped a half a pint of Ram Tam, and told us all about life at university in London.

It was perhaps two years since I'd last seen Lucy, and she had changed, imago-like, from a shy teenager into a confident, self-possessed young woman in her late teens.

She was studying xeno-biology and international relations, preparatory to leaving Earth. She had discussed her decision with her father: it was the thing she most wanted to do, and though Dan had found it hard to accept that soon, within two years, she would be light years away among the stars, he could not find it within him to deny her dreams.

She looked around the group and said, "Did you know that the university is Kéthani-run?"

"What?" Richard Lincoln quipped, "the dons wave tentacles or pseudo-pods?"

Lucy laughed. "Perhaps I should say it's Kéthani administered. All the courses are geared to students who have made the decision to leave Earth and work with the Kéthani."

"I suppose it makes sense," Sam said.

"There's a wonderful atmosphere of... not only of learning, but of camaraderie. We're about to do something wondrous out there, and the excitement is infectious."

Andy Souter, our resident sceptic, said, "What exactly will you be doing out there, Lucy?"

She smiled and looked into her drink. When she looked up, I saw the light of... dare I say *evangelism*... in her eyes. "We'll be taking the word of the Kéthani to the universe, Andy. We'll be endowing as yet uncontacted races with what the Kéthani have given us; I'll be working with pre-industrial, humanoid races, bringing them to an understanding of the Kéthani, rather than have them learn about the Kéthani as we did, with the sudden arrival of the Onward Stations. Other students will be liaising between disputing races or helping races who have fought to the point of extinction. Oh..." she beamed around the table, "there's no limit to the work to be done out there!"

I could see that Andy remained unconvinced, but her enthusiasm won me over.

I said, "The human race has certainly evolved since the Kéthani came, Lucy."

"Evolved," she said. "Yes, that's the word, Khal. Evolved. Everyone has changed, haven't they, not only the returnees, but those who haven't yet died." She looked round the group. "We no longer fear death, do we? That curse has been lifted from our psyches. We can... for the first time in existence, we can look ahead and enjoy being alive."

I smiled. Years ago, I would have labelled her optimism as the product of youth; but now that optimism had infected all of us.

The door opened, and someone hurried into the bar and ordered a drink, a young man in a thick coat and walking boots. Lucy turned quickly and smiled at the new arrival, and it was wonderful to see the unmistakable light of love in her eyes.

I recognised the man as Davey Emmett.

Lucy said, in almost a whisper, "I, more than most, have so much to thank the Kéthani for..."

Davey carried his pint across the room and joined us. He kissed Lucy and sat down beside her, and I noticed that immediately Lucy found his hand with hers and squeezed.

Davey smiled across at me. "Khalid, it's been a long time."

I nodded. "Almost a year? How are you?"

He laughed. "Never better. I enrolled at the London uni. A mature student." He looked at Lucy and grinned. "Amazing, isn't it, that I had to travel two hundred miles in order to meet someone from the same village."

I looked at Lucy; she seemed hesitant and oddly nervous. She cast a quick glance across at her father. Davey, beside her, gave her a subtle nudge, and I guessed what was about to happen.

She said, "Dad..." She coloured prettily, and turned and looked at Davey. "Dad, everyone, I thought it'd be nice to announce it among friends. Davey and I are planning to get married later this year..."

We cheered, and Richard Lincoln ordered a bottle of champagne, and we took it in turns to kiss Lucy and shake Davey's hand.

It was the start of a long night, one of the best among many I'd experienced in the Fleece with my friends.

I thought back almost a year, to the last time I had met Davey Emmett and his remarkable mother.

Even now, not all the citizens of Earth chose to be implanted. Katherine Emmett had been one of these people.

For the most part I viewed these mavericks as misguided, or as short-sighted religious crackpots—though not Katherine Emmett. I had nothing but respect for the old lady and her decision to remain without an implant.

It's a testament to the power of her faith, and her humanity, that she allowed her son the opportunity to make his own choice.

NINE

A Choice of Eternities

I was in the Fleece on Tuesday night when Richard Lincoln buttonholed me about old Mrs. Emmett. I'd arrived at seven and ordered a braised pork chop with roast potatoes and a pint of Landlord.

Sam was serving behind the bar. "You're early, Khalid."

"Hard day at the mill," I said. "I need to wind down."

"Well, the Landlord's on form tonight. I'll just go put your order in."

She disappeared into the kitchen and I took a long draft of ale. Sam was right: it was nectar.

I'd had a tiring day at the hospital. Usually the implantation process went like a dream, but that afternoon, just as I was about to start the last implantation, the patient decided that he'd had second thoughts. He wanted a little time to consider what he was doing. It had been after six before I'd been able to get away.

I was the first of the Tuesday night crowd to arrive, but the others were not far behind. Ben and Elisabeth came in first, looking frozen stiff after the long walk through the snow; then the ferrymen Richard Lincoln and Dan Chester blew in, talking shop as usual, followed by Jeffrey Morrow. Next came Doug Standish and Andy Souter, and last of all Samantha's husband, Stuart Kingsley. Samantha finished her shift at the bar and joined us.

I thought of Zara and the many happy Tuesday nights we'd spent at the Fleece with our friends, before my wife walked out on me and I killed myself, over ten years ago now.

I was on my third pint when Richard Lincoln returned from the bar with a round and sat down beside me.

Richard wore old-fashioned tweeds and liked his beer, but far from being the conservative country type he so much resembled, I found him liberal and open-minded. He lived next door to me along the street from the Fleece, and I considered him my best friend. Certainly he was the only person I'd told about what had really happened ten years ago.

"Cheers, Khalid," Richard said, dispatching a good quarter of his pint in one swallow. "I wanted to talk to you about something. Another reluctant customer."

On my return from Kéthan, I had told Richard that I'd decided to stay on Earth and spread the good word about the implantation process. From time to time he put me on to people he came across in his line of work who were reluctant, for various reasons, to undergo the implantation.

"Old Mrs. Emmett, up at High Fold Farm," Richard said. "She has a son, Davey. He's mentally handicapped."

"And he isn't implanted, right?"

"That's the thing. Mrs. Emmett isn't implanted, either. She's no fool, Khalid. No addled hermit living on the moors. She might be in her seventies, but she's all there. A retired university lecturer. She isn't implanted on religious grounds."

"Always the hardest to convert," I said.

"The thing is, Davey is dying. Lung cancer. He was diagnosed a couple of months ago. I sent a counsellor from the

Onward Station to talk to Mrs. Emmett last week, but she was having none of it."

"And you think I might be able to talk her round?"

"Well, she does think highly of you," Richard said.

I looked at him, surprised. "She does?"

"You treated her in hospital way back. She remembers you. I saw her in town last week and happened to mention your name. Actually, I asked her if you could come and talk to her about the Kéthani."

I smiled at his presumption. "And she agreed?"

"When she heard your name, she relented. I was wondering, if you didn't have a lot on..."

"Why not? You never know..." I thought hard, but couldn't put a face to the name. It had been years ago, after all, and the workload of your average intern even back then had militated against the recollection of every patient.

Last orders were called and the final round bought, and it was well after midnight before the meeting broke up.

When I said goodbye to Richard outside my front door, I told him I'd visit Mrs. Emmett at the weekend.

High Fold was no longer a working farm. Like many once-thriving sheep farms in the area, it had suffered in the economic recession in the early years of the century. Its own-ers had sold up and moved away, and Mrs. Emmett had bought the farm, converted it at great expense, and lived there now in retirement with her son.

The snow was so bad on the Saturday morning that I had to leave the car on the main road above the farm. I struggled down the snow-filled track, towards the sprawling stone-built house on the hillside overlooking Oxenworth. By the time I reached the front door I knew I would never be cut out to be an Arctic explorer.

Mrs. Emmett answered my summons promptly, took one look at my bedraggled figure, and smiled. It was only then that I recalled the woman I had treated as a patient all those years ago.

The smile. Some people smile with just their mouths, others with all their faces. Mrs. Emmett's smile encompassed all her face and emanated genuine warmth. I recalled the experience of feeling like a favourite nephew as she welcomed me.

"Dr. Azzam!" she said. "Khalid, it's lovely to see you. Come in. It's terrible out there."

I stepped into a spacious hall, removed my coat, and stamped the snow from my boots on the mat, then followed her into a lounge where a wood-burning stove belted out a fierce, furnace heat.

"I seem to remember you prefer coffee. I'll just go and put it on. You know Davey of course."

She left the room, and I sketched a smile and a wave at the man seated at a small table beside the stove.

He looked up briefly, but didn't respond. He was absorbed in a world of his own. Davey Emmett was nearing thirty now, a chubby, childlike man, in both appearance and manner. I had never treated Davey—his affairs were looked after by a local doctor— and I had no idea of his medical history, whether his condition was congenital or the result of some childhood illness.

He rarely spoke, as I recalled, and had the mental age of a young child. He was obsessed with collecting stamps—he was poring over a thick album now. I remembered looking at one of his albums years ago when he'd come to the hospital with his mother. He collected stamps not by country or subjects depicted, as is common with philatelists, but by size and shape and colour.

Now he lowered his head short-sightedly over the page, a big Tweedledee absorbed in the polychromatic pattern of stamps before him.

As I watched him, I wondered if Davey was aware of his life-threatening illness.

Mrs. Emmett returned bearing a tray. For a woman in her seventies, she was remarkably upright and spry—and mentally sharp, as I found out.

She sat down and poured two coffees, then gave me a penetrating sidewise glance. "It must be very hard for people wholly convinced of the benefits the Kéthani have bestowed," she said, "to comprehend the stance taken by the few dissenters amongst us." She spoke eloquently, in a soft voice free of accent or dialect.

I found myself smiling. "Well, we do live in an increasingly secular age," I began.

"The two sides cannot be reconciled," she went on. "We with faith are wholly convinced of the truth of our views, while those that hold with the Kéthani pity us for our ignorance, for our choice of passing up the opportunity of certain immortality." She paused and smiled. "Those with scientific certainty fail to understand the certainty of those with true faith."

I smiled. "You're telling me, politely, to mind my own business."

She laughed, the sound like a cut-glass chime. "Of course not, Khalid. I'm merely stating my position. I'd be genuinely interested in hearing your argument."

I took a sip of the excellent coffee. "Well, it's an argument based not so much on faith or theory," I said, "as on my own experience."

She inclined her head. "I understand that you now work on the implant ward at Bradley."

"I do, but that isn't the experience I was referring to. You see..." I paused, choosing my words carefully. "Over ten years ago, Mrs. Emmett, I died." I elected to leave out the messy personal details of my death. "I was resurrected on the home planet of the Kéthani and... instructed, I suppose is the best way to put it. I've only a vague recollection of what happened in the Kéthani domes, just nebulous memories, images. What I do retain is the sensation of rebirth, the wonder of renewed life, and the sense of rightness that accompanied my resurrection. I knew so much more. I became—and this is ironic, as it's the result of an alien process—more humane. I was convinced of the rightness of what I had undergone and the genuine sense of destiny I was to undergo. I knew I had to return to Earth and spread the word of the implantation process—"

Mrs. Emmett interrupted, "If you don't mind my saying, Khalid, what you have said so far sounds not so much a matter of reason, but of faith."

I smiled. "I suppose it does." I paused, marshalling my thoughts. "But the Kéthani believe that the process of resurrection after death is the only true hope of continued existence." I wondered, then, how much my words had been influenced by my own prejudices.

"Or that," she said, again with that sweet smile, "is what they told you."

"Not so much told," I said, "as showed. I find it hard to explain, but at the end of the process, I *knew* they were right."

"Just as, at the culmination of my years of instruction with my Rinpoche," Mrs. Emmett said, "I *knew* that the way of Buddha was, for me, the true and right path." Her bright blue eyes twinkled at me. "Faith, Khalid."

I had to smile. "Touché," I said.

"But..." she said.

I looked up at her.

"But?" I echoed, encouraged.

"But, Khalid, I presume you didn't come here to try to save *my* life." She was ahead of me, and knew it, and I couldn't help but admire her intelligence.

I looked across at Davey, who was thoroughly absorbed in his stamp collection. "Richard told me that Davey is ill," I began, uncomfortable about discussing the man in his presence.

"And you think I should have Davey implanted for his own good?"

I looked her in the eye. "Irrespective of your own beliefs," I said, "I think you should give Davey the chance to decide for himself whether he would like the opportunity of virtual immortality."

She looked at me sharply. "The opportunity?" she said. "But if I agree now to have him implanted, how would that be giving Davey the chance to decide for himself?"

I smiled. I could see the way ahead, the chance to save Davey from the imposition of his mother's trenchantly held beliefs. Was that arrogant of me, small-minded?

I went on, "You see, if Davey is implanted, then when he dies and is taken to Kéthan he will be resurrected not as he is now, but with certain... how should I put it?... *changes*. He will still be Davey, still intrinsically himself, but his intelligence and understanding will be boosted. He'll be the Davey who you would have had if not for..."

I stopped, for I saw a flicker of pain in her expression.

She said, "That might be a difficult fact to face, Khalid. To have Davey as I might have had him for all these years."

"But," I persisted, "wouldn't it be better for him to be cured, to live a full and extended life?"

"That is to assume that what he experiences now is not full and rewarding, Khalid. All experience is relative and valid, as Buddha teaches us."

"Then perhaps it would be a valid experience to allow Davey the opportunity of resurrection," I countered.

She looked at me, assessing. "But, Khalid, forgive me—you haven't answered my question. You said that I should give Davey the opportunity to make his own choice. But if I did agree to have him implanted, then I would be making the choice for him."

I moved forward, sat on the edge of the chair in my desire to win the argument. "But you see, when Davey returns from Kéthan, resurrected, he would still be implanted. Returnees aren't suddenly rendered immortal. They still have the implant which will keep them alive should they 'die' again, before they are taken to Kéthan for a second, or third or fourth, resurrection."

"And..." Mrs. Emmett began, a dawning light in her eyes.

I nodded. "That's right, when Davey returns from Kéthan, he will be implanted—and if he so wishes he can have the implant removed. If he shares your faith, then he can make a choice based on a full understanding of all the factors involved."

I stopped there and watched Mrs. Emmett closely to see how she had taken my argument.

She was staring at her empty coffee cup, frowning slightly. At last she looked up and nodded. "You present a very interesting scenario, Khalid," She said at last. "It is certainly something I need to think about."

I nodded and finished my coffee. I should have realised that nothing I could have said would have made her change her mind there and then.

I wondered if, when I left, she would rationalise the discussion and allow her faith to maintain the status quo.

As she showed me to the door a little later, she touched my arm and said, "Buddha taught that there is no objective truth, Khalid. Each of us carries within us a subjective truth, if only we can find it."

I smiled.

She went on, "I've tried so hard, Khalid, but the truth is that I'm not a very good Buddhist."

"What makes you say—?" I began.

She smiled, sadly. "Attachment is wrong, Khalid. I am being selfish in my love for Davey. I should be able to look past my attachment and see what is best for Davey."

I made the long trek back to the car and drove home, happy with the morning's work.

I had quite forgotten about Mrs. Emmett and Davey when, three days later, my secretary received a call. She put her head around the door. "There's a Mrs. Emmett on the line," she said. "She won't be put off. Shall I tell her you're busy?"

"Emmett? No, put her through."

I picked up the phone. "Mrs. Emmett?" I fully expected her to tell me that she had had second thoughts, and that our conversation had done nothing to change her mind. "How can I help?"

She came straight to the point. "Khalid, I've been giving due consideration to our little talk the other day. I've been reading my Buddhism... and under the circumstances I think it would be in Davey's best possible interests if he were implanted."

I refrained from punching the air in triumph, but I could feel myself grinning idiotically. "That's good news, Mrs. Emmett."

"Davey's at home with me at the moment," she said. "But he's taken a turn for the worse and he's due to be admitted into Bradley General tomorrow."

"I'll arrange for him to come straight to the implant ward," I told her.

She hesitated. "Would I... That is, could I be present when Davey is implanted?"

"By all means. I'll arrange everything and see you tomorrow."

"Thank you very much for your help, Khalid."

I smiled and cut the connection.

* * *

The following afternoon I ushered Mrs. Emmett and Davey into my surgery and explained the implantation procedure. Davey sat clutching a stamp album, oblivious that we were discussing his future.

Mrs. Emmett was surprised that the operation would be over so quickly. "I thought it would be performed under general anaesthetic," she said.

I smiled. "No, local. It takes about ten minutes. I simply make an incision in the skin of the temple and insert the implant. I seal the wound, and the implant does the rest. It releases nano-machines into the subject's body, which monitor the metabolism. When the subject 'dies', the implant takes over and revives the system."

Mrs. Emmett was shaking her head. "And then, when Davey is returned, he can make his decision as to whether or not he wishes to retain the implant?"

I nodded. "That's right. Now, if you'd care to step this way."

Davey proved to be a docile patient. A nurse administered a sedative and a local anaesthetic, and while Davey lay on the couch with his head turned to the left, I made the slit in his right temple, eased the implant home, and sealed the wound.

Mrs. Emmett perched on a stool, watching intently.

I looked up and smiled. "There, done."

"Quite amazing, Khalid."

While Davey was drinking a cup of sugary tea, Mrs. Emmett confided her concerns to me. "It will be a very strange experience, Khalid, when Davey returns, to see him as he might have been if not for..." She smiled, sadly. "You see, so much of my life has been taken up with his welfare. I retired early in order to keep him with me. I could have sent him to a care home, but after my husband died... well, Davey was all I had."

She fell silent, her gaze distant, perhaps considering how her life might have worked out had it not been for Davey's handicap.

I realised, then, that Davey's return would be at once a cause for celebration and, for Mrs. Emmett, much soul searching.

Once Davey was implanted, he was spared the treatment he would have undergone for his condition. A month after his implant, he was admitted to Bradley General where he died peacefully. Richard Lincoln, accompanied by Mrs. Emmett and myself, drove the body up to the Onward Station. There was a small, secular ceremony of leave-taking, and then Davey was beamed aboard the orbiting Kéthani starship. I drove Mrs. Emmett home, promising to accompany her to the ceremony that would greet Davey's return to Earth in six months' time.

That year, winter hung on well into April. There was a late fall of snow at Easter, transforming the land with its total and pristine beauty. Life proceeded as normal, a round of work and Tuesday night sessions at the Fleece. They were the highlight of the week, a few hours of relaxation among good friends.

I saw Zara once in Bradley, and that was painful. She was walking arm in arm with her new husband, on the opposite side of the street. They didn't see me, for which I was thankful. The sight of her, tall and beautiful and seemingly happy, released a slew of painful memories. I went over and over our final days together, and Zara's accusations. I was a bastard, she had said, a domineering, selfish, bigoted, sexist bastard.

And then I had killed myself and been resurrected—remade, as it were, by the Kéthani. I became a new man.

A few months after Davey Emmett's death, Richard Lincoln took me to one side in the Fleece and told me that Mrs. Emmett was in hospital.

"I saw her yesterday while I was making a pick up," he said. "She has cancer. It's terminal. She said she wanted to see you."

I looked at him. "You don't think…?" I began.

"What, that she wants to be implanted? A conversion at the eleventh hour? I doubt it, not our Mrs. Emmett."

"I'll drop by and see her tomorrow," I promised, and returned to my pint, wondering what the old lady might want to see me about.

She was in a private room on the oncology ward, sitting upright in bed and hooked up to a bank of machines. If I had expected a feeble, self-sorry old woman who had given up all hope, then I had grossly underestimated Mrs. Katherine Emmett.

She gave a cheery smile when I hesitantly entered the room. "Khalid, pull up a chair. How are you?"

I smiled and shook my head. "Isn't it me who should be asking you how you are?"

She laughed. "I'm fine, Khalid. Oddly enough, given the circumstances, I've really never felt better."

I took her hand. "You're an amazing woman," I found myself saying.

She laughed again, mockingly this time. "I'm seventy-six, Khalid, and I've had a full and eventful life. I'm quite prepared for the end of this stage of existence."

I gestured at the equipment surrounding the bed. "They're doing their damnedest to keep you alive."

She leaned forward and whispered, mock-conspiratorially, "It's because I'm not implanted, Khalid. They're frightened to death of death. They're trying to do everything they can to squeeze a few more weeks of life from me. But as I've told them over and over, I'm ready to go."

"They haven't tried to get you to agree to an implant?"

"Of course they have. I had some young thing down here just yesterday. He didn't know his theology, though—I tied him up in knots."

"So it'd be useless if I tried to…"

"Absolutely and categorically futile, Khalid, my friend."

I tried another tack. "How long do they give you?"

"Perhaps a month. The liver, you see."

"But you won't be around to see Davey when he returns…"

She allowed a few seconds to elapse before she replied—sufficient time to make me regret the statement.

"No," she said, "I won't be around. And do you know something? I don't want to be around, to be honest."

I stared at her. "Surely—" I began, and stopped myself.

She leaned forward. "Khalid, I want to tell you something. I've never told another living soul this, and I want to get it off my chest before I go." I squeezed her hand, wondering what I was about to hear.

"Khalid, do you know what was wrong with Davey? I mean, what was responsible for his condition?"

I shook my head. "His medical records would have been privy only to his own doctor," I began.

She smiled, returning the pressure of my hand. "It was an accident, Khalid. When he was two years old. I'd taken him out shopping. If only I'd delayed going out or not gone at all… But we can't undo the past, can we? Oh, I've often wondered how what happened might have been the repercussions of sins I might have committed in a previous life. That was the only part of Buddhist theory that I found hard to accept." She laughed. "For obvious reasons, Khalid! Anyway, you see, it was my fault… the accident. We had stopped at the side of the road, and Davey got away from me… ran straight into the road, in front of…" She paused, gathering herself, and then went on. "The doctors said it was miracle that Davey survived, even though he was severely brain damaged."

She stopped, and the silence seemed to ring like an alarm. When I looked up at her, I saw tears streaming unchecked down her wrinkled cheeks. I found a tissue and passed it to her, and she blotted the tears with a gesture at once dignified and pitiful.

"I've had to live with the guilt for so long," she said, "even though my acceptance of karma should lead me to be able to see guilt for the illusion it is. As I said, I'm not a very good Buddhist."

I began to protest.

She gave a sigh and went on, "So do you see why I couldn't bear to see Davey when he returned? He will be how he would have been, were it not for my neglect. And the sight of him, so changed, will remind me not only of my foolishness, but of the Davey I should have been able to love, growing up like other children."

She was crying again, and all I could do was grip her hand.

At last, tentatively, I said, "But if you were to be implanted, you would be able to share his life from now on."

She smiled at me through her tears. She lifted my hand and kissed my knuckles. "You're a good man, Khalid. You mean well. But Davey would be a stranger to me. It wasn't meant to be. Did you know," she said, more brightly now, "that scientists opposed to the Kéthani have developed a new theory of consciousness?"

I smiled. "They have?"

She nodded, enthusiastic. "You see, they posit that our consciousness, the very essence that makes us ourselves, resides on some infinitesimally small, quantum level, a level that permeates the cosmos. And when we die, we don't just fizzle out like a spent match, but our consciousness remains integrated with the matrix of existence..." She laughed to herself. "It's what Buddha said all those hundreds of years ago, Khalid!"

"Well, what do you know, Mrs. Emmett," I smiled.

Before I left, promising to pop in the following day, she restrained me with a fierce grip. "Khalid, when Davey returns, will you meet him at the Station, explain what happened, why I couldn't be there for him? Will you make sure that he understands, Khalid?"

"Of course I will."

"And... something else." She reached across to the bedside table, and gave me a sealed letter. "Will you give this to him, Khalid? It's an explanation of my belief. I want him to consider everything, so that he can decide for himself whether he wants to retain his implant."

I squeezed her hand and promised that I would give him the letter, then said goodbye and slipped from the room.

I did return the following day, only to learn that Mrs. Emmett had died peacefully in the early hours of the morning.

Three months later, in the middle of October, a heavy fall of snow heralded Davey Emmett's return to Earth.

I was just one of three people gathered at the Onward Station to greet him. The other two were care assistants who had worked with Davey over the years. They had never, they said, met a returnee; I refrained from telling them that I had died and been resurrected by the Kéthani.

I recalled my own transformation, both mentally and physically, and wondered how the Kéthani might have remade Davey Emmett.

Five minutes later we found out. We were in a small reception lounge furnished with a few chairs and a table bearing wine and fruit juice. Normally, more people would attend a returning ceremony, and a larger lounge would be required: but Davey had made few friends during his thirty years on Earth.

The sliding door at the back of the room opened, and Davey stepped through. The woman beside me gasped, and I understood her reaction. Even I, who had been expecting a marked metamorphosis, was taken aback.

Gone was the overweight adult-child, the sallow-faced, balding misfit unable to establish eye contact or hold a conversation.

Davey Emmett seemed taller, slimmer. His face was lean, even handsome; he appeared to be in his mid-twenties. He wore a neat suit and strode purposefully into the room, smiling.

He shook our hands, greeting us by name. "It's good to see you, Khalid."

We exchanged inane pleasantries for a while. I recalled my own resurrection ceremony, and the mutual inability of the returnee to express quite what he had been through, and the circumspection of the celebrants faced with the miracle of someone returned from the dead.

"Director Masters informed me of my mother's passing," Davey said. Masters was head of the Onward Station. "Khalid, if you could drive me home via the cemetery...?"

"Of course."

The meeting broke up five minutes later and I drove Davey from the towering crystal obelisk of the Station, through the snow-covered landscape towards Oxenworth.

After a minute, I broke the silence. "I saw your mother during her illness, Davey. She wasn't in pain, and didn't fear death. She had her own strong faith."

Davey nodded. "I know. I remember her telling me all about it."

I glanced across at him. "How much do you recall from... from before?"

He considered for a second or two, frowning. "It's strange, but I recall everything. Who I was, my thoughts and reactions. But it's very much like an adult looking back on his childhood. We have only a refracted, blurred image of who that person was. It's almost like looking back at the life of a stranger."

He was silent for a while, staring out at the snow-softened landscape undulating to the distant moorland horizon.

"The Kéthani remade me completely, Khalid. They took what they had, the fundamental David Emmett, and rebuilt a fully functioning, intelligent human being from the unpromising raw material. The odd thing is, I feel that they maintained a continuity. I am David Emmett, but whole, now."

"I think I know what you mean, Davey. I died ten years ago. The person who came back... well, he was much changed, too."

We came to the cemetery and I turned into the long drive.

We climbed from the car, into the teeth of the sub-zero wind, and I led Davey across to where his mother was interred.

Her grey marble headstone projected from the fleecy snow, bearing her name, date of birth and death, and a line from a Buddhist text: *We each of us have a choice of eternities.*

There were few deaths these days, and the cemetery was little used. The headstone next to Mrs. Emmett's recorded that Claudine Hainault had been buried there twelve years previously.

I felt tears stinging my eyes.

Davey stood at the foot of his mother's grave, head bowed, hands clasped behind his back. The cold wind stirred his full head of black hair.

I said, "Your mother asked me to explain why she couldn't be here to meet you, Davey. And she asked me to give you this." I passed him the letter.

He took it and looked at me. "You mean, why she couldn't face the person I would be—the person I might have been, but for the accident?"

I smiled to myself. He was ahead of me and had saved me from an awkward explanation.

"Do you understand how it must have been, from her point of view?" I said inadequately.

"I understand," he said. "I just wonder how much her belief system was a result of the guilt she felt after the accident. I wonder if she rationalised that she was atoning in this life for sins accrued in a previous one... and if she believed in reincarnation in the hope that my next existence might be a better one." He smiled to himself. "This was all before the coming of the Kéthani, of course."

I shook my hand and shrugged, smiling sadly at the thought of Mrs. Emmett.

"The terrible thing was," Davey went on, "that my mother wasn't responsible for the accident. We were standing at the side of the road and I just pulled my hand from hers and ran off, into the path of a car... Thanks to the Kéthani, I remember everything." He paused, then said, "My mother blamed herself, of course."

He lifted his head and stared into the heavens, and I saw that his eyes were filmed with tears.

"I wonder if she'd forgive me?" he asked at last.

"Your mother was a good and forgiving person," I said.

He stared at the cold, grey headstone. "Would things have turned out differently, for her, but for that incident?"

I said at last, "Who can tell?"

"I wonder if she is happy, wherever she is?"

I let that question blow away on the cold wind, and said instead, "Can I drive you home?"

He hesitated. "No. No, thanks, Khalid." He pointed across the valley, to High Fold Farm. "It's not far, I'll walk."

I shook his hand and made my way back to the car.

I thought of the way the Kéthani had remade us, and then it came to me that, since my return, I had never contacted Zara to apologise for how I had treated her over the years. I knew in my heart that it was my duty to do so, but even then I honestly doubted whether I would be man enough to go through with it.

The Kéthani improve us all, to varying degrees.

I drove from the cemetery, then braked on the road that climbs over the moors. I gazed down on a desolate scene of continuous snow and rank upon rank of headstones, those terrible reminders of the dead.

Davey Emmett was the only living figure in the vast and inimical landscape. As I watched, he opened the letter from his mother and read it slowly. Then he raised his head and stared into the sky, at the stars just beginning to appear in the heavens.

I looked at the road ahead, then started the car and drove towards Oxenworth and home.

INTERLUDE

Over the twenty years since the coming of the Kéthani, the Tuesday night group of friends at the Fleece had grown, evolved, and become for me a second family... or even a first family, if the truth be told. I came to love these quiet, ordinary people, and I was heartened by the fact that my acquaintance with them would continue far into the future.

I arrived late at the Fleece that night, after a busy shift on the implant ward. It was almost ten o'clock by the time I shrugged off my coat, grabbed a welcome pint, and eased myself into my customary seat beside the fire.

Sam said, "Khal, we were beginning to think you'd never make it."

"I was beginning to worry, too," I laughed, taking a swallow of the amber nectar.

Over the years, my actual workload at Bradley General had decreased—there were fewer citizens to be implanted, these days, as more and more people elected to go out among the stars, or to stay out there immediately after their resurrections. I had cut down my hours in the ward to just four a day: today's rush had been a statistical blip.

Dan Chester said, "I've just had this from Lucy. They're..." he smiled and shook his head, as if in wonderment. "I find this hard to believe, but they're aboard a Kéthani faster-than-light-ship beyond the Nilakantha Stardrift, en route to their second posting on an Earth-like world orbiting a super-massive red giant... Anyway," he finished, passing me an information pin and a screen.

I pressed play and stared at the screen.

Lucy smiled out at me, surrounded by passing humans in one-piece suits. She appeared to be in some kind of bar. It reminded me for all the world of a scene from one of the space opera shows I'd watched as a kid.

Davey sat beside her, an arm around her shoulders.

"Dad, everyone in the Fleece—if you're still drinking there! Silly question! Where else would you be? Well, we're aboard an FTL cruiser heading for Kalopia VII, to bring the word of the Kéthani to a race of just-post-industrial humanoids. We're well, and looking forward to the posting." She talked about their work for a few minutes, then turned and looked into Davey's eyes. "We're very happy. It's... I can't begin to describe how amazing it is out here... Look, we've got to rush—can't miss the last post. I'll be in touch again soon. Love you, Dad. Take care!"

Davey waved and smiled, and Lucy reached out and cut the recording.

I shook my head as I passed Dan the screen. "My God... It doesn't seem two minutes since the wedding."

"Four years, Khal," Dan said.

We were silent for a while after that, each of us lost in our own thoughts.

I looked round the bar. It was quiet, which was not surprising these days. Oxenworth was quiet. Half the houses stood empty. Not everyone had gone to the stars; many people had moved to the cities, replacing those who had decided to leave Earth.

Stuart Kingsley said, as if reading my thoughts, "I was in Leeds yesterday, and do you know... It seemed busy, but I was in a bookshop and I happened to look at a local history book, and a photograph of the Headrow in 2006. The crowds! There were thousands of people in the streets..."

Richard Lincoln finished his pint and said, "The world's population has fallen by five per cent in the past five years, and the predictions are that it'll continue like that for the foreseeable future."

Elisabeth shook her head. "So... I'm no mathematician... how long before the world is empty?"

Stuart said, "Roughly a century, Lis. If the exodus continues at this rate."

Ben looked at me and said, "What is it, Khal?"

I must have appeared to be miles away. I shook myself and said, "I don't know... but for the past couple of years I've felt... I find it hard now quite how to describe the feeling..." I shrugged. "I *know*, on some subconscious level, that all I've taken for granted, all that's familiar, is drawing to some kind of close."

"Things are changing," Jeffrey said. "Little by little, inevitably. Nothing is as it was before. Our way of life, which we've taken for granted for so long..."

That gave us pause for thought. We stared into our drinks, for once collectively silenced.

Something that Lucy had said in her communiqué from the stars repeated itself in my head: *Dad, everyone in the Fleece—if you're still drinking there! Silly question!*

I felt, oddly, very old then, as if we were the preservers of a way of life that was soon to change. I had the feeling that we were treading water, waiting... All we needed was something, or someone, to urge us on.

We didn't know what that might be, at the time.

We didn't know that we were waiting for a catalyst, and that that catalyst should prove to be a man called Gregory Merrall.

TEN

The Farewell Party

Gregory Merrall had been part of our group for just three months by the time of the Farewell Party, though it seemed that we had never been without his quiet, patriarchal presence. He was a constant among the friendly faces who met at the Fleece every Tuesday evening, our confidant and king, some might even say our conscience.

I remember his arrival amongst us. It was a bitter cold night in early November and the village had been cut off for two days due to a severe fall of snow. When I saw him stride into the main bar— an anachronistic figure in Harris tweeds and plus fours—I assumed he was a stranded traveller.

He buttressed the bar and drank two or three pints of Landlord.

There were nine of us gathered about the inglenook that night, and as each of us in turn went to the bar to buy our round, the stranger made a point of engaging us in conversation.

"There are worse places to be stranded in than Oxenworth," I said when it was my round. "The Fleece is the best pub for miles around."

He smiled. "I'm not stranded—well, not in that sense," he said, offering his hand. "Merrall, Gregory Merrall."

"Khalid Azzam," I told him. "You've moved to Oxenworth?"

"Bought the old Dunnett farm on the hill."

I knew immediately—and I often look back and wonder quite *how* I knew—that Merrall would become part of our group. There was something about him that inspired trust. He was socially confident without being brash and emanated an avuncular friendliness that was endearing and comforting.

I noticed that he was nearing the end of his pint. "It's my round," I said. "Would you like to join us?"

"Well, that's very kind. I don't mind if I do."

So I introduced him to the group and he slipped into the conversation as if the niche had been awaiting him: the niche, I mean, of the quiet wise man, the patriarchal figure whose experience, and whose contemplation of that experience, he brought to bear on our varied conversations that evening.

It was a couple of weeks later, and I'd arrived early. Richard Lincoln and Andy Souter were at the bar, nursing their first pints. Richard was in his late sixties and for a second I mistook him for Gregory.

He frowned at my double take as he bought me a pint.

"Thought for a second you were Merrall," I explained.

"The tweeds," he said. "Bit out of fashion." I'd always thought it paradoxical that someone who worked so closely with the Kéthani regime should adopt so conservative a mode of dress.

We commandeered our table by the fire and Andy stowed his cornet case under his stool. Andy was a professional musician, a quiet man in his late thirties with a cornetist's pinched top lip. He conducted the local brass band and taught various instruments at the college in Bradley. He was the latest recruit—discounting Merrall—to our Tuesday night sessions. He ran a hand through his ginger mop and said, "So, what do you think of our Gregory?"

"I like him a lot," I said. "He's one of us."

Richard said, "Strange, isn't it, how some people just fit in? Odd thing is, for all he's said a lot, I don't know that much about him."

That gave me pause. "Come to think of it, you're right." All I knew was that he was from London and that he'd bought the old farmhouse on the hill.

Andy nodded. "The mysterious stranger…"

"He's obviously well travelled," Richard said.

That was another thing I knew about him from his stories of India and the Far East. I said, "Isn't it odd that although he's said next to nothing about himself, I feel I know him better than I do some people who talk about themselves non-stop."

For the next hour, as our friends hurried in from the snow in ones and twos, conversation centred around the enigmatic Mr. Merrall. It turned out that no one knew much more than Richard, Andy and me.

"Very well, then," said Doug Standish, our friendly police officer, "let's make it our objective tonight to find out a bit more about Gregory, shall we?"

Five minutes later, at nine o'clock on the dot—as was his habit—Gregory breezed in, shaking off the snow like a big Saint Bernard.

He joined us by the fire and seconds later was telling us about a conversation he'd had with his bank manager that morning. That provoked a round of similar stories, and soon our collective objective of learning more about our new-found friend was forgotten in the to and fro of bonhomie and good beer.

Only as I was wending my way home, with Richard by my side, did it occur to me that we had failed abjectly to learn anything more about Gregory than we knew already.

I said as much to the ferryman.

He was staring at the rearing crystal pinnacle of the Onward Station, perched miles away on the crest of the moors.

"Greg's so friendly it seems rude to pry," he said.

A week later I accidentally found out more about Gregory Merrall and, I thought, the reason for his insularity.

I arrived at the Fleece just after nine, eager to tell what I'd discovered. The group was ensconced before the blazing fire.

Ben and Elisabeth—in their fifties now and still holding hands—both looked at the book I was holding. Ben said, "Tired of our conversation, Khalid?"

Andy Souter laughed, "If we're all doing our own thing, then I'll get my cornet out and practice."

Dan Chester made to cover his ears. "Spare us, Andy, please!"

I smiled. Everyone turned my way as I held up the novel, my hand concealing the name of the author.

"*A Question of Trust*," Samantha Kingsley said. "I didn't know you were a great reader, Khalid."

"I'm not. I was in Bradley today, and this was in the window of the bookshop."

"So," Richard said. "Who's it by?"

"Three guesses," I said.

"You," Stuart Kingsley said. "You've retired from the implant ward and started writing?"

"Not me, Stuart. But you do know him."

Sam cheated. She was sitting next to me, and she tipped her stool and peeked at the author's photo on the back of the jacket.

"Aha!" she said. "Mystery solved."

I removed my hand from the byline.

Dan said, "Gregory!"

"This explains a few things," I said. "His experience, his reluctance to talk about himself—some writers are notoriously modest." I opened the book and read the mini-biography inside the back flap. "Gregory Merrall was born in 1965 in London. He has been a full-time freelance writer for more than thirty years, with novels, collections, and volumes of poetry to his name."

Five minutes later Gregory hurried in, hugging himself against the bone-aching cold. He crossed to the fire and roasted his out-stretched hands before the flames.

He saw the book, which I'd placed on the table before me, and laughed. "So... my secret's out."

"Why didn't you tell us?" Richard said, returning from the bar with a pint for our resident writer.

Gregory took a long draft. "It's something I don't much like talking about," he said. "People assume a number of things when you mention you're a scribbler. They either think you're bragging, that you're incredibly well-off—would that that were so!—that you're some kind of intellectual heavyweight, or that you'll imme-diately start regaling them with fabulous stories."

"Well," Sam said, "you have told us some fascinating tales."

Gregory inclined his head in gracious assent. "It's just not something I feel the need to talk about," he went on. "What mat-ters is not so much talking about it, but getting it done."

The evening unfolded, and at one point someone asked Gregory (it was Stuart, a lecturer at Leeds and something of an egghead himself), "How do you think the coming of the Kéthani has affected how we write about the human experience?"

Gregory frowned into his pint. "Where to begin? Well, it's cer-tainly polarised writers around the world. Some have turned even further inwards, minutely chronicling the human condition in the light of our new-found immortality. Others have ignored it and written about the past, and there's a vast market for nostalgia these days! A few speculate about what life might be like post-death, when we take the leap into the vast inhabited universe."

Richard looked at him. "And where would you put yourself, Gregory?"

Merrall picked up his novel and leafed through it, pausing occasionally to read a line or two. "I'm firmly in the speculative camp," he said, "trying to come to some understanding of what life out there might be like, why the Kéthani came to Earth—what their motives might be."

That set the subject for the rest of the evening: the Kéthani and their *modus operandi*. Of the nine regulars around the table that night, only three of us had died, been resurrected on the home planet of the Kéthani, and returned to Earth: Stuart and Samantha Kingsley, and myself.

I looked back to my resurrection and what I had learned. I had become a better human being, thanks to the aliens, but in common with everyone else who had been resurrected and returned to Earth, I found it difficult to pin down precisely *how* I had become a better person.

At one point Andy Souter said, "I read a novel, a couple of years ago, about a guy who was really a Kéthani disguised as a human, come among us to change our ways."

Gregory nodded. "I know it. *The Effectuator* by Duchamp."

"I've heard rumours that that happens," I said. I shrugged. "Who knows?"

"There are rumours up at the Station," Dan said. "Some of the backroom staff up there are pretty remote. Isn't that right, Richard?"

Richard smiled. "They're just cussed Yorkshire folk," he laughed.

Sam lowered her pint of lager and asked Gregory, "Do you think that happens? Do you think the Kéthani are amongst us?"

Gregory considered. "It's entirely possible," he said. "No one has ever seen a Kéthani, and as they obviously possess technology far in advance of anything we know, then passing themselves off as human wouldn't pose that much of a problem."

Andy said, "But the morality of it... I mean, surely if they're working for our good, then they could at least be open about it."

"The Kéthani work in mysterious ways..." Sam said.

Andy went on, "We take them for granted... we assume they're working for our good. But we don't really know, for sure."

Six pints the worse, I turned to Gregory and said, "Well, you write about the... the whole thing, the Kéthani, death and revival... what do you think?"

He was some seconds before replying. He stared into the fire. "I think," he said, "that the Kéthani are the saviours of our race, and that whatever they have planned for us when we venture out there—though I don't presume to know what that might be—will be wholly for our good."

After that, talk turned to how things had changed due to the coming of the Kéthani. I said, "The change has been gradual, very gradual. I mean, so slow it's been hardly noticeable." I looked around the table. "You've all felt it: it's as if we're treading water, biding our time. It's as if a vast sense of complacency has descended over the human race." I'd never put these feelings into words before—they'd been a kind of background niggle in my consciousness. "I don't know... Sometimes I feel as if I'm only really alive among you lot on Tuesday nights!"

Richard laughed. "I know what you mean. Things that once were seen as important—everything from politics to sport—no longer have that... *vitality*."

"And," Stuart put in, "England is emptying. Come to that, the world is. I don't know what the figures are, but more and more people are staying out there when they die."

And with that thought we called it a night, departed the cosy confines of the main bar and stepped out into the bracing winter chill.

The Onward Station was like an inverted icicle in the light of the full moon, and as I made my way home a brilliant bolt of magnesium light illuminated the night as it ascended to the waiting Kéthani starship.

A couple of weeks later the conversation returned to the perennial subject of the Kéthani, and what awaited us when we died.

Richard Lincoln posed the question: would we return to Earth after our resurrections, or would we travel among the stars as the ambassadors of our alien benefactors?

Gregory looked across at me. "You returned to Earth, didn't you, Khalid? Why, when all the universe awaited you?"

I shrugged, smiled. "I must admit... I was tempted to remain out there. The universe... the lure of new experience... it was almost too much to refuse. But—I don't know. I was torn. Part of me wanted to travel among the stars, but another, stronger part of me wanted to return." I looked across at Richard Lincoln; he was the only person I had told about the reasons for my suicide. "Perhaps I feared the new," I finished. "Perhaps I fled back to what was familiar, safe..." I shrugged again, a little embarrassed at my inarticulacy under the penetrating scrutiny of Gregory Merrall.

He turned to Stuart and Sam. "And you?"

The couple exchanged a glance. Stuart was in his mid-forties, Sam ten years younger, and they were inseparable—as if what they'd experienced, separately, in the resurrection domes on that far-off alien world, had brought them closer together.

Stuart said, "I hadn't really given much thought to my death, or resurrection, before it happened. I naturally assumed I'd come back to Earth, continue life with Sam—we'd been married just over a year when I had the accident—go back to my lectureship at the university. But while I was in the dome I... I learned that there was far more to life than what I'd experienced, and would experience, back on Earth."

"And yet you returned," Gregory said.

Stuart looked across at his wife. "I loved Sam," he said. "I was tempted... tempted to remain out there. But I reasoned that I could always return to the stars, later."

Sam said, looking at Gregory almost with defiance, "Two days after Stu died, I killed myself. I wanted to be with him. I couldn't live without him, not even for six months." She stopped abruptly and stared down into her drink.

"And?" Gregory prompted gently.

"And when I got up there, when I was resurrected... I mean... I still loved Stu, but something... I don't know—something was *different*." She smiled. "The stars called, and nothing would be the same again. Anyway, I decided to come back, see how it went with Stu, and take it from there."

I said, "And look what happened. 'Happily ever after', or what?"

"We both felt the same," Stuart said. "It was as if our love had been tested by what we learnt out there. We considered going back, but... well, we fell into the old routine, work and the pub..." He laughed and raised his pint in ironic salutation.

"That's very interesting," Gregory said. "I've done some research. In the early days, only two in ten who died and were resurrected chose to remain out there. The majority opted for what they knew. Now, out of every ten, seven remain. And the average is rising."

"Why do you think that is?" Ben asked.

Gregory pursed his lips, as if by a drawstring, and contemplated the question. "Perhaps we've come to trust the Kéthani. We've heard the stories of those who've been to the stars and returned, and we know there's nothing to fear."

"But," Elisabeth said, with a down-to-earth practicality, "surely the draw of the familiar should be too much for most of us, those of us who want to return and do all the things on Earth that we never got round to doing."

But Gregory was shaking his head. "You'd think so, but once you've experienced resurrection and instruction by the Kéthani, and gone among the stars—"

Stuart interrupted, "You sound as if you've experienced it first-hand?"

Gregory smiled. "I haven't. But I have interviewed hundreds, maybe even thousands, of returnees from life among the stars, for a series of novels I wrote about the Kéthani."

"And?" I said.

"And I found that the idea of a renewed life on Earth, for many, palls alongside the promise of the stars. And when these people experience life out there, they find life on Earth well-nigh impossible." He smiled. "'Provincial' was the word that cropped up again and again."

We contemplated our beers in silence.

At last I said, "And you, Gregory. What would you do?"

He stared at us, one by one. "When I die, which I think won't be long in happening, then I'll remain out there among the stars, doing whatever the Kéthani want me to do."

A few days later I received a package of books through the post. They were the Returnee trilogy, by Gregory Merrall, sent courtesy of his publisher in London.

That week at the pub I found that every one of us in the group had received the trilogy.

"I don't know what I was expecting," Stuart said, "but they're good."

"More than good," said Elisabeth, who was the literary pundit amongst us. "I'd say they were excellent, profoundly moving."

Dan nodded. "I'd second that. I'm more of a non-fiction man myself, but I found Gregory's books compelling stuff."

Gregory was away that Tuesday—visiting his publisher—so we didn't have the opportunity to thank him. That week I devoured the books, and like Stuart and Elisabeth and Dan found them a heady experience.

He had the ability to write about ideas and the human experience in such a way that the one complemented the other. His characters were real, fully fleshed human beings, about whom the reader cared with a passion. At the same time, he wrote about their experiences in a series of philosophical debates that were at once—for a literary dunce like myself—understandable and page turning.

I canvassed Stuart's opinion on the following Tuesday. I wondered if he, as an intellectual, had been as impressed by Gregory's books as I had. He had, and for an hour that evening before the man himself turned up, all of us discussed the Returnee trilogy with passion and something like awe that we knew its author.

At one point Stuart said, "But what did you all think about the finale, and what did it mean? Gregory seemed to be saying that life on Earth was over, that only humankind's journey among the stars was what mattered."

Ben nodded. "As if Earth were a rock pool, which we had to leave in order to evolve."

At that point Gregory came in with a fanfare of wind and a swirl of snowflakes. We fought to buy him a drink and heaped praise on his novels.

I think he found all the fuss embarrassing. "I hope you didn't think it a tad arrogant, my having the books sent."

We assured him otherwise.

"It was just," he said, "that I wanted you to know my position." He smiled. "And it saved me giving a lecture."

Elisabeth asked, "What are you working on now, Gregory?"

He hesitated, pint in hand. "Ah... Well, I make it a rule never to talk about work in progress. Superstition. Perhaps I fear that gabbing about the book will expend the energy I'd use writing it."

She gave a winning smile. "But on this occasion..."

Gregory laughed. "On this occasion, seeing as I'm among friends, and I've almost finished the book anyway..."

And he proceeded to tell us about his next novel, entitled *The Suicide Club*.

It was about a group of friends who, dissatisfied with their routine existence on Earth, stage a farewell party at which they take their own lives, are resurrected, and then go among the stars as ambassadors of the Kéthani.

Over the course of the next few weeks we became a reading group devoted to the works of Gregory Merrall.

We read every novel he'd written, some fifteen in all. We were enthralled, captivated. We must have presented a strange picture to outsiders: a group of middle-class professionals continually carrying around the same books and discussing them passionately amongst themselves. We even arranged another night to meet and discuss the books, to spare Gregory the embarrassment, though we didn't forgo our usual Tuesday outings.

Only Andy Souter absented himself from the reading group. He was busy most nights with his brass band, and he'd admitted to me on the phone that he'd found the novels impenetrable.

One Saturday evening I arrived early and Stuart was already propping up the bar. "Khalid. Just the man. I've been thinking..." He hesitated, as if unsure as to how to proceed.

"Should think that's expected of you, in your profession," I quipped.

"You'd never make a stand-up comedian, Azzam," he said. "No, it struck me... Look, have you noticed something about the group?"

"Only that we've become a devoted Gregory Merrall fan club—oh, and as a result we drink a hell of a lot more." I raised my pint in cheers. "Which I'm not complaining about."

He looked at me. "Haven't you noticed how we're looking ahead more? I mean, at one point we seemed content, as a group, to look no further than the village, our jobs. It was as if the Kéthani didn't exist."

"And now we're considering the wider picture?" I shrugged. "Isn't that to be expected? We've just read a dozen books about them and the consequences of their arrival. Damn it, I've never read so much in my life before now!"

He was staring into his pint, miles away.

"What?" I asked.

He shrugged. "Reading Gregory's books, thinking about the Kéthani, what it all might mean... It brings back to me how I felt immediately after my resurrection. The lure of the stars. The dissatisfaction with life on Earth. I think, ever since my return, I've been trying to push to the back of my mind that... that niggling annoyance, the thought that I was treading water before the next stage of existence." He looked up at me. "You said as much the other week."

I nodded. After Zara left me, and I killed myself and returned to Earth, I withdrew into myself—or rather into my safe circle of friends—and paid little heed to the world, or for that matter to the universe, outside.

The door opened, admitting a blast of icy air and the rest of the group.

For the next hour we discussed an early Gregory Merrall novel, *The Coming of the Kéthani.*

Around ten o'clock a familiar figure strode into the main bar. We looked up, a little shocked and, I think, not a little embarrassed, like schoolkids caught smoking behind the bike-shed.

A couple of us tried to hide our copies of Gregory's novel, but too late. He smiled as he joined us.

"So this is what you get up to when my back's turned?" he laughed.

Elisabeth said, "You knew?"

"How could you keep it a secret in a village the size of Oxenworth?" he asked.

Only then did I notice the bundle under his arm.

Gregory saw the direction of my gaze. He deposited the package on the table and went to the bar.

We exchanged glances. Sam even tried to peek into the brown paper parcel, but hastily withdrew her hand, as if burned, as Gregory returned with his pint.

Maddeningly, for the rest of the evening he made no reference to the package; he stowed it beneath the table and stoked the flagging conversation.

At one point, Stuart asked, "We were discussing your novel." He indicated *The Coming of the Kéthani*. "And we wondered how you could be so confident of the, ah... *altruism* of the Kéthani, back then? You never doubted their motives?"

Gregory considered his words, then said, "Perhaps it was less good prophecy than a need to hope. I took them on trust, because I saw no other hope for humankind. They were our salvation. I thought it then, and I think so still."

We talked all night of our alien benefactors, and how life on Earth had changed since their arrival and the bestowal of immortality on the undeserving human race.

Well after last orders, Gregory at last lifted the package from beneath the table and opened it.

"I hope you don't mind my presumption," he said, "but I would very much like your opinion of my latest book."

He passed us each a closely printed typescript of *The Suicide Club*.

Two days later, just as I got in from work, Richard Lincoln phoned.

"The Fleece at eight," he said without preamble. "An extraordinary meeting of the Gregory Merrall reading group. Can you make it?"

"Try keeping me away," I said.

On the stroke of eight o'clock that evening all ten of us were seated at our usual fireside table.

Stuart said, "I take it you've all read the book?"

As one, we nodded. I'd finished it on the Sunday, profoundly moved by the experience.

"So... what do you think?"

We all spoke at once, echoing the usual platitudes: a work of genius, a brilliant insight, a humane and moving story...

Only Andy was silent. He looked uncomfortable. "Andy?" I said. He had not been part of the reading group, but Gregory had posted him a copy of the manuscript.

"I don't know. It made me feel... well, uncomfortable."

A silence ensued. It was Sam who spoke for the rest of us, who voiced the thought, insidious in my mind, that I had been too craven to say out loud.

"So," she said, "when do we do it?"

Andy just stared around the group, horrified.

I tried to ignore him. I wondered at what point I had become dissatisfied with my life on Earth. Had the ennui set in years ago, but I had been too comfortable with the easy routine to acknowledge it? Had it taken Gregory Merrall's presence among us to make me see what a circumscribed life I was leading now?

Sam and Stuart Kingsley were gripping each other's hands on the tabletop. Sam leaned forward and spoke vehemently, "Reading Greg's books brought it all back to me. I... I don't think I can take much more of life on Earth. I'm ready for the next step."

Beside her, Stuart said, "We discussed it last night. We're ready to... *go*."

They turned to look at Doug Standish, seated to their left.

He nodded. "I've been waiting for *something* for ten, fifteen years. Unlike you two," he smiled at Sam and Stuart, "I haven't been resurrected, so I've never experienced that lure... until now, that is. I'm ready for... for whatever lies ahead."

He turned to Jeffrey Morrow, on his left. "Jeff?"

The schoolteacher was staring into his drink. He looked up and smiled. "I must admit I've never much thought about my own leaving. I had all the universe, and all the time in the universe, ahead of me—so why rush things? But... yes, it seems right, doesn't it?"

Beside him, Richard Lincoln said in a quiet voice, "Earth holds very little for me now. I suppose the only thing that's been keeping me here is..." he smiled and looked around the group, "the friendship of you people, and perhaps a fear of what might lie ahead, out there. But I feel that the right time has arrived."

Ben and Elisabeth were next. They glanced at each other, their hands locked tight beneath the table. Elisabeth said, "We're attracted to the idea. I mean, you could say that it's the next evolutionary stage of humankind—the step to the stars."

Ben took up where his wife had left off. "And we've noticed things on Earth... The apathy, the sense of limbo, of waiting for something to happen. I think by now it's entered our subconscious as a race—the fact that life on Earth is almost over. It's time to leave the sea."

I looked across at Dan Chester. "Dan?"

He stared into his drink, smiling. "Ever since Lucy and Davey left, five years ago... Well, I've often thought I'd like to follow them. So... yes, I'm ready, too."

A silence ensued. I was next to give my view.

"Like Sam and Stuart," I said, "I experienced the lure while on Kéthan. And like Ben, I've noticed something about the mood on Earth recently, as I said a while back." I paused, then went on, "And it isn't only that more and more resurrectees are electing to remain out there. Increasing numbers of people are actually ending their lives and embarking on the next phase."

Sam said, smiling at me, "You haven't actually said, Khalid, if you want to be part of this."

I laughed. "I've been your friend for years now. You're a massive part of my life. How could I remain on Earth when you're living among the stars?"

I paused and turned to Andy. "Well... what do you think?"

He was rock still, silent, staring down at his pint. He shook his head. "I'm sorry. It's not for me. I... there's a lot I still need to do, here. I couldn't possibly contemplate..." He stopped there, then looked around the group. "You're serious, aren't you?"

Stuart spoke for all of us. "We are, Andy. Of course we are."

Sam nodded. "There... that's it, then. I suppose the next thing to do is discuss how we go about it?"

Andy retreated into his pint.

Richard said, "Perhaps we should ask the man who initiated all this, Gregory himself?"

"I don't know about that," I said. "Don't you think he might be horrified by what he's started?"

Stuart was shaking his head. "Khalid, remember what he said a couple of weeks ago—that he was ready to go? And he wrote the book which endorses the group's decision, after all."

I nodded. Richard said, "So... tomorrow we'll buttonhole Greg and see what he says."

We fell silent and stared into our drinks. We were strangely subdued for the rest of the evening. Andy said goodbye and left before last orders.

The following day on the ward I could not concentrate fully on my work; it was as if I were at one remove from the real world, lost in contemplation of the future, and at the same time remembering the past.

It was almost ten by the time I arrived at the Fleece. The others were ensconced at our usual table, illuminated by the flames of the fire. It was a scene I had beheld hundreds of times before, but perhaps it was the realisation that our Tuesday nights were drawing to a close that invested the tableau with such poignancy.

Significantly, Andy Souter was conspicuous by his absence. No one commented on the fact.

The contemplative atmosphere had carried over from the previous evening. We sat in silence for a while, before Richard said, "Odd, but I was thinking today how insubstantial everything feels."

Jeffrey laughed. "I was thinking the very same. There I was trying to drum the meaning of metaphor in Bogdanovich's *The Last Picture Show* into a group of bored year tens... and I couldn't help but think that there's more to existence."

"I feel," Sam said, "that we'll soon find out exactly how much more."

I voiced something that had been preying on my mind. "Okay, I know you're going to call me a hopeless romantic, but it'd be nice... I mean, once we're out there, if we could remain together."

Smiles and nods around the table reassured me.

Before anyone could comment on the likelihood of that, Gregory Merrall strode in. "Drink up. I seem to recall that it's my round." He stared at us. "What's wrong? Been to a funeral?"

Sam looked up at him. "Gregory, we need to talk."

He looked around the group, then nodded. He pointed to the bar.

While he was away, we looked at each other as if for reassurance that we did indeed agree to go ahead with this. Silent accord passed between us, and Sam blessed us with her radiant smile.

"So," Gregory said two minutes later, easing the tray onto the tabletop, "how can I help?"

We looked across at Sam, tacitly electing her as spokesperson.

"Gregory," she began, "we were all very affected by your novel, *The Suicide Club*. It made us think."

Gregory smiled. "That's always nice to hear. And?"

"And," Sam said, and hesitated.

Gregory laughed. "Come on—out with it!"

"Well... we've come to the conclusion, each of us, independently, that there was something lacking in our lives of late..." She went on, neatly synopsising what each of us had expressed the night before.

She finished, "So... we've decided that we need to move on, to make the next step, to go out there."

Gregory heard her out in silence, a judicial forefinger placed across his lips.

A hush fell across the table. It was as if we were holding our breath in anticipation of his response.

At last he nodded and smiled. "I understand," he said, "and to be honest I've been thinking along the same lines myself of late." He looked around the group, at each of us in turn, and continued, "I wonder if you'd mind if I joined you?"

The party was set for the first Saturday in February, which gave us less than a fortnight to settle our affairs on Earth and say our goodbyes. I resigned my internship at Bradley General and told my colleagues that I was taking a year's break to travel—which was not that far removed from the truth. I had no real friends outside the Tuesday evening group, so the farewells I did make were in no way emotionally fraught.

I considered contacting Zara, my ex-wife, and telling her the truth of my going, but on reflection I came to realise that she was part of a past life that was long gone and almost forgotten.

I put my affairs in order, left instructions with my solicitor for the sale of my house, and bequeathed all I possessed to Zara.

Gregory Merrall insisted that he host the farewell party, and it seemed fitting that this should be so.

I would attend the party along with Sam and Stuart but, as we had died once and been resurrected, we would not take part in the ritual suicide. I wondered what I might feel as I watched my friends take their final drink on Earth.

On the day before the party, the doorbell chimed. It was Andy Souter. He stood on the doorstep, shuffling his feet, his ginger hair aflame in the light of the porch. "Andy. Get in here. It's freezing!"

He stepped inside, snow-covered, silent, and a little cowed. "Coffee?" I asked, uneasy myself.

He shook his head. "I won't stay long. I just..." He met my gaze for the first time. "Is it true? You're all planning to... to go, tomorrow night?"

I showed him into the lounge. "That's right. We've thought long and hard about what we're planning. It seems the right thing to do."

Andy shook his head. "I don't know. I have a bad feeling about it."

I smiled, pointed to the raised square of the implant at his temple. "But you're implanted, Andy. You'll go when you die..."

He smiled bleakly. "I know, but that's different. I'll die of natural causes or accidentally. I won't take my life at the behest of some stranger."

I said, "Gregory's no stranger, now."

He stared at me. "Isn't he?"

"You don't like him, do you?"

"I don't know. Put it this way, I'm not wholly convinced."

I laughed. "About what, exactly?"

He looked bleak. "That's just it. I don't know. I just have this... *feeling.*"

I said, "Look, we're going to the Fleece at nine for a last drink. Why don't you come along, say goodbye."

He shook his head, "I've said goodbye to everyone individually." He held out his hand. "Take care, Khalid."

* * *

The following evening Richard Lincoln knocked on my door, and I left the house for the very last time. We walked in silence past the Fleece, through the village, and up the hillside towards the beckoning lights of Merrall's converted farmhouse.

Our friends were already there, armed with drinks.

There was, unlike our last few nights in the Fleece, a party atmosphere in the air, a *fin-de-siècle* sense of closure, of new beginnings.

We drank and chatted about the past. We regaled Gregory with incidents of village life over the past twenty years, the emotional highs and lows: the break up of my marriage, the resurrection of Ben's father, the going of Father Renbourn... It was as if, with this incantatory summoning of the past, we were putting off the inevitability of the future.

Then we ate, seated around a long pine table, a lavish meal of roast beef and baked potatoes. Conversation turned to the Kéthani and our mission as ambassadors among the stars.

A little drunk, I laughed. "It seems impossible to reconcile my life so far, the insignificance of my existence until now, with what might happen out there." And I swung my wine glass in an abandoned gesture at the stars.

Gregory said, "We will be taken, and trained, and we will behold wonders we cannot even guess at."

Beside me, Sam said, "I wish Andy was coming with us."

A silence settled around the table as we pondered our absent, sceptical friend.

We finished the meal and Gregory poured the wine. He went around the table, clockwise, and tipped an exact measure of French claret, laced with cyanide, into each glass.

Sam, Stuart, and I sat together at the end of the table. I felt a subtle sense of exclusion from the act about to take place. Later tonight we three would report to the Onward Station, would be beamed up in the same transmission as our friends, and begin our journey to the stars.

I was aware of my heart thudding as I watched my friends raise their glasses and Richard Lincoln pronounce a toast. "To friends," he said, "and to the future!"

"To friends and to the future!" they echoed, and drank.

I watched Richard Lincoln relax, smiling, and slump into his seat, as if asleep, and I reached across the table and gripped his hand as if to ease his passing. I looked around, taking in the enormity of the fact that my friends of so many years were dead or dying... Jeffrey leaned forward, resting his head on his arms; Doug Standish sat upright, a smile on his stilled face; Ben and Elisabeth leaned towards each other, embracing, and died together; Dan Chester had fallen sideways in his seat, head lolling. At the head of the table, Gregory Merrall slumped in his seat, chin on chest.

A silence filled the room and I felt like weeping.

Someone was clutching my hand. I looked up. Sam was staring at me through her tears.

We stood and moved towards the door. Already, our friends' implants would be registering the fact of their death. In minutes, the ferrymen from the Onward Station would arrive to collect their bodies.

I took one last glance at the tableau of stilled and lifeless remains, then joined Sam and Stuart and stepped into the freezing night.

Stuart indicated his car. "We might as well go straight to the Station."

I said, "Do you mind if I walk?"

They smiled, understanding. I sketched a wave and set off along the footpath that climbed across the snow-covered moorland to the soaring tower of the Onward Station in the distance.

Their car started and drove away, and soon the sound of its engine died and left a profound silence in its wake.

I strode across the brow of the hill, my boots compacting snow, my head too full of recent events to look ahead with any clarity.

At one point I stopped, turned, and looked down at the farm-house, dark against the snow. The lights glowed in the windows, and it reminded me of a nativity scene.

I was about to resume my march when, from the corner of my eye, I saw movement at the back door. At first I thought it was a ferryman, arrived early—then realised that I had heard no car.

I stared and caught my breath in shock.

A figure stepped through the kitchen door and strode out into the gravelled driveway, and in the light of the gibbous moon I recognised the tweed-clad shape of Gregory Merrall.

At that moment I felt very alone. I wanted Sam and Stuart beside me, to affirm that I was not losing my senses.

As I watched, he stopped in the middle of the drive and stared up at the stars, and my mind was in chaos.

Why? I asked myself... Why had he—

And then the explanation came, falling from the heavens.

Gregory raised his arms above his head, as if in greeting or sup-plication, and from on high there descended, across the dark night sky like the scoring of a diamond point across a sheet of obsidian, what at first I thought was a shooting star. The vector it took, however, was vertical. It fell like a lance, heading for the farmhouse below, and I could only gasp in wonder, breathless, as it struck Gregory Merrall.

He vanished, and the light leapt up and retraced its course through the night sky, heading towards the waiting Kéthani starship.

My face stinging with tears, I set off towards the rearing obelisk of the Onward Station. I thought of Andy Souter, and his suspi-cion of Gregory Merrall, and his decision not to join us... and I wondered if Andy had been right to turn his back, this time, on the new life that awaited us.

I was sobbing by the time I reached the Station. I paused before its cut-glass perfection, this thing of supernal alien beauty on the harsh Yorkshire landscape.

I wondered whether to tell Sam and Stuart that we had been lured to the stars by an... an impostor. Did it matter, after all? I tried to marshal my emotions, to decide whether what Merrall had done could be considered an act of betrayal or of salvation. I wondered if I should go ahead with what we had planned.

I turned and stared out over the land that had been my home since birth, a land slowly emptying due to the ministrations of a mysterious alien race. Then I looked up at the stars, the million pulsating beacons of light, and I knew that there was only one course of action to take.

I hurried into the Station, to join my friends and to begin the new life that awaited me out there among the beckoning stars.

CODA

Diaspora

A thousand years have passed since the events described in the preceding documents.

We went among the stars and experienced wonders beyond our wildest dreams; we each of us beheld sights almost beyond description, and certainly beyond the understanding of the humans we once were. We became the ambassadors of the Kéthani, and in so doing completed the next stage of our evolution, became more than human and at the same time more *humane*. We did the bidding of the Kéthani among the teeming races of the universe and learned that the reason our benefactors selected us for the task was a little more complex than we first thought. But that is another story.

Tomorrow I am meeting my old friends and we are returning to Earth, to the location where we first met, all those hundreds of years ago.

Earth is depopulated now; only a handful of wardens live among its petrified treasures, its overgrown vales, guardians of the cradle of humankind. Despite all the early objections, despite the scepticism and pessimism, the religious and philosophical opposition, time has worked to erode our fears and prove wrong the voices of dissent.

The galaxy is now the true home of humankind, though people do return to Earth from time to time, so I've heard, to dwell in the past and relive old memories, before renewing their lives out there.

We will meet among the tumbled stones of the village we once called home, perhaps trace among the crumbled foundations the dwellings where we lived, the places where we met. We might even find the ruins of the Fleece...

We will recount our exploits on alien worlds, catching up with the deeds of friends we have not seen for dozens of years, in some cases a century or two. Then, talk will turn to the past, to life on Earth, when we were so very young and thought ourselves so experienced and wise.

And we might even shed a tear or two before we part again and return to our rightful place among the distant stars.

ACKNOWLEDGEMENTS

Portions of this novel appeared in the following publications:

"Ferryman" first appeared in *New Worlds*, 1997.

"Onward Station" first appeared in *Interzone* 135, 1998.

"The Kéthani Inheritance" first appeared in *Spectrum* 7, 2001.

"Thursday's Child" first appeared in *Spectrum* 9, 2002.

"The Touch of Angels" first appeared in *Threshold Shift*, 2006.

"The Wisdom of the Dead" first appeared in *Interzone* 186, 2003.

"A Heritage of Stars" first appeared in *Constellations*, 2005.

"Matthew's Passion" (written with Tony Ballantyne) is original to the collection.

"A Choice of Eternities" first appeared in *Postscripts* 1, 2004.

"The Farewell Party" first appeared in *The Solaris Book of New SF*, 2007.

The sections entitled "The Coming of the Kéthani" and "Diaspora", and the linking material, are original to the collection.

I'd like to take this opportunity to thank the editors of the anthologies and magazines where these stories first appeared: David Garnett, David Pringle, Paul Fraser, Gary Turner, Peter Crowther, and George Mann. The chapter entitled "Matthew's Passion" was written with Tony Ballantyne, and I'd like to take this opportunity to thank him for his input and hard work.

ABOUT THE AUTHOR

Eric Brown's first short story was published in *Interzone* in 1987, and he sold his first novel, *Meridian Days*, in 1992. He has won the British Science Fiction Award twice for his short stories and has published twenty-five books: SF novels, collections, books for teenagers and younger children, and he writes a monthly SF review column for *The Guardian*. His latest books include *Revenge*, and the novel, *Helix*. He is married to the writer and mediaevalist Finn Sinclair and they have a daughter, Freya.

His website can be found at *www.ericbrown.co.uk*

Eric Brown makes a triumphant return to hard Science Fiction
in a stunning new series

Necropath
Book One of The Bengal Station Trilogy

The Pride of Vanderlaan

Vaughan stood on the windswept deck of the spaceport, his stomach knotted with apprehension as he waited for the freighter to complete its transfer from the void.

It was all very well planning to board the ship in the comfortable safety of Nazruddin's, but the fact of what he was about to do—the danger he might face aboard the ship—only became real as the time to act approached.

As he watched, the *Pride of Vanderlaan* appeared briefly to the south of the 'port, a grey ghost in the darkness, and then disappeared. For fifteen seconds it flickered like an image on ancient film, before it mastered the slippage and appeared finally, solid and substantial, in this reality. The ship engaged auxiliary burners and moved in slowly across the sea, a stylised wedge of gunmetal grey carapace, company colours excoriated by the void.

Across the 'port the loudspeaker system relayed orders, the bored woman's voice duplicated in Vaughan's earpiece. "Okay... twenty-three hundred hours. This one's ahead of schedule. Coming in due south, estimated docking: four minutes. Berth twelve prepare lines. Hauliers at the ready. Emergency services on stand-by. Class-3 freighter out of Verkerk's World, Vega, terminates at the Station. It's all yours, boys and girls. Out." The drawl clicked off abruptly, the silence immediately replaced by the dull drone of the freighter's engines.

Vaughan stood beyond berth twelve, an oval crater of raised steel flanges. Fuel lines, coloured cables and leads, turned the berth into a snake pit. The freighter swung in over the superstructure of the terminal building, its stanchion legs braced akimbo, landing lights sequencing along its sleek flank. Behind lighted lozenges of viewscreens, crewmembers could be seen chatting casually around tables or leaning against the rails and staring out with the relaxed postures of travellers at journey's end.

Around the berth, one by one, 'port authority vehicles drew up: a fire truck, an ambulance, a tanker to siphon off unused fuel, and three or four other specialist juggernauts. Their personnel climbed down, stood around in bored cliques, chatting and mopping their faces in the relentlessly humid night. Vaughan could not help but read their thoughts, just as he would have overheard music played loud. Without concentrating, he caught only fragments of verbalised cognition from a nearby engineer: >>>*Last one this shift, thank Allah. Home... Parveen...*

Then non-verbal thoughts of security, warmth, sex, and accompanying mental images.

His handset chimed. He accessed the call. "Jimmy?"

Chandra's smiling face looked up at him. "Mission accomplished."

"You took your time."

"Weiss was a bastard. He kicked up a fuss when I hauled his flier down and demanded to see his papers. Called the odds— you know these big shots. He nearly gave me an excuse to arrest him for abusive behaviour to a police officer. He's in interrogation now and demanding a solicitor. He's here for a good three, four hours. Hope that gives you long enough. Catch you later." The screen blanked.

The first job would be to assess the level of security around the ship, and then put his plan into action. He doubted that Weiss would have overlooked the possibility that he would not always be on hand to shunt his telepaths to other duties; he would have posted guards.

The **Vanderlaan** came in over the berth and turned slowly on its axis, lowering itself gradually to the deck. Muscular, ram-rod stanchions took the impact and the ship dipped a quick, hydraulic curtsy.

Minutes later the ramp came down, hitting the deck with a clang like a bell tolling the hour. Two big Sikhs in the light blue uniforms of a private security firm ascended the ramp and positioned themselves on either side of the exit.

Vaughan scanned. The men had been hired by Weiss and instructed to let not a living soul aboard the freighter. Weiss had used some vivid language to get his message across, and the guards had taken notice. They were tensed-up and vigilant, as if expecting a terrorist strike at any second.

He strolled casually around the freighter. From the minds of the 'port workers gathered in the berth beneath the ship he detected not the slightest flicker of suspicion at his presence. He paused on the lip of the berth, staring down at a group of three engineers as they accessed the emergency exit cover.

One engineer was consulting a screader, reading off a reference number to his deputy. Vaughan scanned.

>>>*Twenty minutes should see this through—small ship, no maintenance work reported. Where's that damned code...?*

The engineer found it on his screader, and Vaughan memorised the code. He would wait until the ground crew had finished their work and departed, and the ship's crew disembarked, then enter the freighter through the emergency exit.

A roadster veered around the ship and headed towards Vaughan. He felt the power of the driver's mind, the thoughts strengthening as the car drew up alongside him. >>>*Fuck Weiss having me do his running about. What the hell's he doing... should be here by now. Don't like these damned sneaking teleheads... unnatural. Don't trust the bastards.*

The security officer leaned through the roadster's open window, an olive-skinned southern European. "Vaughan—just got word from Director Weiss. Don't bother with this ship—just cargo, anyway. He wants you to go over some files at Terminal Three."

>>>*If the bastard's reading me...* Followed by nebulous images of violence.

"Fine. I'll make my way over now."

"Look, don't ask me why... Weiss told me to make sure I delivered you there." >>>*Don't know what you done wrong, telehead, but Weiss doesn't trust you.* Thoughts of uneasiness, the desire to be elsewhere. >>>*Can't say I blame him...*

Vaughan climbed into the roadster, doing his best to ignore the miasma of unease leaking from the driver, the irrational urge to strike out at Vaughan because of what he was. As the car set off, he leaned forward and disengaged the augmentation-pin. He had no desire to be corrupted by the thug's primitive mind-set.

"Relax," he said. "I'm no longer scanning."

The officer glanced across at him, smiled uneasily. "Hey, no sweat. I can handle the idea of 'heads. Just doing your job, after all."

Vaughan smiled. He recalled the words of a fellow psi-positive at the Ottawa Institute ten years ago, "Prepare yourself for a lonely life, bud. No one likes a telepath."

The officer dropped him off at terminal three. Vaughan climbed from the car and began walking towards the building, and the officer watched him all the way. Just carrying out orders.

He entered the office and, ignoring the three clerks busy at their screens, crossed to the bank of terminals ranked beneath the windows overlooking the deck. He accessed the report files he'd been completing over the past week and feigned diligence. From time to time he glanced over the screen and watched the activity in the glare of halogen lights around the freighter.

The numerous service teams performed their duties and departed; the bowser finished first, sucking the excess fuel from the tanks and then trundling off across the 'port, lights flashing. Teams of engineers came and went, disappearing beneath the underbelly of the freighter to perform their routine checks. Technicians swarmed over the carapace of the ship, expertly utilising the purpose-built footholds in the sloping flanks.

As he watched, a shuttle beetled out from the terminal building beneath him and zipped across the deck, pulling up before the ramp and waiting patiently. Minutes later the crew disembarked, ten men and women in the stylish black and silver uniforms of the Vega Line. They boarded the shuttle and it looped around the ship then headed back towards the terminal.

Vaughan stood and stretched, then casually left the office.

He strolled across the deck, heading away from the Vegan freighter. To his right, the officer's roadster was parked outside the security wing of the terminal building. Vaughan increased his pace, putting the bulk of a voidliner between him and the terminal.

He turned left, making his way towards the freighter. As he walked through the humid night, he slipped his pin from its case and inserted it into his skull console. Although he often strolled around the deck between jobs, and his presence here tonight would not be considered amiss, he nevertheless felt self-conscious—as if the few engineers and security guards he passed were aware of his intentions. Swift scans told him that their thoughts were as banal as ever.

He approached the freighter, becalmed now in the aftermath of its landing. He made sure that he went unobserved—it was not within his duty remit to board ships through their emergency exits. The coast was clear. There was no one in the vicinity, other than a team of engineers busy working on a nearby ship, and they were too engrossed in their work to notice him.

He hurried to the lip of the berth and descended a ladder into the shadowy pit beneath the belly of the freighter. He paused, regaining his breath and his composure. That was the first stage of the operation successfully completed. All that remained was to board the ship. He scanned, probing behind the sleek curved lines of the freighter. He detected a single mind, too high up in the ship to be read with any clarity.

He found the emergency exit cover and tapped the entry-code into the lock. The cover sighed open, extruding steps.

He climbed into a small, darkened compartment. At his presence, sensors activated and a hatch above him slid open. Low lighting came on, illuminating a corridor. He hauled himself into the ship and stood. He was in the working end of the freighter: the corridor was spartan, uncarpeted. He set off in the direction of where he judged the cargo hold to be. First, he would inspect whatever goods the ship was hauling; later he would investigate the source of the distant mind-noise in the crew-cabins high above.

The cargo holds were situated on either side of the corridor. He pressed the sensor panel on the hatch to his left, and it eased open to reveal a small, dimly lit hold, empty but for hauling trolleys and lifting equipment. He closed it and crossed the corridor, palming the sensor on the opposite hatch. The dull steel cover slid open and Vaughan saw that this hold was occupied.

He stepped into the vaulted chamber, poorly illuminated by sporadic strip-fluorescents. A bulky, oval case stood in the centre of the bare steel floor. It was the approximate size of a flier, shoulder high at the rear, sloping to around waist high where Vaughan stood. It seemed to be constructed of some brass or copper-like material, engraved with an intricate pattern of spiral and curlicue striations. He walked around the case; the random design of whorls was repeated on every facet, and nowhere could he make out a seal, lid, or hatch.

The most remarkable aspect of the casing, however, was the fact that it was shielded. When he scanned, he detected the strange emptiness—an **absence**—that denoted a powerful mind-shield. He touched the cold surface of the case, lay his cheek against the inscribed patterning surface. He scanned again, read nothing.

He backed off a pace, contemplating the case and wondering what it contained. If Weiss was transporting illegal immigrants to Earth from Vega, why do so like this? Why not just have them travel as foot passengers? Weiss would have called off his telepaths anyway, so there would have been no threat of discovery.

Animals, then. Was Weiss smuggling some proscribed species of fauna to Earth—and, if so, why?

There had been two earlier freighters Weiss had warned him off. Vaughan wondered how many shielded containers Weiss had successfully smuggled into the Station.

He recalled the mind situated high above him. As he hurried from the cargo hold and took the elevator to the upper-decks, it occurred to him that he should have felt pleased that he had uncovered the illegal operation—satisfied that a hunch had hit the jackpot. Instead, he experienced a subtle uneasiness at the discovery and its ramifications.

As the elevator climbed, the contents of the mind above him came into focus. He realised that it was the mind of a child, a young girl, and that she was distressed.

The lift door opened onto the third floor. A red tiled corridor dwindled into the distance, archways opening onto other passages at regular intervals. He set off at a jog along the main corridor. The cerebral signature became louder as he ran, then modulated almost imperceptibly: he had passed the turning down which the kid was located. He retraced his steps, took the turning. The mind cried out.

>>>*Help—someone please help!*

Even as he moved towards the girl, something told him to ignore the cry and leave the ship. He tried to analyse the desire. The cry was human, in need of help, and yet his initial impulse was to run.

He arrived at an archway leading into a bedchamber. The girl was in the room, hiding in a storage unit.

Vaughan stepped into the room, crossed to the stack of units. He touched the control panel on the unit, and the door whirred open. A young girl, perhaps ten years old, hugged her shins and stared at him. She had straight, dark hair, brown eyes. Her resemblance to Holly struck him like a blow.

He probed and found her name: Elly Jenson.

He knelt before her, trying to block her sudden surge of fright, and held out a hand. "Please, don't be frightened. I can help."

She whispered, "Who are you?"

"Don't worry. I'll get you out of here. Please, trust me."

He probed, and her mind entered his in a kaleidoscopic whirl of fragmented images. He sorted through them, discarding extraneous thoughts and memories, picking out only what he needed to know. He shared her fear, her memories of life on Verkerk's World. He identified the image of her father, and read her incomprehension at why he had allowed her to be taken away. He relived the day two strangers came to her father's house and took her, and shared with the girl her bewilderment when her father tried to explain that she had been Chosen, and must go.

He reached out for the girl's hand. She flinched at his touch, but did not pull away. She watched him with wide eyes, wanting to trust him and yet fearing to do so.

"I'm not with the people who took you," he said. He sensed that part of her confusion was that she did not know where she was. She had been told that she was going to Earth, but her young mind had been unable to encompass the idea.

He said, "You're on Earth now. You came through the void from your world. I want to help you."

"Please, take me home. Can you take me home?" The words were clean and sharp with the ice of Scandinavian intonation. "Please, take me away from here!"

He thought through the situation, considered his options. He could always take her from the ship, back through the emergency exit, then contact Chandra and deliver her into the care of the police.

He wondered if the presence of the shielded container and Elly Jenson aboard the freighter was anything more than a coincidence.

He scanned her again, tried to read the whereabouts of the people who had escorted her to Earth. He read a name—Freidrickson—caught the image of a man in the black and silver uniform of the Vega Company.

He took Elly's hand and pulled her to her feet. "It's okay, Elly. You're safe now—"

Something in her wide-eyed expression of surprise alerted him. Vaughan tried to turn, to follow the direction of her gaze, but the neural incapacitator hit him before he caught sight of his assailant. He arched as voltage stabbed him in the back and coursed through his body. In the fraction of a second before he lost consciousness, he scanned but read nothing.

He seemed to come to his senses almost immediately, but even as he struggled to his feet, his body protesting with spasms of pain, he knew that minutes had elapsed.

Elly Jenson was no longer in the unit.

He staggered to the entrance of the chamber and sent out a probe. There was no sign of the girl's harried cerebral signature—but he did pick up, approaching him at speed, the minds of the Sikh security guards. Whoever had attacked him—Freidrickson?—had alerted them to his presence.

He ran down the corridor in the opposite direction. The guards were ascending in the main elevator. He made his way to the auxiliary shaft at the back of the ship, his muscles jarring with every step.

He read the guards as they emerged from the elevator and ran along the corridor to the chamber he'd just left. He slammed a palm against the lift sensor, willing the doors to open. He scanned the guards. They were in the bedchamber, searching for him, their minds loud with anger. Three seconds was all it took for them to ascertain that he was no longer there. They exited and split up to search the ship. One headed away from Vaughan; the other ran down the corridor towards him.

He prepared himself for a fight, knew the futility of the idea. The Sikh was a matter of metres away, about to turn the corner and discover him, when the elevator doors sighed open. He dived inside, thumbed the sensor panel. The doors whirred shut and the lift carried him down into the belly of the ship.

A minute later he dropped through the emergency hatch into the hot night. He climbed from the berth, made sure his way was clear, and jogged from the shadow of the Vegan freighter. He scanned the deck for Elly Jenson in vain. Beyond the terminal building, fliers took off and banked into the red and blue airlanes above the Station. He realised, with a sudden, plummeting despair, that the girl and her captor might be aboard any one of them.

He slipped the augmentation-pin from his skull console. If taken beyond the boundaries of the spaceport, the pin activated an alarm back at stores, detailing the device's precise position: augmentation-pins were valuable commodities, dangerous in the hands of the wrong people. He would have to waste precious seconds and return it to stores: the last thing he wanted was for Weiss's henchmen to find him now.

He was running across the deck when his handset chimed. He halted and quickly pressed the caller code—if it was Weiss, he would not answer.

The code was Jimmy Chandra's. Vaughan accepted the call.

Chandra stared up at him. "Jeff. Can you get over here?"

"Sure. I need to see you, too. I found something aboard the ship."

Jimmy looked grim-faced. "Later."

"What's wrong?"

The cop shook his head. "Not now. I'll tell you when you get here, okay?"

Vaughan handed his pin to the clerk in stores and hurried to the flier rank.

Original stories from some of the world's best loved SF writers

Featuring stories by
Peter F Hamilton
Stephen Baxter
Paul Di Filippo
Ian Watson
Neal Asher
and more...

ISBN: 978-1-84416-448-6

The Solaris Book of New
SCIENCE FICTION
Edited by George Mann

All-new stories by
Peter Watts
Kay Kenyon
Michael Moorcock
Karl Schroeder
David Louis Edelman
Dan Abnett
Eric Brown
Robert Reed
and more...

The Solaris Book of New
SCIENCE FICTION
VOLUME TWO
Edited by George Mann

ISBN: 978-1-84416-542-1

The Solaris Book of New Science Fiction volumes 1 & 2 are short story anthologies of the highest order, showcasing the talents of some of the world's greatest science fiction writers. The eclectic stories in these collections range from futuristic murder mysteries, to widescreen space opera, to tales of contact with alien beings.

www.solarisbooks.com

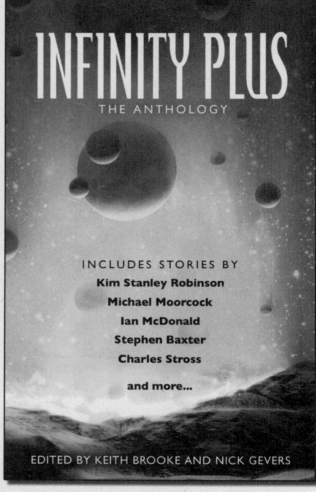

"The king of high-concept SF." — *The Guardian*

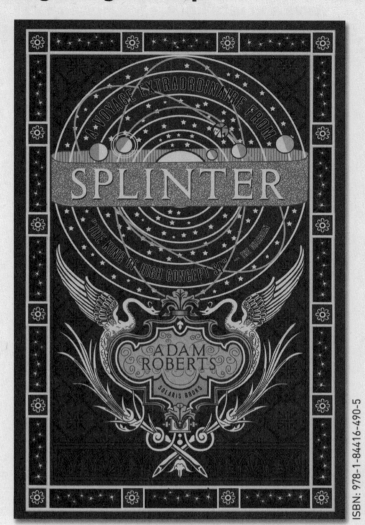

When Hector discovers his father has channelled the family fortune into a bizarre survivalist sect who await the imminent destruction of the Earth, he is wracked by feelings of betrayal and doubt. Things change, however, the night an asteroid plummets from space and shatters the planet, leaving Hector and the remnants of the human race struggling for survival on a splinter of the Earth.

www.solarisbooks.com

ISBN: 978-1-84416-490-5

SOLARIS SCIENCE FICTION

"Deadstock is a gripping page-turner written with verve and intelligence." — *The Guardian*

ISBN : 978-1-84416-447-9

Punktown, crime-ridden metropolis on the colony world, Oasis, is home to the scum of countless alien races. Stalking its mean streets is Jeremy Stake, the private detective with chameleon-like abilities he does not want and cannot control. When Stake takes on a new disturbing case, things in Punktown are about to get very nasty indeed...

www.solarisbooks.com

"For a wild ride, readers will be hard-pressed to find a better vehicle than Thomas's bizarre multiverse." — *Publishers Weekly*

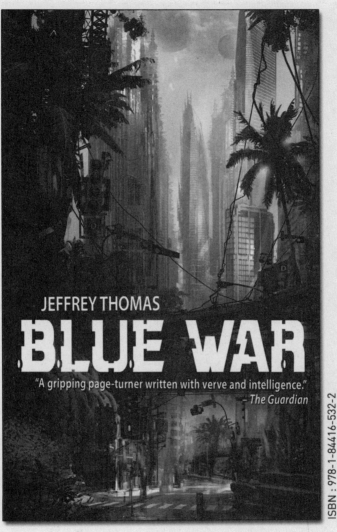

JEFFREY THOMAS

BLUE WAR

"A gripping page-turner written with verve and intelligence."
– *The Guardian*

ISBN : 978-1-84416-532-2

A jungle of blue vegetation in another dimension. Cloned human remains discovered in an otherwise empty city. The impending threat of a second inter-dimensional war. Just another case for private investigator Jeremy Stake, the man with chameleon-like abilities he does not want but cannot ignore.

www.solarisbooks.com

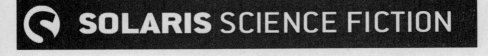

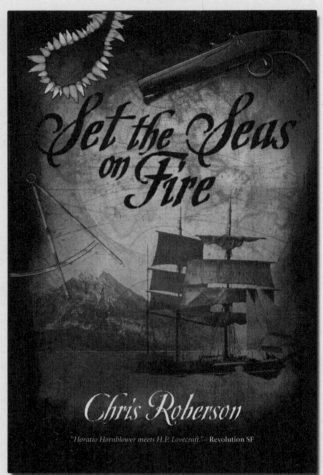

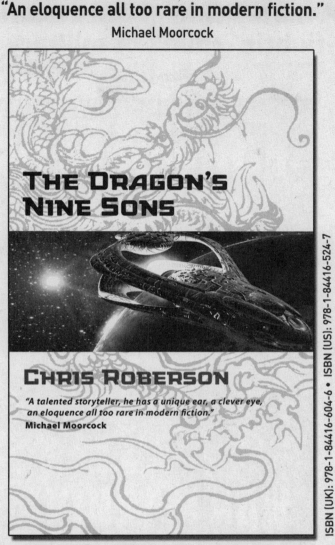